I0766954

Trafalgar and Boone
in the
Drowned Necropolis

Geonn Cannon

Supposed Crimes LLC • Matthews, North Carolina

www.supposedcrimes.com

This book is typeset in Goudy Old Style, licensed by
Ascender Corporation.

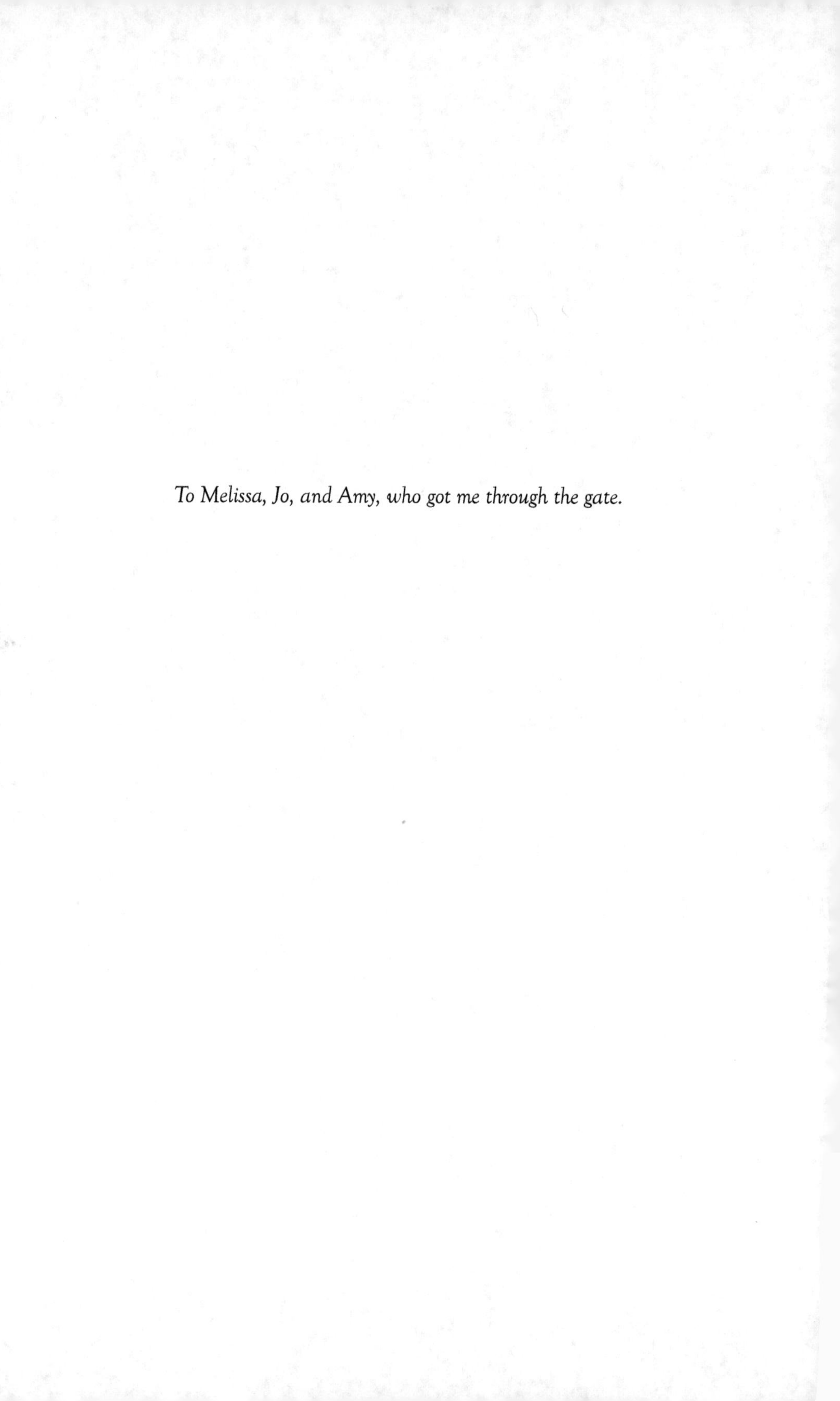
To Melissa, Jo, and Amy, *who got me through the gate.*

When last we visited our intrepid heroes...

LADY DOROTHY BOONE and **MISS TRAFALGAR OF ABYSSINIA** were both targeted by a deadly group known as the Watershed Society. Twenty years ago, members of this society kidnapped Trafalgar from her home to use her in a profane ritual meant to bring forth an ancient evil. Faced with an enemy neither of them could confront alone, Trafalgar and Boone agreed to temporarily put aside their differences for the greater good. Teamed with Dorothy's stalwart majordomo **BEATRICE SEK**, invisible private investigator **IVY SEVER** and Trafalgar's associate **LEOLA KIDANE**, the erstwhile enemies boarded the *Skylarker*, the airship of ARAMINTA "MINTY" CROOK.

Their pursuit led them to Rome, where the women were taken hostage by **ORVILLE** and **DANIEL WEEKS**. The brothers uncovered the location of the mythic labyrinth where they believed they would find the means to summon their new god. They required Trafalgar and Boone's skills to navigate the maze and defeat the Minotaur. Forced to work together to survive the Weeks brothers and the Minotaur, Trafalgar and Boone were indeed successful in surviving the mission and preventing the summoning. With one brother dead and the other lost in the labyrinth at the mercy of its bovine protector, the women return to London.

With many of their allies dead due to the Weeks brothers' schemes, there is more than enough work to keep them both busy. But Dorothy lacks the funding to outfit an entire expedition on her own, and Trafalgar suddenly finds herself without either of her most trusted companions. With no other options, and reluctantly aware of how well they work together, the two women decide to combine their resources to take on whatever trial comes next, wherever it might take them.

It was just a short stroll from the train station to the County Mental Hospital, Wraysbury, which was fortunate as there were no cars for hire when the travelers arrived at their destination. The group took a flight of stairs to a narrow footbridge that stretched over the tracks and went on their separate ways. One of the disembarking passengers was a young gentleman in a bowler hat and eyeglasses shaded lavender. He wore a bespoke suit that fit his slender frame perfectly. His sidewhiskers were neatly trimmed and connected above his lip with a tidy ginger mustache.

The man hummed as he walked, hands in his pockets and shoulders back as he took in the scenery. Wraysbury was perfectly idyllic. It was precisely what people had in mind when reminiscing about the English countryside. It was just over a mile before he arrived at a wall of bleached stone. The road branched off and was blocked by an arch of vertical iron bars. There was a secondary, man-sized gate to one side of the main entrance, and a guard was station between the two points of ingress.

"Good afternoon," the traveler said, his accent revealing him to be from America's east coast. "My name is Alvin Peck. It's come to my attention you've admitted the cousin of my business associate. He's asked me to look in on her while I was in London on business."

The guard took Peck's papers and looked them over. He snorted when he saw the name of the patient. "Oh, her. The 'adventuress.'"

Peck smiled beneath his mustache. "I hope she hasn't been causing you much trouble."

"Pain in the arse, that one," the guard said as he handed the papers back. "She just got back from some expedition overseas, digging around in old tombs or whatever. No wonder she cracked as soon as she got back. No job for a woman, that's for sure. Constitutions can't handle it."

Peck smiled but said nothing.

"Go on. A nurse or an orderly will be at the front desk, they'll show you the rest of the way."

The American touched the brim of his hat, nodded in thanks, and continued through the smaller gate. His shoes crunched on the gravel of the main drive as he followed its curve. The entrance of the asylum was a red-brick clock tower, with wings extending out to either side before they curved back in around a central courtyard. The grounds were rolling stretches of well-manicured green lawn. He saw patients in white waistcoats and drawers moving along the hills under the attention of similarly-attired staff. As he ran his gaze along the arched windows of the building, he imagined he could hear the wails of the incarcerated within.

As promised, a young man named Gerald looked at Peck's information and escorted him for the rest of his trip. The central space of the asylum seemed to be a common area where men and women were allowed to interact. Gerald led Peck through a recreation area and the mess hall before he turned right and unlocked the door to the women's ward.

Peck noted that the floors were polished to a fine gleam. While wheelchairs and gurneys were stationed rather haphazardly outside the private rooms, the linens all seemed crisp and clean. There was a sharp smell of antiseptic and bleach, the odors of institutional health, and it burned Peck's nostrils. He reached up and touched a finger to his nose in an attempt to block out some of the sting. His eyes watered behind the lenses of his glasses.

"The guard seemed to know my friend's cousin quite well," Peck said. "Has she been a hellion?"

Gerald laughed. "Oh, no. She just likes telling stories about all her travels. She's an explorer, did you know? Treasure hunter. Did all sorts of incredible things. Sometimes she gets the patients a little riled up when she gets carried away. She doesn't mean any harm."

The American nodded. When they reached room 183, Gerald rapped his knuckles on the doorframe and waited for a response before he turned the knob. He stopped just over the threshold, and Peck followed to stand behind him. The room wasn't large, but it seemed comfortable. A neat and tidy bed next to a window that looked out over a small pond, a shelf of books, and a sitting area with two chairs separated by a table. The table bore the trappings of a tea service. The room's occupant was standing by the window with her back to the room.

"You have a guest."

"I haven't the time nor the inclination for guests, Gerald."

Peck said, "Come now. Not even for your cousin's favorite business associate?"

The patient turned slowly at the sound of the American's voice. She narrowed her eyes suspiciously and then chuckled under her breath. She turned back to the window.

"It's all right, Gerald. Leave us."

Gerald looked at Peck. "You'll be able to find your way back out?"

"Oh, I'm certain."

Content the guest wouldn't end up wandering the halls unescorted, Gerald closed the door behind him as he left. As soon as the latch clicked, the woman at the window laughed out loud and shook her head.

"You make a beautiful man, Dorothy Boone."

"I thought I was quite dashing." Dorothy took off her glasses, the Alvin Peck persona dissipating like fog as she moved into the room. Cora was round about Dorothy's age, give or take a few months, with black hair and eyebrows men had often called severe. She was the sort of woman who could quell a storm with a stern look and a wave of her hand. Dorothy was accustomed to seeing her old friend in suits, in the turtlenecks and wool skirts of academia. To see her clad in what amounted to pajamas, with her fine silken hair haphazardly pinned back, was quite shocking. She put past her alarm and tried to retain her calm.

"So what did you think of the accent?"

"Passable. But it could use some work."

Dorothy nodded and took a seat in one of the chairs. "Needs must, I'm afraid. The flatness of it forces me to lower the register of my voice. It's easier to pass as male that way."

Cora took the other seat and leaned forward to check the teapot. "Ah, splendid. Plenty to offer you a cuppa, if you're so inclined."

"Please."

"While I pour, you can tell me the meaning of this ruse."

Dorothy said, "Why... your emancipation, of course. I took stock of the premises when I entered. I can arrange for a boat to be waiting on the shores of the river, but we must get there first. I have some thoughts about the kitchen. You've probably had more time to determine the layout, so I'll defer to your judgment on some of my plans."

Cora paused in her pouring. "You mean to free me? Dorothy, I... I'm sorry, I thought I was quite clear in the letter. I admitted myself to Wraysbury."

"I thought that was just a ruse. Your brother~"

"Lawrence is dastardly as ever, yes. I've made arrangements so he can't get his grubby hands on my assets while I'm here. Oh, dear, I do apologize for the miscommunication. For you to have wasted all this time on an unnecessary rescue."

Dorothy said, "I suppose it wasn't a complete loss. It is wonderful to see you again."

"And you!" She took Dorothy's hands. "I know the letter said I didn't want guests, but to see your face is simply the best surprise. Even if it is hidden behind those whiskers."

"But why here? Why would you lock yourself away in an asylum?"

Cora said, "It's not as bad as you're thinking. I know we've all heard stories of women who were institutionalized for the high crime of thinking or having lewd thoughts. I did my research before choosing this place. The patients are well cared for. The staff is knowledgeable and compassionate. I am here for the very reason these hospitals were built in the first place. I needed... time. I needed a rest."

"Was your latest expedition so harrowing to require this?"

Cora began to answer but, instead, sighed heavily and fell back into her chair. Dorothy could see now that her skin was pale and gray smudges had taken up residence below her eyes. "What do you know about Khirokitia?"

"Not even how to spell it."

"Cheeky," Cora said, allowing a small grin. "It's on Cyprus. It was the site of a sudden and unexplained vanishing event. Nearly four hundred people suddenly gone without a trace. There are countless examples of things like this happening throughout prehistory. No one wrote anything down. They could have been victims of a flood or a drought, there might have been a virus, or an epidemic of child deaths that depleted the population. My goal was to discover which event caused the abandonment of Khirokitia."

She reached up and pressed her fingers to the bridge of her nose. Dorothy moved to the edge of her chair and touched her friend's arm.

"I'm sorry. I came here without warning. You must be overwhelmed..."

"No. No, it's quite all right." She sandwiched Dorothy's hand between hers. "We were there seven weeks before a member of my team discovered the entrance to a cavern running below the main village. It was a crevice so narrow that half the men with me were unable to join us on the descent. I went with three other women. We measured the depth to approximately three hundred yards before we found ourselves in a wide cavern. There were a series of archways in the stone. Too perfect to be natural formations. One of the women with me..." She looked down at their hands. "Her name was Ada. She was a brilliant and brave young girl. She offered to explore one of the tunnels and report back. We let her go into the darkness with a rope around her waist. To help prevent her from getting lost."

She fell silent. Dorothy patted her friend's hand, willing to give her as much time as necessary.

"There was something down there with us. We've seen creatures before, as I know you have. The Minotaur..." She smiled weakly, but the expression died as soon as it was birthed. She swallowed a lump in her throat and pulled her hands away from Dorothy. "This was something different. I could hear it in my head. In my soul. This was something darker. We never saw it. We never even heard it, not out loud. We only knew it was there because of a creeping dread in our chests. We called for Ada, but she never responded. So we started pulling on the rope. After several seconds, there was a vicious tug. And then the rope went slack. When we got it back to us, the loop was still tied. And it was bloody."

Dorothy said, "My God, Cora. I'm so sorry."

"None of us were brave enough to venture into the darkness. We knew it was a lost cause. The worst part was that we could only ascend one at a time. The girls insisted I go up first. I was stronger, you see, and they felt I could assist pulling the others up. Once I was on solid ground we sent the rope back down. The other two... the other two girls never took it. They never responded to us when we called down to them."

"Did anyone go back down to find out what happened?"

"I was the only one on the expedition slender enough to make the descent. I couldn't... I couldn't bring myself to..." A tear rolled down her cheek. "I knew it would leave us without answers but I-I..."

"Of course not," Dorothy said softly. "Hush. Anyone in your position would have done the same thing."

Cora said, "None of us could sleep that night. Not that we tried very hard. And to be honest, I haven't slept very well since. We stayed near the crevice in case anyone called for help. But it was utterly silent. We left in the morning and came home. I started looking for this place right away. I knew I needed something to... forget... or... move on..." Her voice trailed off, and she looked toward the window.

"If you should need anything, Cora, all you need do is ask."

"Thank you, Dorothy. For now I believe the only thing that will help is solitude. And perhaps medication." She bit her bottom lip. "I apologize, since you came so far to see me, but it's easier to try sleeping during the day."

"Of course." Dorothy stood and bent down to kiss Cora's forehead. "No distance is too far. If you need anything, even someone to sit beside you and silently serve you tea, you have my number."

Cora nodded her gratitude, then gripped Dorothy's hand. Her fingers were trembling, but her gaze was steady and focused. "The thing in the caverns below Cyprus. It's just one of many strange occurrences and encounters being reported in recent years. We both saw monsters under the earth in the Mediterranean. I fear this is only the beginning. There is a world beyond this one, a veil that conceals wonders and horrors we can't even imagine. I believe every time magic is used, we pierce that veil just a little bit further. During the War... so much magic was spent on the Continent. Spells cast every hour of every day on both sides. I fear we may only now be seeing the consequences of those actions. Be careful, my friend."

"And you as well. I'll come back to see you again as soon as you're ready. I'll dress more appropriately then."

Cora managed a smile. "It would be appreciated. I'm finding myself oddly attracted to you in this garb, and I'm confused enough as it is."

"Flatterer."

Cora winked and stood to escort Dorothy out of the room. Though she hated leaving her friend behind, Dorothy trusted that Cora best knew her own needs. If she said solitude was required for her peace of mind, then Dorothy would let her have it. She adjusted her hat and glasses as she walked back through the asylum, nodding a farewell to the desk clerk and the gateman as she passed. Once she was back on the road she peeled away her beard and removed her hat to let down her hair. She didn't care if anyone on the train was scandalized by the sight of a woman in a suit; she was more concerned about her friend's welfare.

She couldn't help but think Cora was right. Since the end of the War, the world seemed more unsettled than ever before. There had always been mysteries and creatures that should only exist in nightmares and fairy tales. But Dorothy knew the occult had been on the rise in recent years. The texture of reality did seem more fractured than ever before.

If there was a preternatural threat in the offing, she could take some comfort in the knowledge that she wouldn't have to face it alone.

Chapter One

There was a special kind of anxiety to being left alone in someone's home. Leonard Keeping graciously invited Trafalgar in when she arrived, but a bell summoned him upstairs as soon as she'd been escorted to the study. His wife, Agnes, had fallen ill on their last sea voyage and she found it unseemly to be tended by their manservant, Mr. Elmer. She of course granted him leave to see to her needs and found herself unattended. She had gotten to know the Keepings fairly well in the past year, but their acquaintance was nowhere near intimate enough to make her comfortable in their private rooms.

Her attention was captured by a bowl of fruit sitting on the table. Trafalgar crossed the room and picked up the orange. The first time she'd seen one was in Cairo after her ordeal on Enoch Solomon's ship. She was a child alone in a strange and frightening world with no guide or guardian. She'd seen the orange in a marketplace stall and was drawn to its shape and color. It reminded her of the sun but felt like a stone in her hands. She had stared at it, turning the strange thing over in her hand a few times before a tall man with a face burned red by the sun tapped her on the shoulder. He smiled at her, gestured with an orange of his own, and demonstrated how to break its skin with his teeth. Trafalgar did the same but bit too deep. She was startled by the juice spilling into her mouth and made a squeak of surprise.

The man had laughed at her reaction. He paid the stall owner for his items, then gestured at Trafalgar and added a coin. "I'll buy that one, too."

"Thank you," Trafalgar had said. He seemed surprised that she spoke English. "I have my own money." That is, she had money she'd found in Solomon's coat pocket. It wasn't much, but it would buy her an orange without incurring a debt to this strange man.

He shook his head and gestured with his orange. "Consider it a gift, young lady. Enjoy your treat." He smiled again and disappeared into the crowd.

Decades later, in the Keepings' study, Trafalgar brought the orange to her face and breathed deeply. Even now, citrus reminded her of the dust and crush of the Cairo marketplace. It was the first act of kindness in her new life, and it helped give her the courage to keep moving. There were kind people in the world; she just had to learn who to trust and who to be wary of.

Leonard Keeping swept back into the room and glanced in her direction on his way to the large walnut partners' desk in front of the window. "I've heard those can also be eaten, if one is so inclined."

Trafalgar smiled. "But then its simple beauty would be lost to us forever. Best to enjoy it while we can."

"There will always be oranges."

"But there is no guarantee we will always be here to enjoy them."

He took a seat and nodded. "Then take it, with my compliments."

"Thank you." She slipped the orange into her jacket pocket and approached the desk. "How is Agnes faring?"

"Better than she would lead you to believe," he said under his voice. He checked the doorway as if to make sure she hadn't followed him downstairs. "She can get very dramatic when she's ill. Of course I encourage that behavior by jumping to attention whenever she calls."

Trafalgar smiled. "Give her my best."

"I shall." He opened the humidor on his desk and removed a cigar. Out of deference for his guest, he simply held it in his hand without lighting it. "To what do I owe the pleasure of this visit? I hope you or Lady Boone weren't intending to ask for our aid for as you can see~"

"You have other priorities," Trafalgar said. "But no, this has nothing to do with an expedition. Rather, it's related to the events of last year when you and Mrs. Keeping, along with myself, Lady Boone, and a host of others in our profession were targeted by the Weeks brothers."

He grimaced. "I remember it well. We lost some good people that day."

"Yes." Trafalgar thought briefly of Adeline, her dear friend who had been a casualty of that awful endeavor. "Dorothy and I have continued working together over this past year, and it occurred to me that the Weeks' scheme could never work now. It only came close to succeeding because we were distrustful of each other. Our partnership would have made the deception impossible to believe. Just as we've become closer, we have become friends with you and your wife. That relationship doesn't preclude us from competing against one another, but it does give us allies should we require assistance in a future endeavor. I believe that in the grand scheme, we have more to gain by being friendly competitors rather than true rivals."

Leonard had leaned back in his chair to listen to her. He dragged a finger along his jaw, tracing the line of his beard. "You suggest we enter into a partnership? Like the one you formed with Lady Boone?"

"No, nothing like that. You and Agnes would remain independent, just as you've always been. You would have your expeditions and we would take our commissions. Competitors in the field just as always. But here on the home front, we would support one another. We would meet infrequently, discuss our work, support one another..."

"Like Doyle's Diogenes Club?"

"With less of an emphasis on 'gentlemen,' of course," Trafalgar said.

"Of course," Leonard said. "I fear this club would create a conflict of interest among its members. We do like our secrets and our exclusive knowledge."

Trafalgar said, "Competition is the lifeblood of any endeavor, it's true. But we could at the very least learn how to be civil to one another. Perhaps if such a club existed, we could have ferreted out Orville and Daniel Weeks before they became a threat. Dubourne, Mummery, Whitmore... my friend Adeline, they might all still be alive."

"And Lady Boone would take part in this? I only ask because, in the past, she's been rather adamant about working better on her own."

"I believe her partnership with me has changed her mind on that front." She laughed at his disbelieving look. "I wouldn't have believed it myself but we seem to work well together. We haven't yet had cause to work extensively as a pair, but we've met often to do research or archive our collections. We've gone on what she calls training missions so we can learn each other's foibles. She can be abrasive and self-centered but I'm sure she would say the same about me. We're both getting better at finding our footing."

Leonard nodded slowly, then shrugged. "I would have to discuss it with Agnes. And of course I would want insurance that it's not just the four of us in this guild. What you're proposing would do little good if it's only a handful of us."

"I quite understand," Trafalgar said. "We shall endeavor to recruit as many people as possible. If they should ask about who else we've spoken to, I trust I can share your names?"

"If it helps, yes."

Trafalgar stood up and extended her hand. "I thank you, Mr. Keeping. If we are to prevent another tragedy like the one we faced last year, we require unity rather than conflict."

Leonard took her hand and squeezed gently. "You and Lady Boone are sterling examples that it can be done. If the two of you have buried the hatchet, well... I suppose it must be possible for all of us."

Trafalgar smiled. "Lead by example, as they say. Thank you for meeting with me. And for the orange."

"My pleasure on both counts. I'll show you out."

He escorted her to the foyer, opening the door and peering out at the sky to make sure the looming clouds hadn't yet begun to spill. He faced her again as she buttoned up her coat.

"About the orange, Miss Trafalgar. It's fine to enjoy its presence. The scent and the weight of a thing, it's all worthy of appreciation. But if you wait too long, it begins to rot. The beauty fades and the fruit is useless to eat."

Trafalgar narrowed her eyes. "Are you certain Mrs. Keeping is doing well?"

He smiled and nodded. "She is fine. Now, at least. But there were moments at the on-set of the illness when I must confess I harbored some very dark thoughts. Enjoy the beauty, Miss Trafalgar, but do not ignore when the time for action has arrived."

"I will keep that in mind, sir. And I recommend heeding your own advice in terms of what I proposed today. You never know when the next Orville and Daniel Weeks may show their awful face."

"Your warning is heeded." He looked out into the street. "Has your driver been summoned, or...?"

"I walked. It's a beautiful day, after all."

Leonard looked at the storm clouds again and raised an eyebrow. "To each their own, I suppose. Good day, Miss Trafalgar."

She nodded and left the Keeping house. The storm was still well south of London. She would have plenty of time to make it home before the rains came even on foot. She began to walk and, at the corner, paused to retrieve the orange from her pocket. She hefted its weight in her hand and ran her thumb over the pebbled surface of its skin. There would always be oranges, she thought, and she intended to be around long enough to enjoy them for many years to come. But if the worst happened and her life was cut short, she would be loath to die with an orange uneaten in her pocket.

Trafalgar brought the orange to her lips and bit into the skin as she started across the street.

Dorothy was in her private office, her stockinged feet up on an ottoman as she held two maps up to the light. It had been three weeks since her visit with Cora, and she'd spent the intervening days trying to find some corroborating evidence of the network of underground caverns she believed existed under the Mediterranean. The labyrinth where she and Trafalgar had nearly been entombed was massive and, though Crete and Cyprus were nearly eight hundred kilometers apart, she felt the two had to be connected. A minotaur at one end, a beast that killed anyone who dared enter its territory at the other, and who knew what lay between?

She had drawn a map of Crete upon their return, and she had borrowed a map of Cyprus from a friend of Desmond's. The Mediterranean had been a sea for millions of years, but there was a theory that it must have dried up at some point. All it would take is the right factors occurring at the same time. If the sea was cut off from the Atlantic Ocean near Gibraltar, the heat and dryness of the region would evaporate the water in the blink of an eye. The Sahara would stretch all the way up into France, and the entire seabed would be exposed. Crete and Cyprus would be connected by a long stretch of salty and empty land. When she thought of it that way, eight hundred kilometers was practically right next door.

Three floors down, she heard someone enter the house. "Trix!" she called. "I'm in my private office. Would you mind coming up here, please?"

"I'm afraid I'm not Miss Sek," Trafalgar said.

"Oh. Come up regardless." She sat up straighter and put the maps down. It was still eminently odd to have Trafalgar enter her home unbidden and unannounced, but it quickly became a pain to make her ring the bell and summon Beatrice just to let her in every time she visited. There were very few people in London who were afforded that kind of access to Dorothy's home, and she was surprised every time she was reminded she'd extended that courtesy to a woman she'd once considered her nemesis.

Trafalgar nudged the door open and peered inside before stepping over the threshold. "I hope I'm not intruding."

"Only brainwork," Dorothy said. "Sometimes those tasks must be placed on the back burner in order to find a solution. I'm happy for the distraction. I assume you're returning from the Keepings' residence?"

"I am. I spoke to Leonard, but Agnes was under the weather. Unfortunate for them, but also for us. He was reluctant to give an answer one way or the other without her input."

Dorothy sighed. "I suppose I understand. That's one reason I hope to never be married. Casting my lot in with someone else, making every decision a democratic ordeal... it sounds harrowing. To be avoided at all costs."

Trafalgar said, "If anyone else heard you speak like that, they might feel very sorry for poor Professor Tindall."

"Ah, poor Professor Tindall and our never-ending engagement. It makes one wonder why he puts up with me at all." She smiled and winked as she returned the maps to their proper places behind her desk. "Leonard is a good man. And Agnes is intelligent. They'll decide that our idea has merit. We are stronger together than if we are constantly at each other's throats."

"He suggested that you and I are sterling examples of what we hope to accomplish. If the two of us can work together..."

Dorothy laughed. "What a cheeky bugger he is. Agnes would have thumped him if she'd heard him talking that way. I do hope she was well…"

"He seemed to believe the worst was past, yes."

"Excellent. I'll call on her myself later. We can be friendly while still competing. The world is large enough and history so vast that there are treasures enough for everyone to find."

Trafalgar moved toward the window. "When I came in, you thought I was Miss Sek. I would have expected her to be here at this time of day."

"As would I." Dorothy furrowed her brow to show her consternation. "She's become annoyingly unreliable of late. Long and unexplained absences, reluctance to discuss where she's been or who she's meeting with. If things don't change soon, I may have to take drastic action."

Trafalgar looked at her with concern. "You don't mean you'd fire her."

"Of course not!" Dorothy said. "Perish the thought. I'd be lost without my Trix. No, I simply meant that if she doesn't explain herself soon, I may have to resort to following her. I would not like to violate her trust in that manner, but if she is in some manner of trouble, then I must do everything in my power to let her know I can help."

"Surely she would come to you for help."

"She can be stubborn."

Trafalgar laughed.

"Oh, shut up." She sighed and shook her head as she examined the papers scattered across her desk. "In the meantime, my correspondence has gone woefully awry."

"Would you like some help sorting it?"

Dorothy squared her shoulders and gave Trafalgar a playfully skeptical look. "Hm. Speaking of trust…"

Trafalgar rolled her eyes and picked up one of the letters. "Yes. The whole of this past year has been a diabolical plot simply so I could discover your grocery bill is very overdue."

Dorothy smirked as she snatched the paper away and took a seat. Trafalgar sat across from her and discarded the grocery invoice for something she hoped would be a bit more interesting.

Chapter Two

LESS THAN two miles from the opulent comforts of Dorothy Boone's townhouse on Threadneedle Street, Beatrice Sek navigated the warren of Bethnal Green's slums in search of a specific address. It was harder than it might have been in other parts of the city. Intersections were unmarked and numbers had faded or been removed from buildings. The day was prematurely dark due to the storm clouds, and long shadows stretched out from every ragged awning and threatening alleyway. A discarded couch had been moved to block one of the alleys, innards bursting from its seams. Two grimy boys in filthy clothing were perched on the back of it and eyed her carefully as she passed. Beatrice met their gaze as she passed and resisted a smile as their defiant expressions turned to wariness and then something close to fear.

Not long ago these had been her streets. Anyone who dared cross her soon learned their mistake. She was a thief and a pickpocket, a grifter and a confidence artist. She knew her time with Dorothy hadn't softened her - some of her most brutal fights occurred after she moved into the townhouse - but living a life of privilege had put her at a disadvantage to those who had to fight for everything they had.

She was dressed in an old work shirt and pants so worn that the patches overlapped in several places in an effort to blend in, but there was only so much she could do. She could hide the affluence of her current situation but it was harder to disguise her Chinese features. Rich or poor, she stood the risk of being assaulted simply for being an immigrant. She ignored the comments she heard muttered as she passed. People who were out of work and assumed she or her family had arrived to steal jobs, people who were just hateful to outsiders on principle, or those who combined the two and added the extra sin of being a woman. The hate and fear radiated off of everyone she passed, but she wasn't afraid of what they might do. She was worried about the damage she might cause if one of them chose to start a fight.

The narrow street she was on dead-ended at a sharp right angle with the connecting road blocked by a plywood wall and a metal dumpster. A group of men were seated in front of the building to her left. Most of the windows were boarded over, with those that weren't leading out onto hazardous-looking fire escapes. When Beatrice left the street to approach the building, one of the loitering men stood up to block her path. She continued walking until she risked colliding with him. Only then did she meet his gaze. He was a few inches taller than her, forcing her to lift her chin. His cheeks were hollow, his nose long and thin with a bulb at the end, and he wore his cap pushed forward to shade his eyes.

He examined her for a long moment. "You have the English?"

"If you're asking whether I speak the language, the answer is yes," Beatrice said. "I speak English, among others."

"There's nothing for you here, little girl. Turn around and walk away now or else leavin' will cost you. Ya twig?"

Beatrice said, "I have business inside. There's someone I need to speak with."

He smiled to reveal he was missing his front tooth. "We're the friendly ones. Whyn't you stay out here 'n' see if you can handle us 'fore you go disturbing anyone inside?"

"I don't have time for this." Beatrice reached into the man's jacket and removed the brass knuckles he had stashed there. When he grabbed her wrist, she spun around and threw her weight against him. He stumbled and she hooked her foot around his leg, then kicked forward. He fell and sprawled on the grass, and Beatrice dropped her knee onto his chest. Now she could see the revolver that had been hidden under his arm and she sneered as she pulled it from the holster. The grip was clammy with sweat, but a disgusting weapon was better than nothing.

By now the other men had risen to defend their comrade. Beatrice punched the man she had pinned and got to her feet as the first attacker reached her. He swung a knife and she used the brass knuckles to knock it out of his hand. She stepped forward and forced him into a violent embrace, but he wasn't prepared for her to drop her knees and wrap her arms around his waist. She lifted him off the ground and surged forward with him as a battering ram. A bullet from one of his friends sank into his shoulder, and one man inadvertently stabbed him because he had been leading with the blade of his knife.

Beatrice tossed him aside and dropped into a crouch to await the two men left standing. One man landed a punch, something Beatrice found impressive even as his friend took advantage of her distraction to pin her arms behind her. She struggled against him but found he was far too strong for her to break his grip. The puncher stood in front of her, so close she could smell his rotten breath as he grabbed the front of her clothes.

"Huh. She's a woman, all right. Don't fight like one, that's for sure."

Beatrice let her knees go limp and threw herself toward the ground. The man holding her fell forward and head-butted the man who had been groping her. Both men cried out as one man's nose was broken by the other's chin. Beatrice's arms were freed, so she punched her would-be rapist between the legs. He folded and she stood up, turning to face the man who had been holding her arms. His upper lip and chin were smeared with blood.

Beatrice held out her hand palm-up and magicked one of the fallen guns to her. She wrapped her fingers around the weapon and aimed it at his head.

"If this fight is to continue, I'll be forced to use every weapon at my disposal. How do you think you would fare in that encounter?"

His answer was to flee. Beatrice waited to make sure he was truly retreating, examined the men she had left bleeding or otherwise indisposed on the yellow grass, and stuck the gun into her belt as she stepped over them.

"Don't bother getting up, gentlemen. I'll show myself inside."

She had only taken two steps into the darkened lobby before she heard a chorus of weapons clicking. She froze where she was on the broken tile and held her hands out to either side. Directly ahead of her was a door that had been nailed and painted shut. The ground floor had four apartments, none of them with doors and all of them too dark to see inside. To her left was a staircase leading up to the first story landing, and it was from these shadows that the voice of Dov originated.

"You have three weapons trained on you right now. You're good, but I don't think you're quite that good."

"I've faced worse odds. Renata Koessel, I presume? The Dove?"

"Dah-v, darling," the woman said. "A subtle but important difference. It sounds like the bird of peace, but in my father's tongue it means bear. It is a word whose true danger lurks beneath the surface. Where did you hear my name?"

"From a man in Whitechapel. It didn't come cheap. I received his name from a soldier who fought in the Great War. I've been searching a long time for someone with the intelligence and wisdom to provide the answers I seek."

There was nothing but silence from above for nearly a full minute. Then at last, following a signal Beatrice didn't notice, the weapons leveled at her were disarmed.

Dov said, "Come up."

Beatrice lowered her hands. She crouched slowly, making sure her hands were visible as she removed the gun from her belt by pinching the grip. She put it down on the tile, then placed the brass knuckles next to it.

"I did not require you to disarm yourself."

"I would never enter your inner sanctum with tools of violence."

Dov said nothing. Beatrice stepped over the weapons and ascended the stairs. As soon as she reached the landing she was greeted by a strong wave of jasmine undercut by a bitterer, earthier scent she couldn't identify. There was only one door and it stood open, revealing a lavish office space. Her feet sank into the carpet when she entered and city sounds she hadn't been aware of hearing through the walls were suddenly muted by the thick curtains.

There was a sitting area in the middle of the room, and Dov sat facing the door in one of the massive wingback chairs. She was younger than Beatrice had expected, only barely in her forties, with dark hair pulled back to frame a strong, square jaw and a slender throat. Her eyebrows were thick and regally arched, leaving her with a haughty and judging expression. She wore a red dressing gown that was open at the throat to reveal the ruffled collar of the blouse underneath.

"Tell me your name."

"Beatrice Sek."

Dov said, "Your true name. The name you were born with."

She hesitated. Names had power, but everything she'd heard of this woman led her to believe it would be safe. "Bao Tai Sek."

Dov rolled her eyes. "Your *true* name."

"That is the only name I know."

"Hm." Dov brought her hands up to steeple the fingers. "You've obviously gone to a lot of trouble to find me. What do you expect in return?"

Beatrice said, "I'm told you're a witch."

Her lips curled ever so slightly. "I won't cast spells on those who have wronged you. Judging from your display downstairs, you wouldn't need my help with that, anyway. You're a powerful creature in your own right."

"I barely did anything."

"You took out a group of men who intended to cause you bodily harm without resorting to your magic until the end. A weaker practitioner would have flattened them where they stood. You have discipline. That is important. It's the main reason I had my security officers hold their fire when you came in."

Beatrice said, "There was no security downstairs. I heard the weaponry and felt their sights on me, but they didn't really exist. That was you."

One eyebrow arched, her green eyes narrowed, and her smile widened. "Once again, you impress me, Miss Sek. I can only imagine what you seek."

"As you said, I'm adept at magic. I've always been able to draw and manifest energy. But last year while I was drawing a large amount of power, something unprecedented happened. I have a large tattoo on my back. While I was conjuring, the ink began to glow. I felt no pain, but the energy burnt through the clothes

I was wearing. I was told you're the most learned practitioner in London. I've jumped many hurdles just to attain an audience with you."

Dov said, "The tattoo's design... what is it?"

"A tree."

Beatrice opened the pocket of her coat and withdrew a drawing she'd had made of the tattoo. It had been on her back in her earliest memory, a tree that seemed to grow from her hairline to spread its branches over her shoulders and down her spine. It seemed to grow as she did; the design never faded or stretched as her body changed over the years. Until the incident on Knossos, she'd thought it was just some peculiar artwork, perhaps a way for her birth parents to eventually identify her, but now she was afraid it had a deeper purpose.

Dov refused to take the drawing. "I need to see it with my own eyes."

Beatrice scoffed.

"Miss Sek, if I wished to see your naked body, I would not play coy. I would simply ask." She gestured. "I'm only interested in answering your question to the best of my ability. I cannot do that from a potentially flawed duplication. If you want my expertise..."

"Fine." Beatrice loosened the tie at her throat and tugged at her collar. She pulled the shirt over her head and bundled the material in front of her chest as she turned around. The chair creaked as Dov stood up and moved closer. Beatrice looked over her shoulder and saw Dov held a ball of light over her cupped hand. When she brought it close to Beatrice's back, she felt just a hint of warmth from it. Any humor she'd seen in Dov's expression was now replaced with a stern professional curiosity.

"How many branches? Have you ever counted?"

"Four hundred and twenty-six."

Dov clicked her tongue against her teeth. "It's a focus. But I've never seen one so intricate. May I touch it?" Beatrice nodded. A moment later she felt a cool finger tracing one of the lines. She tensed to avoid shivering.

"Sorry."

"It's all right."

Dov said, "How old is this?"

"At least thirty years. It was done when I was a child."

Dov's finger stopped moving. "When you were a child? Who did it?"

"I don't know. I don't have any memories of~"

"Stop." Dov dropped her finger and stepped back. "I cannot help you."

Beatrice pulled her shirt up to cover herself as she turned to look at the witch. "What are you talking about?"

Dov crossed the room quickly, her gown parting around her legs like a bird taking flight. She stopped at a bookshelf next to the window and took a moment to run her fingers along the spines before she found what she was looking for.

She took it from the shelf and cradled it with one hand as she flipped pages with the other.

"There are only fragments of this story that still exist. When magic was first identified, when the first groups of adepts were found, they had histories and prophecies. One of those prophecies told of four harbingers who would signal the beginning of a great magical age. Each would represent an aspect of being. Earth, wind, water, and fire. When these four elementals are brought together, they would bring about the fifth element: void."

Beatrice said, "They would destroy the world?"

"That is unclear. All that's known is that each child would be born into the world with a mark identifying them. A mark like a tattoo in the shape of a tree to signify the earth element."

Beatrice became cold. "You're saying I'm one of these elementals?"

"That, I cannot tell you." She closed the book and held it against her chest. "The prophecy is incomplete and we have only your tattoo as evidence. But you asked for my insight and I have given it to you. There is the matter of the prophecy being Japanese whereas you are Chinese. Maybe it traveled, maybe it was spread throughout that corner of the world, or maybe it's completely unrelated. I only know one thing for certain, and that is what I felt when I touched your tattoo." She held up her finger. "You are powerful, Miss Sek. You terrify me."

"I should go."

Dov put a hand on Beatrice's arm. "If you come back, it won't be necessary to cripple my guards. I would very much appreciate a chance to explore your tattoo in depth."

There was no doubt now that she was being flirted with. She arched an eyebrow as she finished buttoning her blouse and smoothed down the material. "I thought you said you were terrified of me."

Dov smiled. "Yes. And that excites me."

Beatrice didn't know how to respond to that, so she simply nodded and stepped out of the other woman's reach. She had much to think about, and Dorothy was most likely wondering where she was.

Chapter Three

Eventually the gloom grew so deep that Dorothy was forced to turn on the lamps just so they could see. Trafalgar excused herself so she could try reaching home before the rain started. Dorothy wished her luck and moved to the library. Her mind was full with Cora's account of what happened to her last expedition. She had a vague memory of reading an archaeological theory implying the Mediterranean Sea had been dry some millions of years earlier when a tectonic shift caused the Strait of Gibraltar to cut it off from the Atlantic Ocean. Civilizations could have built cities on the salt plains of the newborn desert, and those lost cities could be key to understanding where the Minotaur and its ilk had come from.

She wasn't aware the storm had finally broken until the room's temperature dropped low enough for her to want a shawl. She looked up from the book and smiled at the irony of not hearing rain because she was so absorbed with reading about a desert. Now it was all she could hear; pelting on the windows and the roof, a steady and comforting sound that helped fill the empty house. After her grandmother died but before Beatrice moved in, Dorothy had tried to get used to the silence. She'd never succeeded.

Leaving her books open on the table, she went to retrieve a shawl from her bedroom. She was halfway across the landing when the front door opened. She stepped to the banister and looked down, knowing even before she looked who she would see. The clothes threw her at first, but it quickly became apparent that it was indeed Beatrice dressed in a raggedy, neglected outfit. She was soaked to the skin and paused in the foyer to attempt drying off before venturing further.

"Trix," Dorothy said. "I'll get you a towel."

Beatrice glanced up and said nothing. Dorothy went to the linen closet and retrieved a pair of towels, tucking them under her arm before she descended the stairs. She put one down and Beatrice obediently stepped onto it so she would stop dripping on the carpet. Dorothy wrapped the towel around Beatrice's hair and rubbed it vigorously as Beatrice undid the ties and catches of her clothes.

"Thank you," Beatrice said.

"Of course. If you were going to be out, you could have used the car."

"I wasn't going very far."

"Regardless..." She stepped back and helped Beatrice out of the sopping-wet clothes. They let them fall onto the towel at Beatrice's feet rather than transferring the wetness to Dorothy's outfit. "Come with me. I'll take you upstairs and find you something dry to wear."

Beatrice followed Dorothy upstairs without a word. Her silence was alarming. She would have expected a self-deprecating comment, a joke about being in her underwear, anything.

Beatrice's bedroom was at the far end of the second floor, a cozy space with a slanted roof and a view of the courtyard between her home and the back of the building on the neighboring street. Beatrice went to the closet and removed a boxy pink chemise. She stepped into it and drew the straps up onto her shoulders as Dorothy opened the curtains to let in the meager light allowed by the storm. Beatrice sat on the bed and Dorothy knelt on the carpet in front of her.

"My hypothesis is that whatever you've been seeking has either yielded results you didn't expect, or you have reached a dead end and don't know where to turn. Whichever it is, I hope you know you can come to me. Whatever you need."

Beatrice touched Dorothy's cheek and let her palm linger. "I know."

Dorothy turned her head and kissed Beatrice's wrist. "Whenever you're ready, I'll be here to listen. I love you, Trix."

"I love you, Dorothy."

Dorothy put her head down in Beatrice's lap, and Beatrice loosened the ties of Dorothy's hair until it was spread across her lap like a spill of crimson ink. Dorothy closed her eyes as she was petted by Beatrice's long, slender fingers. This dashing and heroic woman came into Dorothy's life intending to rob her. Instead she had been trapped by an artifact carelessly left out in the open. When Dorothy finally came home, she freed Beatrice from her prison. Since then Beatrice had felt indebted to her savior, even though she was responsible for saving Dorothy multiple times as well.

And now Beatrice was sneaking out of the house on secretive missions, dressed in outfits she would have worn as a cat burglar. Whatever her purpose, Dorothy knew she could either handle it on her own or would ask for help as soon as it became necessary. She stroked Beatrice's thighs, her fingers easing up the lace edge of her chemise. Beatrice lifted up off the mattress and pulled the smooth material up to her waist, accepting Dorothy's offer without speaking. Dorothy pressed her lips to Beatrice's thighs as she eased her legs apart. She couldn't apply her expertise or problem-solving skills to whatever was concerning her dearest friend, but there was a way she could ease the tension in her.

Dorothy flicked her fingertips against her tongue, then rubbed them against Beatrice's sex. Her index and middle fingers parted Beatrice's lips, and she used her thumb to massage the sensitive pink skin she had exposed. Lowering her head, she used her tongue and thumb in concert. Beatrice had helped her relax after enough expeditions; it was the least Dorothy could do to repay the favor.

Beatrice kept her hands in Dorothy's hair and began moving her hips against Dorothy's mouth. She made quiet noises of pleasure, grunts and gasps that occasionally trailed off into muttered oaths and curses. Dorothy smiled as she used the tip of her tongue to tease. Beatrice was usually so in control of herself that it was fun to take her to the edge and hold her over without letting her fall. She extended her middle finger and pushed it inside, then joined it with a second.

"Oh, Lady Boone..."

A thrill ran through her at the use of her proper title, and she redoubled her efforts. Beatrice twisted strands of Dorothy's hair in her hands and pulled as she climaxed, arching her back before collapsing onto her pile of blankets and pillows. Dorothy turned her head and brushed her cheek against Beatrice's thigh, kissed her sex once more, and then pushed herself up. Beatrice twisted on the mattress and watched as Dorothy reached under her dress to remove her undergarments without actually undressing. She let the thin materials fall before she straddled Beatrice's hips.

"I hope you know I'm here if you need me."

Beatrice licked her fingers before easing her hand under Dorothy's skirts. "I've never been more certain of anything in my life, ma'am."

Dorothy closed her eyes as Beatrice's hand explored her most sensitive areas. She put her hands on Beatrice's shoulders and bit her bottom lip, arching her back as she rocked forward against Beatrice's touch. She sank down and kissed Beatrice, whose free hand slid up the outside of Dorothy's leg. Their lips and tongues met, and Beatrice twisted to blaze a trail down Dorothy's throat.

"You smell like the library."

"What does that entail...?"

"Dust. Smoke and candlewax. Old books." She sucked the skin just below Dorothy's ear, making her shudder. "Inkwells and paper. What were you up to before I arrived, Lady Boone?"

Dorothy shivered again. "In good time, Miss Sek. For now, perhaps you can tell me what else I smell like. Be as detailed as possible."

Beatrice chuckled and breathed deep.

Dorothy woke from a light doze to the smell of ozone and petrichor, the sublime smell of dirt after the rain, and the far more unique smell of a sleeping Beatrice Sek. She turned her head and kissed the curve of her lover's shoulder. They were lying tangled together on Beatrice's too-small bed rather than the larger one in Dorothy's bedroom. She took a moment to appreciate how blissful the moment was. Just her, the woman she loved, and a room large enough to hold them. Everything else was an unnecessary complication.

The storm was still pouring down, and it made telling time difficult. Dorothy knew it was well past dinnertime by the rumbling in her stomach, so she kissed Beatrice's lips and carefully extricated herself from the other woman's arms and legs to go in search of sustenance. She stooped to pick up her blouse and was slipping into it when Beatrice stirred and said her name. Dorothy returned to her and sat on the edge of the bed. Curls of black hair had fallen into Beatrice's face so Dorothy brushed them away.

"I've been looking for something," Beatrice said. "You know that my birth is a mystery."

Dorothy nodded.

"The past few months, I've been looking for information. Either about the old man who left me with my parents, or the ship that brought us to France, anything that I could follow back to the source."

"I see. And have you found anything?" Beatrice pressed her lips together and Dorothy deduced the answer. She patted Beatrice's leg through the sheet. "Nothing you wish to share. I understand. In your own time, then."

Beatrice averted her gaze. "What if I discover something about myself that makes you hate me?"

Dorothy bent down and kissed Beatrice's lips, touching her chin to turn her so they were looking at each other again. "I could never hate you, Bao Tai Sek. You could anger me, or frustrate me. You could irritate me with ease or drive me absolutely insane, but I would never hate you." She put her hand over Beatrice's heart. "For as long as you are the same person you've always been, you don't have to worry about losing me."

"Thank you, Lady Boone."

"I like it when you call me Lady Boone during the deed," Dorothy said, "and ma'am is fine for when you're on duty. But I do so enjoy hearing you say my name."

Beatrice smiled. "Dorothy."

"Ah. There it is." She bent down and caught Beatrice's bottom lip between hers. Beatrice lifted her head off the pillow slightly to prolong their contact, then dropped back down. Dorothy chuckled and stroked Beatrice's hair. "You've been worrying me, Trix. These errands you wouldn't tell me anything about, the outfits, your dour moods. I have no doubt you can handle yourself no matter what you're up against. But I feel helpless to think you're facing it alone. So I'll tell you what: if you need anything from me. Money, research, weapons, anything at all, simply ask and you'll have it. You don't need to explain what it's for. You can keep your secrets."

Beatrice said, "Thank you, Dorothy. That means the world to me. Should I need anything, you'll be the first to know."

"Very good. And as it should be." She winked and patted Beatrice's cheek. "I'll go see if I can scrounge up something to eat. Do you feel like fruits or meats?"

"Bread. Something with bread or crackers."

"I'll see what I can whip together." She kissed Beatrice again and left the bedroom. Before going downstairs, she stopped in her bedroom to retrieve her robe. Trafalgar or Desmond might decide to drop by while she was making dinner, and she wasn't keen on providing them voyeuristic thrills. When she reached the ground floor, she went to the front of the house and peered out at the street. The storm had turned the city blue-gray. Bankers held briefcases or newspapers over their heads to provide what scanty protection they could get from the downpour as they hurried past her building.

She imagined what would happen if the rain never stopped. If the swirling streams in the gutter were allowed to swell, would they eventually swallow the entire street? Would they cap the buildings until no evidence of the great metropolis was left? She doubted anything as huge as London was lost beneath the waters of the Mediterranean, but the thought of settlements and civilizations that had been washed away in a great flood was too intriguing to ignore. She let the curtain fall back into place and went to ponder the possibilities as she prepared dinner.

Chapter Four

Trafalgar elected to take the tram rather than walk back to Bankside. Since Adeline's death, she took no pleasure in driving. Her car remained untouched and hidden beneath a tarp in a garage space she spent far too much for. She arrived at her home and office just before the rains began, and she stood for a moment in the doorway to watch as the first hedge washed across the dry grid of granite setts that made up the road. She relished the cool breeze that came with the storm and tilted her head back, eyes closed, to fully appreciate it.

When she finally went inside, she spent a few minutes turning on lamps and lighting candles. She lived in the downtrodden district for the same reason so many others in her profession also hid in the slums. They stored countless historic treasures in their homes, and a modest exterior was the best deterrent to thieves. Dorothy Boone, of course, was one of the many who did nothing to disguise her wealth, but she at least took the precaution of living on one of the most secure streets in all of London. Her townhouse, along with the two on either side she had turned into a vault and library, were surrounded by banks. The whole of England's wealth was at risk on that street, and Dorothy was tucked snug in the midst of every protective measure the government could throw at it.

The truth was Trafalgar had lived in the same place since arriving in London just after the turn of the century. Stolen from her homeland, abandoned in Cairo, she quickly discovered that London was the heart of the world. Getting there was time-consuming and expensive, but she found ways. She earned passage by working in the kitchens of airships and steamers. She worked as a commis waiter and dishwasher and, through those jobs, improved her English by listening to the staff and clients she served. She ate whatever she could sneak off the plates and saved her paltry salary so she could afford housing when she finally arrived at her destination.

London seemed like a fairy tale. She'd never even seen pictures, only heard it described. Streets of gold. Eternal fog. Magic so thick in the air you could practically taste it. She refused to believe the most fantastical aspects of what people said; even at that age, she understood people tended to romanticize their homeland. Still, even if only a fraction of it was accurate, then it was definitely the place she needed to be. She could also count on the fact that every ship she sought passage on - land, sea, or air - all had multiple departures to the capital of the world.

When she arrived she continued looking for work. There was no shortage of jobs to be done by someone who was strong and willing. Compared to the life she'd been taken from, struggling just to stay alive and keep her siblings in one piece, there was no job she considered too menial or taxing. She saved everything she could and was eventually able to buy the tenement she currently called home. Others talked about moving up in the world. Trafalgar tried to find ways to improve the place she already had.

Once she was established enough to relax, she finally went out to see the sights of her new home. She only intended to visit a museum so she could educate herself on the beauty of the world after spending so much time in its cargo bays and washrooms. She quickly became lost and asked a man where she could find the National Gallery.

"Just south, love," he said, "on Trafalgar Square."

It was the first time she'd ever heard of the place, the first time she knew the origin of her name. It was given to her by a sailor who misheard the name "Tall Girl" because her tongue had been dry and numb at the time. Now she knew where the phrase had come from, and the museum was forgotten. She ran to the square, frightening off a kit of pigeons as she arrived. A massive tower she later identified as Nelson's Column stretched into the sky. She stood at its base and looked up at the man it honored.

By that point she was so attached to the name Trafalgar that she couldn't imagine assuming a new one, but she was irked by the fact she shared it with such a well-known tribute. She turned in a slow circle and looked at the fountains and the majestic museum. Now she could see other statues, all of men. One was seated in a chair, the other standing in a relaxed pose. She snorted at the thought of being named after altars to these men. They were all most likely soldiers and colonists whose victories had been won with a sea of blood from native people. She swore to live her life so that, one day, her actions would be brought to mind when people said Trafalgar.

She smiled now when she thought about that goal. She knew she would never achieve that level of fame, but it was no great loss. She was well-known to those who mattered. She was famous in certain circles. That was enough for her.

Trafalgar went to the kitchen and cooked herself a small evening meal. As she prepared her food, she hummed a tune that complimented the rhythm of the rain beating on the windows. Outside she could hear the neighbors shouting to their children to come inside before they caught their death of cold. She smiled and moved to the window. Four children, all under the age of ten, filled the alleyway with their strange formations, like a flock of geese constantly moving toward and away from one another. These families were a big part of why she had never left Bankside. Dorothy chose to utilize existing protection of the financial world, but Trafalgar was forced to protect herself. In doing so, she helped to make the district safer for people like the children currently being dragged back inside by their mother.

When her food was ready, Trafalgar took it into her modest library. It was nothing compared to Dorothy's archive, but it served her purposes well. During her visit, Dorothy had mentioned her current undertaking with the Mediterranean Sea and what might lie beneath it. Trafalgar was skeptical but intrigued at the possibility. She skimmed the spines of her books until she found a collection of journal entries from ship captains and their crews.

The author had collected accounts from across the globe of mysterious encounters at sea, monsters rising from the depths, whirlpools, unidentified creatures spotted on the shore, and the like. It had long been a subject of interest to her; she was desperate to know if anyone had ever encountered anything like what she saw in the Gulf of Aden. So far she hadn't had any luck. But she remembered tales from the Mediterranean Sea and thought it may help Dorothy in her quest.

She sat at a table with the book open to her left, her meal to the right, and she browsed through the pages while she ate. In her mind she held a map of the sea. The Minotaur was one pinned area. Cora Hyde's frightening encounter, which Dorothy had relayed to her, was another. The Gulf of Aden was too far south to be part of the same phenomenon, but it could still be related somehow.

There were a great number of reports from near the sea-port Jaffa, which was speculated to the point of departure for the Biblical character of Jonah. Most translations of the story say he was devoured by a whale, but the more accurate translation was "cetacean," meaning any sea creature larger than a dolphin. Perhaps there was a creature haunting the port of Jaffa which was large enough to swallow a man whole without killing him. Pliny recounted a tale in which Perseus slayed a cetacean and brought its body back to Rome for display. The bones were forty feet long and "taller than an Indian elephant." It was hard to imagine such a creature existing without being seen for thousands of years. Perhaps they had gone extinct. Or perhaps they had gotten better at hiding.

In the book, there were excerpts from eyewitness accounts of giant squids wrapping their tentacles around ships and crushing them into kindling. She read about islands which sank below the surface only to reappear and split in half to reveal a horrendous mouth. Terrified men wrote of huge unseen objects creating a wake wider than a mile as something stalked them across the ocean. Thirteenth century Norwegian explorers warned of "sea-mist" and the kraken. Even as recently as seventy years ago, Melville and Verne had written of giant squids haunting the depths. It seemed that from the moment mankind set out onto the oceans, they'd spoken of monstrous creatures that lived beneath the waves waiting to lay claim to unsuspecting sailors. The waters of the world were over a kilometer deep, in some places far deeper, and they'd barely scratched the surface of what was hidden in those dark depths.

Trafalgar leaned back and rubbed a hand across her face. She'd gone hopelessly off-topic, her intention to learn about a potential link between the Minotaur and Cora Hyde's adversary had led her off into an unexpected direction. But it was fascinating! Who knew how many creatures lurked undiscovered under the surface of their world? How many of them might be monstrous at first glance? The Minotaur had turned out to be a reasonable sort, even if he was irritable and strong as an ox. Dorothy had found a way to reason with it, to earn its favor.

Her meal was finished and she felt she could do no further research without sacrificing her mental faculties. She returned the book to the shelf and carried her dishes back to the kitchen. Sea monsters and underwater caverns, cities lost under the waters of the Mediterranean... there could be entire cultures that had been wiped out by floods just waiting to be uncovered. She'd always thought of archaeology as digging in the dirt, brushing away sand to find something buried ages ago. She never considered the possibility of excavating something submerged.

Trafalgar smiled as she rinsed out her bowl. Dorothy Boone had promised their partnership wouldn't be dull, and she was certainly delivering on that.

The rain continued through the night. Dorothy sat in her study, maps of the Mediterranean and its various shores spread on the table around her. Some of the maps were drawn by her own hand, others were purchased or pilfered from those who had no business owning them. In the center of the maps were her books, adrift on the charcoal-and-ink version of the sea. Pliny the Elder believed the Gibraltar Strait, then called the Columns of Hercules, had been split open by the god to allow the Atlantic Ocean entry. What if some nefarious civilization lived in the salt plains of the Mediterranean? What if someone had intervened? A cataclysmic event that forever changed the face of the planet just to wipe out one country or faction.

In 1867, Karl Mayer-Eymar speculated that the time period for this event was somewhere in the neighborhood of five million years ago. Dorothy tapped her pen against her lip and narrowed her eyes as she mentally did the math. "Around the time the first hominids showed up. Or alternatively... what we think of as the first hominids were actually the survivors of this event. Something disastrous caused this flood and mankind was devastated. It was apocalyptic. The survivors were forced to rebuild from scratch. My God, this could have been the end of the world."

The door to her study opened and she heard Beatrice's soft tread. "I'll be back to bed in a moment, Trix."

"That would be your own bed, I would hope."

"Why..." She looked up at the scent of tea and toast. Her confusion deepened when she saw Beatrice was bathed and dressed for work. She looked toward the window as if it had betrayed her.

"It can't possibly be morning."

Beatrice put the tray down on a side table where it wouldn't affect Dorothy's research materials. "I hate to be the bearer of bad news. It would seem you've lost the entire evening."

Dorothy sighed. "Well, at least it can't be said the time was wasted. I'll have my breakfast and then take a quick nap." She put her hand over the books. "Touch nothing on this desk, Trix. Any attempt at organization would be catastrophic."

"Of course, ma'am. When shall I wake you?"

Dorothy looked at the clock. "Three hours should be more than enough." She stood up and stared down at her books again. "There is something beneath the Mediterranean, Trix. Pieces of it have been coming up for years, but now I fear the hidden things are becoming bolder. The last time they walked the Earth, humanity nearly destroyed itself trying to stop them. I hope we have better luck."

Chapter Five

Just over a week later, Dorothy was forced to stop working for a night out with Desmond. He'd gotten them tickets to the theater and also invited along one of his students. Their guest was a bright young man named Carter Marsh. He was nervous and almost unbearably young, just shy of twenty-one and hesitant to say anything upon his arrival at the townhouse. Desmond was looking sharp in his best duds, and Dorothy accepted the compliments of both gentlemen on her own outfit. She'd invited Clara Levy, a young woman she'd met at the library to serve as Carter's date and the foursome set off for dinner and light entertainment.

"Clara and Carter, Desmond and Dorothy," she had said with a laugh as they climbed into the hackney cab. "Why, aren't we adorable?"

Desmond and Dorothy, the very soon to be Professor and Mrs. Tindall, if gossip was to be believed. They'd been engaged for years, they were the light of the social scene, and everyone wondered when Desmond would officially take her to church and make an honest woman of her. It would behoove everyone if he did it quickly so she could get to work making him a family instead of running off on her "adventures." Every woman needed their hobbies, but a married woman had duties to perform. Whenever the topic came up, Desmond would laugh it off.

"You know Dot. She's only interested in things that happened a hundred years ago, if that recently. Trying to get her to consider the future is like herding cats."

Of course, everyone on that evening's excursion was aware of the true story. Dorothy preferred the company of women, and Desmond was of the exact opposite persuasion. Carter was there was Desmond's date. Ideally the woman they brought along as the fourth member of their little ruse would be someone for Dorothy, but Clara the Librarian was merely an ally who was willing to "suffer" a night of culture to help out a friend. Everyone deserved a nice night on the town, she said, and she didn't understand why it was necessary for one couple to hide while another could flaunt their romance.

Midway through the first act, Dorothy tapped Clara's wrist and indicated they should take a powder. They stepped out of their private box and Dorothy hooked her arm around the younger woman's elbow to guide her to the stairs. She kept her pace slow; it wouldn't do to return prematurely. Clara was dark-haired, with large eyes the color of sweet milk chocolate. Her nose and chin were pinched, and her mouth was a wide bow. Her orientation was a huge disappointment to Dorothy; the things she could have taught this scholarly little virgin...

She forced herself to find a less distracting topic of thought as they ventured downstairs. "I apologize for making you miss the performance."

"Oh, don't apologize. This theatre is a palace. I found it difficult to concentrate on the story anyway, what with those chandeliers, the dome, and oh! Did you see the electric lights?"

Dorothy laughed. "I did, yes."

Clara blushed a bit at her own exuberance. "I'm sorry. I don't get much opportunity to be fancy."

"Well, you should do it more often. It suits you very well. The next time Desmond and I go out on the town, you shall be my first call. Assuming you don't hit it off with Mr. Marsh."

"Truth be told," she leaned in close and lowered her voice to a whisper, "I don't believe he's quite my type."

"Yes, he didn't quite strike me as your kind of man."

Clara grinned as they reached the lobby. A pair of theatre attendants were lingering near the stairs, so Dorothy and Clara lapsed into silence until they were far enough away that their voices wouldn't carry back to the young men.

Clara said, "It's a good thing you're doing for them."

"I benefit from it as well," Dorothy said. "In fact, my rewards are greater than Desmond's. If I were a single woman without a man courting me, I'd have far more headaches to deal with."

"I suppose. And he... does the same for you? For instance, if I were, um, of the persuasion..."

"Then Desmond would offer to drive Carter home on some pretense whereas you would be far too exhausted to leave. And I would offer you my guest room for the night."

"But I wouldn't spend the evening there."

Dorothy smiled at the pink flush rising on Clara's cheeks. "No. It is highly likely you would not."

Clara pressed her lips together and looked around the lobby. They could hear the voices of actors echoing through the historic hallways of the old theatre, but they were too indistinct to understand. It was like being underwater and hearing voices on the surface. Dorothy chided herself for letting her thoughts drift back so easily to her work. For the past few days she had done nothing but research the flooding of the Mediterranean. She was now convinced it had actually happened, a world-changing flood that might even have been the origin of the Noah mythology. An entire sea crashing through the desert. What a sight it must have been. What an awe-inspiring and horrifying thing to experience...

"Lady Boone?"

She realized Clara had been speaking to her. "Yes, I'm sorry?"

"No, I shouldn't have asked. It's not my place..."

"Now I have to know."

Clara worked her lips back and forth and looked down at the carpet. "Is it wrong that I find it... the idea of what Professor Tindall and Mr. Marsh are doing right now... I mean, presumably what they're doing... I find it arousing."

Dorothy laughed and patted the girl's hand. "It's human nature. We're a very voyeuristic species, Clara. There's nothing wrong with you." She leaned closer and lowered her voice to a conspiratorial whisper. "In fact, though nothing about the mechanics appeal to me in the slightest on their own, I've been known to fantasize from time to time myself."

Clara covered her mouth when she laughed. "How long do you think it will take?"

"Desmond will be... efficient. But still, probably best not to rush him. Perhaps a stroll around the lobby."

"Sounds splendid."

They took a slow tour of the theatre lobby before they returned to their box. Desmond and Carter were facing forward to watch the show, but there was a distinct odor in the air that told Dorothy their absence hadn't been wasted. Desmond had a sheen of sweat on his forehead and Dorothy reached over to pat his wrist as she took her seat. Behind them, Clara sat next to Carter and asked him how the show was going. When he told her it was absolutely bloody splendid from where he sat, Dorothy had to bite down on her finger to keep from laughing out loud.

After the show, Desmond braved the crowds and summoned a hackney for the four of them. Their plan was to return to Threadneedle Street for tea and a late dinner, after which Clara would be given the spare room while Desmond and Carter took advantage of Dorothy's room. She would spend the evening with her research. If she got too tired, she would bed down with Beatrice.

They were nearly to Paternoster Square when Dorothy's attention was drawn to the row of offices above the Viaduct Tavern. One of those windows was Cora's office, and Dorothy leaned forward craning her neck to watch it as they passed. The shades were drawn, but a lamp was burning within.

"Cora is still institutionalized, isn't she?"

"Last I heard," Desmond said.

Dorothy patted the roof with the back of her hand. "Stop the car, please."

"What are you doing?" Desmond asked as the driver pulled to the curb.

"If someone is attempting to rob Cora, then it's my duty to stop it."

Carter said, "Forgive me, Lady Boone, but isn't that explicitly the job of the police?"

"Excellent idea, Mr. Marsh. Kindly alert them to the break-in. While you're doing that, I will apprehend the thief myself." She stretched back into the car and kissed Desmond's cheek. "Thank you for the lovely evening, Des. If you choose to continue to my home, Beatrice shall let you in. I shall hopefully not be out too late." She caught Clara's awed look and threw her a wink. "I do hope we meet again, Miss Levy. A curiosity left unexplored can be a dangerous thing."

With that, she stepped away from the cab and gathered her skirts as she hurried across the sidewalk. After a moment she heard Desmond order the driver to continue on their trip. She knew the delay had been his masculinity insisting he stay behind the help her, but they'd had that discussion before. Desmond was no fighter. He would only get in the way. He was best served continuing to Threadneedle Street and either calling the police or sending Beatrice back to offer her assistance.

An exterior entrance revealed a flight of stairs that led up to the third floor, where Cora kept her offices. Before ascending, Dorothy lifted her skirts and removed the gun she had tucked into her boot. She wished she had the opportunity to change into something a bit more intimidating than her finery, but she couldn't allow the thief to escape just because she was uncomfortable.

Dorothy made as little noise as possible as she went up the stairs. Cora's office was the second on the right, its door currently standing ajar. She paused for a moment and heard something crash to the ground within, followed by a muttered curse. There was no response or an admonishment to keep quiet or be more careful, so she assumed she was dealing with a solitary intruder. She pushed the door open with her shoulder and stepped over the threshold.

The office was small to begin with, but Cora had further reduced space with deep bookshelves against three of its four walls and a roll-top desk beside the window. A woman in a black coat was crouched with her back to the door, a stack of papers in one hand while she used the other to clean up the books she'd knocked off the shelf. She was wearing a pageboy cap, but her dark black hair fell across her shoulders like a mantle.

"I believe those items belong to my friend," Dorothy said, "and I would thank you to leave everything where it is."

The woman twisted at the waist and struck out with her leg in the same fluid movement, kicking the gun from Dorothy's hand. Disarmed, Dorothy grabbed the woman's ankle and twisted. Her quarry was thrown off balance and collapsed on the floor. Dorothy reached for her gun, which had fallen onto one of Cora's shelves. Before she could get a grip on it, the woman in black threw herself at Dorothy's waist and knocked her into the doorframe.

"Ah, crumbs!" Dorothy yelped. Pain radiated from her shoulder as she swung her fist like a bludgeon, catching the other woman in the side of the head. The woman absorbed the blow and responded by punching Dorothy in the gut. The air was knocked out of her and she stumbled forward, wrapping her opponent in a sloppy embrace. They both fell hard to the office floor, but the other woman recovered first. She pushed herself up and then dropped her weight down, elbowing Dorothy so that her head cracked against the floor.

"You've got guts, I'll give you that," the woman said in a thick Irish accent. "But do yourself a favor and stay down."

Dorothy saw the woman shoving a book into her belt. "Cora Hyde is my friend. I will not allow her to be robbed." She pushed herself up and grabbed the woman as she was moving for the door. They spun together before the woman growled and threw herself back. She slammed Dorothy against the shelves and caused an avalanche to cascade down onto them. Dorothy cried out at the sharp edge of a book bounced off her crown. The woman turned and punched Dorothy hard in the face twice, again in the stomach, and then threw her onto the floor.

"I'll leave you alive this time, but if you follow me... well. Just don't make me regret it. Ta."

Dorothy was too sore to even think about giving chase. She felt blood trickling through her hair, and she had bit her tongue at some point during the scuffle. For a long moment she lay on the floor taking account of her injuries. She was definitely bleeding from the injury on top of her head, and she knew that there would be a string of bruises along her shoulder and torso come morning. She reached up to touch her shoulder and massaged it through the pain. Not broken. That was a blessing, at least.

After a long moment she managed to sit up. Her abdomen ached, and she pressed a hand against it as she looked around the office. The intruder had certainly made a mess of it. She hoped Cora had some manner of organization that would allow them to discover what had been stolen. There was a box of tissues on the floor next to the desk and she reached out to grab a handful of them. She dabbed at the blood on her cheek and chin, then hissed as she pressed a wad of it against the wound.

Dorothy hated losing. She despised being bested in a fight, but more so when she didn't even know her opponent's name. She felt humiliated and weak. When Desmond and Beatrice arrived, as she knew they soon would, she would have to admit to them that she'd been beaten. They would treat her like a child. The idea was maddening. But fortunately, she knew it was not a feeling she would have to carry for long. She would meet her Black Irish enemy again, and on their second encounter Dorothy would not be dressed for a night at the theatre. She would remember each ache and pain she suffered over the next few days so she could inflict it back ten-fold.

CHAPTER SIX

DOROTHY RETIRED to her study, an ice pack pressed against her head, listening to jazz on the gramophone in an effort to calm her jangled nerves. Beatrice had been a dervish upon arriving at Cora's office to find Dorothy bruised and bloodied. It took her and Desmond both to convince Beatrice not to race off into the night in search of the thief. Her biggest regret was that coming to retrieve her and staying to make the police report required Desmond to cancel his evening with Carter Marsh. Dorothy felt almost as bad about that as she did about letting the Black Irish go. Almost.

There was a knock on the door and she bit back a growl. "Trix, I assure you, I am one hundred percent fine. I don't require anything. Thank you."

"It's me," Trafalgar said. Dorothy furrowed her brow and twisted in her seat as Trafalgar stuck her head around the door. "May I come in?"

"Yes. Certainly." Trafalgar closed the door and took a seat across from Dorothy. "This is quite a surprise. I know Desmond called to let you know what happened, but I wouldn't have expected you to come by in the middle of the night like this."

"I was concerned. If Cora's office was ransacked because of what happened to her in the Med, there's every chance that you and I might also be targeted." She started to say something else, stopped herself, but then shook her head. "And I wanted to see if you were all right. We've been working together for a year. I've grown fond of you, despite my best efforts."

Dorothy smirked. "So sweet, Miss Trafalgar. The worst damage was done to my pride, and that's not permanent. I don't suppose you've ever encountered my attacker before. Female, Irish, black hair, close to my height. Hell of a right cross."

Trafalgar said, "She doesn't sound familiar. Have you contacted Wraysbury?"

"Cora is unharmed. The institute's security has been alerted to the situation and they've assured me they'll keep an eye out."

"I'm a bit wary to trust an asylum."

Dorothy nodded, then winced as the motion caused her headache to flare. "Indeed. I felt much the same, but it's what Cora wants. She was reasonable and seemed to be herself. I just have to take her at her word that she chose to be there."

"I knew a woman before the war," Trafalgar said, "who was institutionalized for political excitement. In my attempts to get her released, I discovered those hellholes were little better than holding pens for women who dared used their mouths and brains in conjunction. As a matter of fact, Lady Boone, you should have been a prime candidate for committal."

"Thank you for the compliment," Dorothy said. "My grandmother did much to protect me from men who would've locked me away. You weren't lucky enough to have a guardian, making your independence much more impressive."

Trafalgar nodded her head in thanks, then looked around. "A woman of loose morals such as yourself must have a wet bar at hand..."

Dorothy chuckled and pointed to the globe in the corner. Trafalgar rose and went to make them both a drink.

"We'll go to Wraysbury tomorrow. Hopefully Cora will have some idea of who her intruder was."

The door had opened and Desmond slipped inside while she was speaking. "I may be able to give you some help with that. Constable Curry questioned the bartender at the tavern below and gave your description of an Irish woman with black hair. He reported a woman who sat in a table facing the window drinking nothing but Jameson on the rocks with ginger and lime. He never heard her speak, but she matched the description. She was there for at least the past three days. He said that was when he started noticing her."

"She was watching the office to see if anyone was using it. From that, we can at least deduce that it wasn't a crime of opportunity. Whoever Black Irish is, she was targeting Cora specifically. The question is why." She fixed her gaze on a random spot across the room and tried to call up the image of the book her opponent stole. "It may have nothing to do with Cora's most recent expedition. We'll know more when we've spoken to her. Trafalgar, you're more than welcome to join me on the trip to Wraysbury in the morning. You may bed down here for the night if you wish. It's extremely late and I won't send you back across the river only to return in a handful of hours. I'm sure there is something here that will fit you so you won't have to wear the same clothes tomorrow." She checked the clock and groaned. "Or rather, later today."

"If you have the room, it would be much appreciated."

Dorothy nodded and told her where she could find the spare room, since it wouldn't be used by the lovely and curious librarian.

"We'll leave at eight, after breakfast. Desmond, would you like to accompany us?"

"I'm afraid I have a class." He bent down and kissed her forehead. "Do be safe. I realize it's not a realistic request, but it makes me feel better to say it out loud. At least then perhaps you'll feel guilty while running headlong into danger."

Dorothy smiled. "I'll have Trafalgar with me."

"Yes," Desmond said, eyeing her warily. "I'm not entirely certain she's a calming influence on you. Last month you went to the countryside for target practice. What were the charges you came home with?"

Trafalgar said, "Trespassing, arson, assault, and felonious wounding."

Dorothy said, "Don't forget cruelty to children."

"That 'child' was fourteen if he was a day. And he certainly gave as well as he was getting."

Desmond cleared his throat and nodded to prove his point had been made. "I leave you to take care of each other. May at least one of you survive."

Trafalgar chuckled as he left. "He's a good man, but he's unfortunately fun to tease."

"Oh, he loves it." Dorothy finished her drink and stood up, stretching her arms out and wincing as her bruises protested the movement. "Ahh. I believe I shall retire. Sleep well, Trafalgar."

"You as well. Shall I make breakfast for the household when I wake?"

"That won't be necessary. But thank you for the offer."

She left the study, well aware that a year earlier she would have forced Trafalgar to leave first to ensure she didn't snoop. Their partnership had been difficult at first. Trust came slowly over a series of small missions. They weren't so much training exercises as they were experiments in trust. She and Trafalgar had spent so much time butting heads and competing that they wanted to be sure they could depend on one another in the field. They both needed to learn how the other thought in order to anticipate in the event of an emergency. Trafalgar was quick to adapt and seemed willing to adjust to Dorothy's way of doing things, but Dorothy didn't think that was fair. She was working hard to meet the other woman in the middle so their endeavor would be a true partnership of equals.

Something clattered in the kitchen. Dorothy turned and went to investigate, finding Trix standing at the sink with her back to the door. She'd removed her uniform jacket and the sleeves of her shirt were rolled up and pinned above her elbows. Her entire body was tense, causing her to drop each dish rather than easing it onto the drying rack. Dorothy crossed her arms over her chest.

"If you break one, I shall be forced to take it out of your pay."

"You should withhold my salary entirely."

Dorothy rolled her eyes. "Don't start."

"I should have been there. If I had been..."

"Stop that right now. There's no use in speculating, and the harm done was minimal."

Beatrice turned, eyes dark with anger. "Shall I help you into your pajamas so we can catalogue just how undamaged you are? You should have waited for me."

"If I'd remained on the street, she may have thrown me in front of a tram. She might have been willing to use a gun. Or worse, she might have gotten away. As it is, I managed to describe her well enough that the constables are close to identifying her. I would change nothing about the way this evening transpired." She reached up to touch her jaw. "Well. Perhaps I would alter a few small details. But you are not to blame."

"I'm supposed to keep you safe."

"As Desmond pointed out before he left, that's a fool's errand. The best anyone can hope to do is pick up the pieces after things calm down. You do that better than anyone ever has."

Beatrice put her hand on the sink and looked at the dishes. "I'll do better in the future."

"An impossible goal, but one you're more than welcome to attempt." Dorothy crossed the room and cupped Beatrice's face. "Will you come to bed with me tonight?"

"You need your rest. And it would probably be more painful than pleasurable."

"True." She pecked Beatrice's lips. "I'll see you in the morning, then. Sleep well, Beatrice."

"And you, Lady Boone."

Dorothy let go of Beatrice and started to leave. "Oh, and Miss Trafalgar is staying here tonight. There's no need to make up her room or fix her breakfast tomorrow, but just in case you heard something odd in the night. I wouldn't want you thinking she was an intruder."

Beatrice smiled weakly. "Thank you, ma'am. I'll try not to attack your guest."

Dorothy winked, blew Beatrice a kiss, and headed upstairs.

Trafalgar found the guest room and shut herself away. It was already abominably late, but she trusted she could get a few hours of sleep before they departed for Wraysbury. Dorothy hadn't mentioned anything about nightgowns, but Trafalgar had slept nude before. She undressed and left her clothes draped over the back of the armchair, unpinning her hair and letting it fall onto her shoulders. She could still hear Beatrice moving around downstairs. Through the window she heard the sounds of cars and buses on the street below. Bankside was nowhere near as active at this time of night. The spare bedroom's window looked out onto the street, but it was high enough that she wasn't worried about anyone looking in at her.

For all the headaches she credited Dorothy Boone for giving her, the woman had become a dear friend when Trafalgar was in desperate need for one. Her years of solitude had proven that she was not comfortable being by herself. Leola and Adeline had filled the void admirably. They served as her aides and her friends, and losing them both in one fell swoop could have been devastating. She wouldn't have been able to continue working without their help. And if she couldn't do her job, she couldn't have remained in her home. She would have been forced to leave London. Her entire life would have been uprooted and she'd have ended up God knew where. In that way, Dorothy was not only her friend but her savior as well.

"But there's no reason to let her know that," Trafalgar said softly to her reflection. She smiled and went to the bed. The blankets were soft against her thighs, and she propped the pillow against the headboard before settling in and looking up at the ceiling. The house creaked and settled around her and, in the silence, she realized at some point Beatrice must have gone to bed as well.

Going from rivals to partners could have been disastrous. There was so much animosity built up between them over the past few years, trying to work together might have ended with both of them dead, in prison, or out of work. But Dorothy was willing to change and Trafalgar had repaid it with her own enthusiasm. She forgot all the times Dorothy caused her strife in the past, just as Dorothy had to forget the times Trafalgar had trumped her on an expedition. Bygones. Water under the bridge.

They had done enough dry runs and small commissions. The time had come to show themselves off as the partners they had become. In the morning they would board the train to Wraysbury and the world would get its first glimpse of Trafalgar and Boone as a singular force. Villains of the world would do well to take note.

Chapter Seven

The morning found Dorothy agitated, moving around the kitchen with a barely disguised anger that was directed at herself. She chided herself for being so focused on the big picture that she missed the obvious, even when it was staring her in the face. While Trafalgar calmly ate the oatmeal Beatrice provided, Dorothy explained that the intruder in Cora Hyde's office might have nothing to do with her previous expedition and everything to do with the fact she was currently residing in an institution.

"Cora's brother Lawrence is a gambler and a cad," she explained. "They've been estranged ever since she cut him off. Rather than try to heal their relationship, he's started attempting to undermine her independence. He wants access to her accounts. It's just like him to hire someone to break into Cora's office. We may not need to disturb Cora at all."

She waited impatiently for Trafalgar and Beatrice to finish eating rather than insisting they leave at once. When they did head out, Beatrice followed them out.

"Trix, I'd like you to remain here."

"Absolutely not."

Dorothy said, "There's a chance I could be wrong and Black Irish is searching for something to do with Cora's last job. She may strike here next. I don't want the house unprotected. As much as I wish you could be in two places at once, I would much rather have you protecting my home."

Beatrice looked as if she wanted to argue. Dorothy put a hand on her shoulder and softened her voice.

"I need you, Trix. God knows I proved that last night. But I need you here, where you'll do the most good."

"Sitting on my bum."

"Guarding my life's work. Everything my grandmother left for me, everything I've spent the last few years working toward. Trix... you do realize that I would never trust this with anyone I didn't trust with all my heart? The woman who came into my life to rob me of these treasures is now the only one I'd want protecting it. You must understand how important that is."

Beatrice nodded stiffly. "Try not to get into any more fights, ma'am."

Dorothy smiled. "I shall do my best."

She kissed Beatrice on the cheek and then joined Trafalgar, who had been standing quietly to one side during their exchange. Lawrence Hyde worked in a tobacconist shop on Cheapside, a short stroll from Dorothy's front door, so they elected to walk to their meeting. Trafalgar had borrowed a suit from the closet Desmond kept stocked for his infrequent nights spent at the house, since she was too tall to fit comfortably into any of Dorothy's outfits. The suit, combined with her standard leather coat, was an altogether masculine look for her. She wore it very well.

"She is fiercely loyal. It's a good quality."

"It can be a bit frustrating at times," Dorothy admitted, "but I wouldn't trade her for anything."

They walked west, passing under the formidable bronze doors of the Bank of England. Motorcars in the streets moved slowly around horse-drawn carriages and pedestrians strolling casually along the thoroughfare. Trafalgar could hear a paddle steamer moving east toward Tower Bridge and, high above, an airship following a similar course. She squinted to see the registration, curious if it was Araminta Crook's ship, *Skylarker*, but it was too far away for her to read.

Other pedestrians walking in the opposite direction moved out of their way as they walked, something Trafalgar noted immediately but Dorothy seemed to take as commonplace. She didn't find it odd that the swarm of male pedestrians would step to one side to allow her passage. When they reached Princes Street, she almost expected the cars to run off the road to avoid hitting her, but they stopped and waited just like everyone else.

"How do you do that?"

"Do what?" Dorothy asked.

Trafalgar gestured behind them. "You moved out of the way for no one."

"Years ago, my grandmother demonstrated that if a woman does not give way to a man, nine times out of ten, he will walk directly into her. Men expect the path to clear itself for them. I decided I would take back that privilege for myself. I was knocked to the ground more than once, but I suppose over time the men wised up. Herd mentality. They might not even know why they're stepping around me, but they do."

"I shall have to walk with you more often."

Dorothy smiled and led them across the street. They joined the crowd pouring onto Cheapside and scanned the storefronts until they found the right name. Fumeur Cigars and Smokes, a name she remembered from Cora mocking how pretentious it sounded. She led the way through the front door, triggering a small bell that hung from a ribbon on its back. The shop was a small room with counters in front of every wall like barricades against assault. The walls were decorated with cartoonish posters, Cubist and Modernist and some other style she couldn't pinpoint. Whatever it was, she found the combination to be garish. As always when she entered a tobacconist shop, she was surprised to find it smelled sweet rather than harsh. There was a fruity element to tobacco that was lost in the finished product.

A door to the back room was covered by a curtain, and a man swept it aside as he came through. He looked enough like Cora that Dorothy didn't have to question his identity. He had the same hair and severe eyebrows, but he was heavier in the face and torso. He glanced at them both as he moved to take what she assumed was his standard position behind the counter to the left of the door.

"How can I help you fine ladies this morning?"

Dorothy moved closer to the counter while Trafalgar wandered toward the back of the shop. "Yes, I was wondering if you carried any Craven A. I seem to have run out despite my best efforts to stock up." She chuckled at her feigned foolishness. "I woke up this morning with a craving. I suppose that's where they got the name!"

Lawrence Hyde smiled weakly and gestured for her to follow him. She moved along the outer edge of the counter in parallel to his movements behind it.

"Craven A are quite expensive. But I can see that most likely won't be an issue for a woman such as yourself, Miss...?"

"Boone," Dorothy said. "Lady Boone, actually."

Lawrence stopped in his tracks. "Dorothy Boone?"

"Oh, crumbs. Your sister must have mentioned me."

Lawrence bolted for the back room, but Trafalgar vaulted over the counter and cut him off. She twisted her wrist and released her emei piercers. She closed her fist around the stem of the weapon and held her hand up so the light glistened off the blades on either end. He skidded to a stop and turned to see Dorothy closing the blind over the front door. She had removed a Colt revolver from somewhere on her person and currently had it aimed in his general direction.

"We're simply here to talk, Lawrence."

"I don't have anything to say to you. My sister put herself in that place, understand? I didn't have anything to do with it. So if this is some kind of revenge deal~"

Dorothy said, "I know all about Cora's decision to stay at Wraysbury. This is about the woman you hired to break into her office last night."

Lawrence gave himself away with a slight widening of his eyes and the bobbing of his Adam's apple. "I don't even know where her office is."

"Then the woman you hired found that out on her own. Who is she, Mr. Hyde? What was she looking for in Cora's office?"

"I don't know anything. You can't make me tell you anything."

Trafalgar, who had been silent up to that point, said, "That's where you're wrong, Mr. Hyde. Did your sister ever mention Trafalgar of Abyssinia?"

He looked warily at her. "No..."

"Oh, good. Then everything that happens will be new for you."

Beads of sweat glistened on Lawrence's forehead. Dorothy managed to hold back her laughter, but only just.

"A name, Mr. Hyde. If it makes you feel better, tell yourself that you're giving a reference. For all you know, we simply wish to hire this woman for ourselves. I saw how well she can fight. Perhaps there's a job I have in mind and she would be the perfect contractor."

Lawrence seemed conflicted for another moment before he decided it was wiser to cave to the threatening women who were present rather than keeping a promise to the threatening woman who wasn't actually there.

"I only know the name she uses for business. Virago. And I didn't hire her, so I can't help you find her. She came to me."

Dorothy said, "She came to you?"

"She wanted access to Cora's offices. She wanted to know if there were any booby traps she would have to contend with. She said if I told her how to get in without being hurt, she would wipe my debts clean. I didn't see what harm it would do."

Trafalgar said, "You claimed not to know where her offices were, and yet you were aware of the precautions she took?"

"She always uses the same security measures."

Dorothy said, "And I'm sure you've kept apprised of any purchases she's made to protect herself as well, haven't you?"

He looked away from her. His voice was quiet when he spoke again. "Cora is in the country, no one was going to be there, so it was an easy decision to make."

"Perhaps for some people," Dorothy said. "Did she give you any clues as to where she could be found?"

"No."

Dorothy took a step closer and steadied her gun on his chest. "Mr. Hyde, surely by now you've realized I can tell when you're lying. Perhaps you would like to save us all a bit of time and effort and simply come clean now."

He swallowed the lump in his throat and said, "The money she gave me to clear my debts. She sent it via wire transfer. I have the receipt in that drawer."

"I thought you said you only knew her business name," Dorothy said.

Trafalgar had moved to the drawer and received the slip of paper. "He wasn't lying. This purports to be from someone named A. Virago."

Dorothy smirked. "Well, then. Point for you, Mr. Hyde. Is there an address on the paper, Miss Trafalgar?"

"There is."

She relaxed and lowered her gun. "Fantastic. Thank you for your assistance, Mr. Hyde."

He remained tense, eyeing Trafalgar's piercers as she snapped them together and secured them up her sleeve again. "You won't tell Cora about this, will you?"

"I have no reason to keep it from her. For your sake, you should hope we can recover whatever this Virago stole from her." Dorothy raised the blind again. "Good day, Mr. Hyde."

She held the door for Trafalgar and together they stepped back outside. Trafalgar held out the wire transfer receipt so Dorothy could read the receipt. "Kentish Town," she read, then checked her watch. "Moorgate is the closest Underground station. I believe we can just make it, if we hurry."

They began walking toward the station. Trafalgar said, "So was this Virago seeking something to do with Cora's latest expedition after all?"

"It's difficult to say," Dorothy admitted. "I was quite thrown when Mr. Hyde revealed she sought him out rather than the reverse. Virago must have been looking for a weak link in Cora's operation and found it in her brother. That receipt proves he wasn't a cheap asset, so we know that whatever was taken from Cora's office must have been rather valuable. At least to her." She clucked her tongue. "Virago. Quite a moniker, I have to say."

"Yes, I was going to comment on that. It's not a name I'm familiar with."

"It's not necessarily a name at all," Dorothy said. "It means a domineering woman. Harridan, shrew, termagant, vixen. They're all words used to describe the same thing: a woman who frightens men. If you ask me, men need to be frightened more often."

"You almost sound approving."

"Of the name, yes. I have a modicum of respect for anyone who takes a slur and wears it with pride. Men most likely used it to dress her down, and she took it for herself as a warning. That said, I'm still aching from our run-in. I can compliment her choices at the same time I'm settling our score."

When they arrived at Moorgate Station, Dorothy led the way underground and paid for both of them. As they waited for the train, Dorothy thought about what it could all possibly mean. Cora's doomed expedition. A potential netherworld populated by monstrous creatures who were beginning to find their way to the surface. And now they were en route to meet with a mysterious thief who had paid a small fortune just for access to Cora Hyde's offices.

She hoped Virago, whoever she turned out to be, was able to shed some light on just what they were dealing with. If not, she and Trafalgar would be forced to set out blindly with no compass to guide them. That, she was certain, would certainly lead to them meeting the same fate as Cora's expedition. It was clear something was brewing underneath the Mediterranean. Something big, ancient, and very deadly. She wanted to have as much information as possible before she went after it.

Chapter Eight

The St. Pancras public baths were an imposing presence rising high over Kentish Town. Dorothy and Trafalgar stood on the corner of Grafton Road and gazed up at its turrets and spires, a red-brick Gothic edifice with demons hidden in its architecture. All told, it was an extremely impressive structure given what it housed. The address on the receipt led them to a boarding house near the Underground where an elderly woman identified Virago as Emmeline Potter and informed them she was currently here, partaking in a bath.

"And me without my suit," Dorothy said as she followed Trafalgar through the women's entrance. They obtained tickets from the office and delivered it to the attendant. As soon as they were through the doors, the sound of gurgling water surrounded them. Dorothy was starting to feel anxious just at the idea of running water, invoking as it did thoughts of a Biblical flood. They entered the main room, where a crowd of people in swimming suits were milling about around the large main pool under the vaunted ceiling.

Trafalgar seemed uncomfortable with the amount of skin on display, but she scanned the women nearby to see if any met Dorothy's description of her attacker. "Do you see her?"

"No one meets all the criteria." Dorothy started moving clockwise around the nearest pool. "Too short, too muscular, too dark..."

"There are private bathing rooms over here," Trafalgar said.

"I'd prefer not to intrude on innocent people unless it's absolutely necessary. If all else fails, we can simply..." Her voice trailed off as she brought her hand up. "There."

The woman was at the other end of the room, a towel draped over one arm as she walked from the changing rooms to one of the private slipper baths. It was the first good look Dorothy had gotten of her attacker, and she was surprised to see Emmeline Potter was older than she had expected. She was closer to fifty than Dorothy's own age, but moved with the grace of a dancer or soldier. She had large and smoky eyes and lips that even from a distance seemed to relax into an easy and sardonic smirk. She wore a white bathing outfit that left her upper chest and legs exposed. Her long brown hair was pinned back loosely to keep it off her neck and shoulders as she walked.

Dorothy hurried without running to catch up with her, bursting into the room just as the woman was lowering herself into the tub. Virago paused and snapped her head toward the intruders, then smiled and continued to sink. She stretched out and let her knees rise out of the water as she rested her arms on the lip of the tub. The bicep of each arm was tattooed with an ornate design Dorothy couldn't quite make out and didn't feel like getting a closer look.

"Miss Trafalgar and Lady Boone," Virago said in a lilting brogue. "This is quite a surprise. I wasn't expecting you until after tea. You must have had a very productive morning."

"So you know us," Dorothy said.

"Word gets around. Last night I was curious about who I was scuffling with. Your name cropped up almost immediately. For the past year, it seems all I've been hearing are fantastical stories about the staunch Miss Trafalgar and the scholarly Lady Boone. It was an honor to leave you bloody in my wake."

"Bruised. Not bloody." She thought for a moment and then said, "Why am I scholarly and she's staunch?"

"Oh," Trafalgar said, "was mine a compliment?"

"At least that means strong. Scholarly... it implies I'm hunched over in a library all day."

Trafalgar said, "Well, there are frequently ink stains on your fingers."

Dorothy harrumphed.

Virago said, "Was there anything else? I'd like to get on with my bath."

"We want to know why you broke into Cora Hyde's office, why it was worth the money you gave to her brother, and what you intend to do with what you recovered."

"Oh, is that all?" She stretched her legs and rested her feet on the edge of the tub. "How much do you know about Cora's last expedition? The one that sent her off to the madhouse?"

"It's not a madhouse," Dorothy said. "But I know enough. She was trying to find the truth about the mass disappearance of Khirokitia's residents. She and her team explored a crevice, which led them underground to a cavern that appeared man-made..."

Virago said, "And that's where everything went wrong. But Miss Hyde and those children should never have been there in the first place. She had everything she needed and she was still missing the big picture. She was looking for the wrong thing. The people of Khirokitia aren't important in the grand scheme of things. They were a walled-off city full of sheepherders and farmers. If Cora uncovered every secret they ever had, she might have found some really boffo tips on how to slaughter pigs. They were remnants. People think that they mysteriously vanished, but that's nonsense. They just went somewhere else. They are really the least interesting thing to waste your time on."

Dorothy said, "Then perhaps you can enlighten us as to what would be worthwhile."

Virago moved one of her hands into the water to watch it drop from her fingers. "Eons ago, Europe and Africa were joined together by a desert. It wasn't entirely barren; there were rivers and lakes and whatnot. But the land was extremely arid. The Sahara desert and the European coast without the benefit of ocean breezes. There were cities in that land, populated by people who chose to live in the most unforgiving environment the planet had to offer."

Dorothy glanced at Trafalgar. On the Tube, they had compared notes on their recent studies. It was bizarre to hear their own theories spoken by this woman they considered their enemy.

"As you can imagine, anyone living like that would have to be tough as nails. They were no hunters or farmers. They struck out across the salt plains to sack their wealthier neighbors. Ancient peoples of Egypt and northern Africa and Italy. This was well before even the earliest hint of history. Think dinosaurs. Think early drafts of the Bible. They were going around tearing shit up and taking whatever they didn't destroy for themselves."

Trafalgar said, "Until someone decided they needed to be wiped off the face of the Earth. They caused the flood by opening the Mediterranean to the Atlantic. Something to do with Gibraltar? An explosion at the strait to allow seawater to flood in and wash away their nemesis."

Virago winked at her. "Very well done. But you can't do something so drastic without consequences. Imagine if the Americans blew up part of their coastline and created a sea across the middle of their continent. The enemy was destroyed, yes, but at the cost of life as everyone knew it. It was such an epic event in human history that every culture has a Flood myth. The Sumerians, the Bible, the Quran, Hindus, name the culture and they'll all have a story about the Earth flooding to wipe out the evils of mankind."

Dorothy said, "So what is it you claim to have found? Evidence of the Flood?"

"No," Virago said with a sly grin. "I know where to find the remnants of a city."

Dorothy tried to cover her excitement at the possibility. "As monumental as that would be," she said with a steady voice, "it hardly seems plausible."

Virago gestured with her hand, flicking water toward them. Dorothy took a step back, but Trafalgar did not. "Believe what you want. I learned Cora had come extraordinarily close to locking down its location when she took a detour. She didn't even know she was off-course. All I needed was what she had already done so I could follow the right path. The journal I took last night detailed every step she's taken over the past three years. I merely have to backtrack, find where she turned left when she should have turned right, and I'll have my answer. A road map to the largest treasure anyone could ever dream of. That's what I stole. The legwork that would have gone to waste otherwise."

Dorothy said, "How altruistic of you."

"Oh, it's one hundred percent selfish. I want to be the one who finds this city. I want to be the first one to pick it clean before I announce my discovery to the world. And once I've chosen what I want from the ruins, I will reveal everything to the world and accept my fame and immortality in the history books."

Trafalgar finally broke her silence. "As I feared."

Virago and Dorothy both looked at her.

"There's no reason for her to tell us any of this. If she truly wants this city and the treasures it surely holds for herself, then she has nothing to gain by telling us this. We're her rivals. So either she thinks we aren't good enough to be concerned, or she has a contingency plan to make sure we don't get in her way."

Dorothy screwed her lips into an irritated expression. "Crumbs. I was so entranced by what she was postulating that I missed that." She looked at Virago again. "So do you mean to kill us?"

"That would be rather difficult, seeing as I'm the one in the bath. You're full-dressed, standing up, and presumably armed. How could I possibly have the upper hand here?"

"You've been researching us since your run-in with Lady Boone last night. You have something in place. A plot of some sort to remove us from the equation."

Virago kept her expression static for a long moment, but then she smiled and aimed a finger at Trafalgar. "You did well teaming with this one, Lady Boone. I may have been able to blind you, but not her. Very clever."

"I've taught myself to sniff out your type. People like you believe that I'm a simple foreigner who won't notice when she's being fooled. So what is your plan, Miss Potter? Assassins on the rooftop to pick us off when we leave? An explosive in the Underground?"

Virago hissed through her teeth and shuddered theatrically. "Oh, so dramatic the both of you." She scooped water into her hand, then drew it up her arm. "Nothing so nefarious, I assure you. I was simply going to leave you with a warning. As of right now, we're colleagues. Three women in the same field with no reason to attack each other." She furrowed her brow. "Just so long as you're not harboring any ill will for our scuffle last night, Lady Boone."

Dorothy narrowed her eyes. "I've been hurt worse."

"Bygones, then." Virago smiled. "And we're all friends having a nice conversation. But if you should interfere with my plans in any way, you will go from colleagues to rivals. I do not treat rivals well, nor do I take betrayal kindly. So it's down to you. Our ongoing relationship relies entirely on your actions, not mine. Perhaps we could even work together at some point. I would very much like to get to know you both."

Dorothy said, "I doubt that."

Virago shrugged. "You and Trafalgar started out as rivals as well, I'm told. Word is last year the two of you brawled in the street, right in the middle of London Bridge."

"It wasn't on the bridge," Dorothy said.

"But you take my meaning." She leaned back in the tub and eyed Dorothy suggestively. "Who knows what sort of relationship you and I might have in a year? Now, if there's nothing else, I would like to bathe in private."

Dorothy glanced at Trafalgar, who nodded to indicate she was willing to leave. "This isn't the last we'll speak," she said.

"Oh, good. Hopefully next time I can be dressed. At least for the beginning of the conversation..." She smiled suggestively and then closed her eyes. "Take care."

Dorothy stepped to the door, then paused and looked down at Virago. "Enjoy your soak. I'll try to take it easier on you next time."

Virago smiled without opening her eyes. "I was the victor in our encounter."

"Yes. And now you're soaking your weary muscles in a warm bath while I've spent the morning finding out everything I can about you, Emmeline Potter. Have a lovely day."

Dorothy and Trafalgar left the private room and moved along the edge of the larger pool. Dorothy's mind raced but she remained silent until they were outside again. The bathing rooms had been humid and left a layer of sticky sweat on her forehead and upper lip. The fresh air immediately cooled her, and she hooked a finger under the collar of her blouse to air her skin out a bit. She turned to look at Trafalgar who seemed consternated but otherwise comfortable.

"What do you think?" she said.

"I think we shall have to be very careful with our next move."

Dorothy nodded and looked at the building as if she could see Virago through the walls. "She's not going to hesitate. As soon as she has an idea of where to search, she will set out to find this lost city. Like the Weeks' brothers last year, we've forced her hand. The only bright side is that this may cause her to be sloppy."

"And that's a good thing?"

"With someone as skilled as Virago appears to be, it's a very good thing. I'm confident in my abilities, but I doubt I would stand much of a chance against her if she had time to plan her attacks." She straightened the cuffs of her jacket and set off down the street. "Come along, Miss Trafalgar. If we're going to beat Virago to the punch, we shall have to get started immediately."

Trafalgar said, "Why are we involving ourselves at all? From the threat she leveled at us, we would be better off ignoring this entirely."

Dorothy said, "Did you not hear what she hopes to discover? A city more ancient than anything we've ever discovered! The possibilities are absolutely endless. But Virago is only interested in the riches she can pull from the ruins. She'll do unbelievable damage and who knows what knowledge could be lost. The origins of life on this planet could depend on what we find in that city." She stopped to catch her breath and shook her head. "I know that I'm being overly dramatic. But we cannot let something with so much potential be destroyed by someone who is only interested in the money she can make from exploiting it."

Trafalgar nodded. "I agree. So where do we begin?"

Dorothy gathered her skirts and started walking back toward the Underground station. "Now we return to our home base and discover everything we can about Emmeline Potter. Know thy enemy, Miss Trafalgar."

"And if she makes good on her threat and attacks us?"

"Let her try," Dorothy said with a sly grin. "I'd love a rematch."

Chapter Nine

On their trip back to Threadneedle, Dorothy and Trafalgar worked out their next move. Dorothy figured that if anyone in London had encounter Virago before, it would be Abraham Strode. He was the most senior of their peers and others often contacted him if they reached a dead end in their own research. He was respected if not well-liked, but his personality didn't matter. The odds were good that if he hadn't encountered her himself, someone had contacted him with information that would be helpful to their cause. Trafalgar volunteered to visit him and see what he knew while Dorothy returned to Wraysbury to discover what Cora knew about their adversary. Virago knew too much about Cora's work to have been an unseen stalker. They parted ways at the station to go about their individual tasks. Strode's manservant received Trafalgar at the door of his home and, after announcing her presence, "regretfully" informed her that he was busy.

"Shame," Trafalgar said as she brushed past the old man to enter the foyer. "Is he in his office?"

"Miss, you cannot go in there." He followed a step behind her, his hands at his sides so he wouldn't be forced to lay hands on a woman.

Trafalgar pushed open the sliding doors. Abraham Strode was seated at the desk cleaning up the remnants of his cocaine hobby. His ash-blonde pompadour was askew, and he brought up both hands to smooth it down when he realized his space was being invaded. He glared at her and then shifted his gaze to the manservant who still stood uselessly in the doorway behind her.

"I am unpleased, Ira."

"I'm sorry, Mr. Strode. I doubted you'd want me to use violence on her."

Trafalgar looked at the older man and smiled. "You're welcome to try." He swallowed hard and took a step back. She looked at Strode again. "I would have expected a much kinder welcome, Mr. Strode, considering what Lady Boone and I did for you last year. We saved your life from Ivy Sever and ensured you would not be falsely arrested for the murder of Mr. Dubourne. Surely that is worth granting me an audience."

Strode grimaced and waved Ira away. "This is not a permanent allowance. But I suppose since you have already interrupted my afternoon, I might as well find out what is so important." He gestured to the seating area and finished putting away his drugs as Trafalgar removed her jacket.

He sniffed dismissively at her attire. "I see Lady Boone has been influencing your wardrobe."

"I wore trousers long before Dorothy came into my life. And my current outfit is a matter of necessity more than choice." She sat and crossed one leg over the other. "Don't take my intrusion out on your man, by the way. I forced my way past him."

Strode grunted. "I hired him after Ivy Sever gained access to my home. Seeing how well he handled a visible intruder, I have little faith in his usefulness against an invisible attacker."

"If it's any consolation, I don't think Ivy has any reason to want you dead these days."

"What a comfort." He looked in the small vanity near the window and finished straightening his hair. "So if this isn't a warning, to what do I owe the... well, let's call it 'pleasure' just for the sake of civility."

"What do you know about a treasure hunter called Emmeline Potter?"

Strode paused in his movements and threw his head back with a laugh. "Oh-ho. First Dorothy Boone and Ivy Sever, and now the Virago. You truly keep remarkable company, Miss Trafalgar."

The way he said 'remarkable' made it sound like a curse. "So you are aware of her."

"More than aware, unfortunately." He offered her a drink and she declined with a shake of her head. He poured one for himself and took a seat across from her. "She predates even Lady Boone. The beginning of my career, I was aboard a steamer heading for Morocco. Supposed to be an eighteen-week expedition. First time on the African continent. I was thrilled, as you can expect. Virago stowed away aboard the ship and spent the first week of our sea voyage stealing information from anywhere she could find it. We never saw hide nor hair of her until the day she revealed herself. She had arranged for another ship to pick her up. Left us stranded and adrift with very little food or supplies." He sighed and shook his head. "My first expedition ended with us slinking back to London with our collective tails between our legs. Virago went ahead to the site we were supposed to explore and gained much of her fortune from it."

Trafalgar said, "Dorothy was concerned that Virago may be more focused on wealth than the historic value of these sites."

Strode laughed again. "She's a bloodhound, Miss Trafalgar. Singular purpose. If she thought there was a fiver behind that wall, she would tear it apart with a hatchet. It wouldn't matter to her if it was plasterboard or a piece of stone carved in the thirteenth century as long as she could get the money out. She wants riches, and everything else is secondary."

"That is alarming."

He finished his drink and bared his teeth as he put the tumbler down on the table. "I will give you this advice, Miss Trafalgar. If you and Lady Boone do intend to go up against this woman, take heed. She will destroy artifacts in her quest for wealth, but she will also destroy people. I cannot prove that she's killed in the past, but it's hardly inconceivable given the tales I've heard from others in our profession."

"Anyone in particular who might have dealt with her?"

He thought for a long moment. "A few, but I believe they passed away in last year's unpleasantness. Perhaps that is why Virago has reappeared. She's been inactive for a while now. But with all the deaths last year..." He sighed again. "The Weeks brothers. Damn them to hell for what they did to our profession. They've changed everything even in defeat."

Trafalgar considered his words. Dorothy hadn't mentioned bringing him into the group they were putting together, but he seemed like a plausible candidate. "Mr. Strode," she began, but she wasn't able to finish before he pushed up and walked quickly across the room. "Is something wrong?"

"A thought just occurred to me. No one knows exactly where Virago hangs her hat, but most assume she resides in the Irish Republic. That accent is difficult to disguise, of course." He was standing at his desk rifling through his papers as he spoke. "There are those who believe she's a member of the Irish Republican Army and the reason she hasn't shown her face is because she's been busy up north with those hooligans."

Trafalgar stood and joined him at the desk. He continued looking through journals, flicking the pages of one book with his thumb before putting it down and lifting another. He took another from his drawer and untied the rawhide string around it.

"Nigel Mummery was up there in 1918 on an unrelated matter. He claimed to have seen her in a pub with a bunch of rabble-rousers. The election was still fresh in everybody's mind and a British fop in their midst was too rich of a target. Aha!" He withdrew a folded sheet of paper and checked to make sure it was the right thing before he handed it over. "He sent that to me when he returned."

Trafalgar unfolded the note and skimmed its contents. "Fortunate to be back in one piece... scuffle with some Volunteers, including one woman I believe is of your acquaintance." What followed was a description that matched the woman she and Dorothy had met at the Kentish Town baths. "I believe it was the Virago you've mentioned because when they were ransacking my supplies, she seemed keenly interested in my journals. She tore out several pages and stuffed them in her back pocket..."

"She's a scavenger," Strode said. "She's willing to do some work on her own, but if it's faster and more efficient to just steal what others have done, then she'll do that. She's only interested in the wealth because she wants to funnel it back to the IRA and their blasted war."

"They're fighting for independence. It means they're passionate about their cause and they'll do anything to further it. It doesn't mean they're wrong."

"You're a supporter?"

"I'm nothing," Trafalgar said. "I know too little about their cause and I'm too removed from the outcome to have a useful opinion on it. All I know is that this particular woman is willing to do anything to get what she wants. I take offense to that, not her politics."

He smiled snidely. "A very politic answer, Miss Trafalgar."

"It has the benefit of being honest as well. Thank you for your assistance, Mr. Strode. I'm sure Lady Boone will find this information illuminating." She held up the note. "May I take this?"

"Of course."

She retrieved her jacket and pulled it on. "And we shall be in touch in the coming weeks. We have a project that we're putting together, and I believe Dorothy would like you to be a part of it."

"Perhaps you can give me a bit more warning before your next visit."

"No promises. I can show myself out."

He said her name just as she was about to enter the corridor. "I've heard rumors of Virago in the past few years. Nothing substantial enough to lead you to her, but enough for me to know that I never want to cross her path ever again. If you and Lady Boone intend to make an enemy of her, then I would suggest... hell, to be honest, I would only advise you to not do it to begin with. But this is the two of you we're talking about."

Trafalgar smiled. "We will take your advice to heart, Mr. Strode. And we appreciate your concern."

"But you won't listen, will you?"

She straightened her jacket. "Good day, Mr. Strode.

"Good luck, Miss Trafalgar."

Ira was waiting by the door when she left, and she touched a finger to her brow in an unfinished salute as he held the door for her. She was sure it made him feel as though he was throwing her out and she saw no reason to disabuse the man of the illusion. She didn't know much about Irish politics. She knew tensions had been rising since before the Great War ended, and things were coming to a head. They would need funds to continue the fight. The Weeks' campaign had left many explorers dead and left the field open for Virago to make her grand return to the profession. She would take the opportunity and take whatever job was the most profitable. She would then rip apart invaluable relics just to make money. History left in the dust and civilizations one step closer to being forever forgotten. The very idea was abominable.

Whatever Cora Hyde was on the verge of discovering, Trafalgar agreed with Dorothy that it had the potential to be something that changed the world. They had the chance to uncover a culture that existed in pre-Biblical times. Humanity from the book of Genesis, maybe even before that. It could hold the key to so many mysteries she didn't even know where to begin. The thought of it being lost was a sin she couldn't abide.

She believed Abraham Strode's warnings about the danger of going up against Virago. But at the moment she didn't care. Virago had to be stopped at any cost.

CHAPTER TEN

CORA PASSED through a quick progression of emotions upon Dorothy's arrival. Exhausted, but happy to see her old friend without a disguise. Then concern when she read Dorothy's expression. As Dorothy explained the events of the past day, Cora was concerned for her safety and grateful for what she'd done. And when Dorothy mentioned the name Virago, the color drained from Cora's face. She stood up and looked at the tea service, then ran her hands through her hair as if she meant to put it in an up-do before she left it lying on her shoulders.

"You're certain it was Emmeline Potter?" she asked, looking out the window rather than meeting Dorothy's gaze.

"Trafalgar and I tracked her down. It was her. And I'm assuming you know how she was aware of your work?"

Cora nodded and cleared her throat. "She tried to seduce me."

Dorothy smiled. "I doubt she made it far in that endeavor." Cora kept her face turned away. "Cora? You're not of that persuasion."

"No, I'm not," Cora said softly. "But I was lonely. Drunk. And the Virago is so beautiful. She touched my hands and my face and told me I didn't have to do anything to her." She swallowed hard. "It had been so long since I was touched that way, Dorothy. I thought there was no harm in letting her do what she wanted. It's not as if I didn't enjoy myself."

"She blackmailed you," Dorothy said.

Cora nodded. "I have investors. Patrons. Clients who would pull their business from me if they thought they were doing business with a..." She finally looked at Dorothy again. "I'm sorry, Dot."

"Don't be. It's not your fault we deal with closed-minded imbeciles, and if someone fails to hire me because of rumors or gossip, then I'm glad they end up with you. But if Virago was blackmailing you, why did she need to break into your offices? Why did she need to pay off Lawrence for access?"

"Because I stopped giving her what she was asking for. Before leaving for Cyprus, I told her to do whatever she wanted with her 'scandal.' I had given her enough. I was more afraid with what she would do with the information I was giving her than I was of the evidence she had of our dalliances. I would rather have been unemployed and destitute."

Dorothy said, "You would have been neither. I would have gladly welcomed you into my employ. In fact... Trafalgar and I are putting together a group. A confederation of those in our profession. I would like to extend an invitation to you."

Cora returned to her seat and took Dorothy's hand. "It sounds lovely. But I want to postpone any sort of long-term decisions until I'm out of this place."

"Of course. I understand. The offer is open-ended."

Cora nodded her thanks. "Whatever you need from me to stop her, I'm at your disposal. I'll return to London at once."

"Absolutely not."

"Easy, Dorothy. The beauty of being self-admitted means I can excuse myself for sabbaticals. I will help you stop this Irish madwoman, and when everything is sorted, I will return to complete my convalescence." She squeezed Dorothy's fingers. "I am sorry that I was ashamed of being called... of..."

Dorothy shushed her. "Think nothing of it, Cora. I understand. I'm not offended by your reaction to it, I'm offended at someone who would use it as a weapon. The more I learn about Miss Potter, the more eager I am to cause her downfall."

Cora said, "As am I. Firstly, we must pack the things I will need upon our return to London."

"Splendid. I'll help." She stood up and put her hands on Cora's shoulders. "And then we will show Miss Potter what a true virago is capable of."

It was dusk by the time Dorothy returned to Threadneedle Street, her whole day given over to trains and seeking information. She was exhausted and starving by the time she finally walked through her own door. Cora was staying in her guest room because, as she explained on the train, she didn't want to go home until she could stay there for good. Dorothy understood and hoped Trafalgar didn't need to use the room for another night. Beatrice responded to their arrival by coming downstairs and immediately took custody of Cora's bag to take it upstairs. Cora excused herself to the powder room and left them alone.

"Thank you, Trix." Dorothy hung up her coat and ran a hand through her hair. "I trust today was uneventful."

"Dull as dirt, ma'am."

Beatrice started up the stairs and Dorothy followed. "I hope you understand why I asked you to remain behind today."

"Understanding and accepting are two different things, Dorothy."

Dorothy winced.

"But I was able to use the time well. I thought perhaps your grandmother may have had some experience with what you and Miss Trafalgar have been researching, so I thought I would see if she mentioned anything in her journals. She was meticulous with labeling, so it wasn't difficult to find journals that corresponded to trips taken to the Mediterranean area. I left the pertinent journals on your desk in chronological order."

"Beatrice." She put her hand on Beatrice's arm to stop her so they could face each other. "Thank you very much. I hadn't yet thought of that but, when I did, it would have taken precious time to gather those journals. I appreciate you taking the initiative."

"My pleasure."

Dorothy stood in the doorway of the guest room while Beatrice put away Cora's suitcase and began preparing the room for her arrival. Some of Trafalgar's things were still present and Beatrice gathered them for later retrieval. As she tidied the room, Dorothy revealed what they had discovered over the course of the day.

When she finished, Beatrice sneered. "This Virago seems to be quite a formidable opponent. If we are going to draw her ire, you'll have plenty of opportunities to defend me in the near future."

"I look forward to it."

Dorothy hesitated before asking her next question. "Perhaps before we embark on a new adventure, you would like to enlighten me as to your extracurricular activities."

Beatrice said, "They're not of any consequence."

"Trix, you know fully well I don't mind if you take another lover. Our physical relationship has never required exclusivity. But you act guilty. You act as if you're terrified I will discover you've been unfaithful." She entered the room and put her hands on Beatrice's shoulders. "I find it very difficult to believe you've betrayed me. I can't even think of a way you would. Please, Trix. Be open with me. What is going on with you?"

Beatrice was quiet for a long moment before she faced Dorothy. "Something happened last year. During the encounter with the Weeks brothers. I drew more magical energy than ever before. I was pushed to my limits."

"I remember. You saved all of us."

"What you don't know is that my tattoo burned with enough energy to burn through my clothes. That's never happened before. So I've been trying to learn where I'm from, hoping to find some answers to who I am. To what I am."

"Have you found anything?"

Beatrice shrugged and shook her head. "I'm not sure yet. I don't want to say anything until I have a solid lead."

"Well, that's understandable." She moved her hands to take Beatrice's. "The moment you know anything, I want you to tell me immediately. Anything I can do to help you."

"Thank you." She cupped Dorothy's face and briefly kissed her lips. "I prepared dinner. I doubt you found time during the day to stop for food."

Dorothy grunted and put a hand on her stomach. "You would be correct in that. So you see, remaining behind has proven useful in three different ways."

"I would still rather have been at your side when you met this Virago woman. I would like her to know what's in store should she come after you."

Dorothy hooked her arm around Beatrice's elbow and led her downstairs. "I'm not so sure I agree with that, Trix. I would like for you to be an unpleasant surprise for her when it's too late for her to retreat. It should be quite a show."

Beatrice chuckled as they reached the ground floor. Cora was waiting for them in the sitting room, and Beatrice ushered both women into the dining room.

"Has there been word from Trafalgar?" Dorothy asked.

"Not as yet. There's enough should she decide to stop by. Should I set a place for her?"

Dorothy hesitated. Trafalgar had been her guest, her backup, her partner, and co-conspirator, but dinner guest seemed like a new intimacy. She wasn't sure she was prepared for that. At the same time, she didn't see any reason to object.

"Yes, Trix, I'd say it would be polite, just in case."

Beatrice nodded and excused herself. Dorothy took a seat at the table with Cora to her right. "I've been thinking about what Virago told you," Cora said, "about my research being on the right track but I worked out something else incorrectly."

Dorothy nodded. "I wish there was a way to get back the journal she stole from your office."

Cora shook her head and tapped her temple. "Unnecessary. I have everything I need in here. The journals are just a way to organize my thoughts and reinforce them if I should need to remember something in a few years. I have a good memory, but it's far from perfect. Still, it should be fresh enough that we hopefully won't need the book."

"Fingers crossed," Dorothy said.

The doorbell rang and Dorothy stood before Beatrice could come out of the kitchen in response. "I'll see who it is, Trix." She pardoned herself from the table and went to the foyer. Even through the narrow fogged glass of the door she recognized the silhouette Trafalgar made; tall and dressed in her standard coat.

"Miss Trafalgar. I think you've been our guest enough times that you can bypass ringing the doorbell and simply come inside."

"Ah. Perhaps one day I shall feel comfortable doing that every time I stop by. But until then..."

Dorothy nodded and gestured for Trafalgar to enter. She had changed into her own clothing and had Desmond's borrowed suit draped over one arm.

"I would have had it cleaned, but a bachelorette taking a man's suit to the cleaners..."

"Of course." Dorothy took the clothes and hung them on the back of the closet door. "Was Mr. Strode as helpful as I hoped he might be?"

"Once I convinced him to speak to me, yes. According to him, Virago is a parasite. She steals rather than doing her own research. As you theorized, she is absolutely only interested in money. Mr. Strode believes she's channeling the funds back to the IRA to assist with their War of Independence."

Dorothy said, "It makes sense. Wars are expensive affairs. My fear is that she'll find something more valuable than gold or silver. If there are indeed creatures under the earth, the Mediterranean seems to be honeycombed with ways to access them. Creatures who haven't seen sunlight in millennia have been drawn back to the surface due to how much magic was expended during the War. What if Virago is able to harness one of those beasts to do her bidding? Would she stop at Irish independence or would she have grander designs?"

Trafalgar said, "Having met her only briefly, I'm still certain she would take as much power as she was able."

Beatrice came out to retrieve them for dinner and Dorothy led Trafalgar through the house. "Virago is a perfect example of why I think an alliance of explorers can only be a good thing. If we are a united front we can stop people like her from gaining footholds in our profession. This used to be a revered occupation. A few more bad apples like the Weeks or Virago and we'll be thought of as little more than treasure hunters."

"On that subject, I spoke to Mr. Strode about joining your club."

"Mr. Strode?" Dorothy said. "Really?"

"I believe he could be valuable."

"Perhaps you're right. He's a bit splenetic, but a good man overall. He wouldn't be my first choice, but he would be a good ally against Virago and her ilk. I'll support your decision to invite him to the group, should we ever get it off the ground."

Dorothy introduced Trafalgar and Cora as Beatrice brought out their dinner. Trafalgar sat across from Cora, and Beatrice had set a place for herself at the opposite end of the table from Dorothy.

Once Beatrice had taken a seat, Dorothy picked up her glass and held it out in a toast. "For now, I believe we've spent far too much time this evening on

Virago. Let us spend the rest on friends and food."

Cora said, "Hear, hear."

Trafalgar, Beatrice, and Cora responded to her raised glass by hoisting their own. There would be time enough for plotting and research in the days to come. A casual dinner among friends was a rare occurrence and should be treasured whenever it was possible.

Chapter Eleven

After dinner, Cora and Trafalgar insisted upon doing the dishes. Beatrice dismissed herself for a bath and reading in bed. Eventually Cora went to bed and Trafalgar departed to spend the night in her own bed. Dorothy, left to her own devices, changed into her pajamas and a robe before she retired to the study with a mug of herbal tea. She turned on the sonic amplifier Desmond had gotten her, though she still wasn't quite sure she trusted the machine. An orchestra could be recorded playing their music, and the sound was recorded onto a thin metal disc. The disc was then placed into the machine, which used some complicated array of pins and armatures to read what was on it. Still, if it could fill a room with music, she was willing to accept its presence in her home.

Gustav Holst's *The Planets* began playing as she took a seat behind her desk. The suite began with Mars, a brutal and warlike piece that fit her mood perfectly. She didn't want to be soothed, although that was coming soon, with the serene arrangement of Venus. She wanted to feel as if she was preparing for war. She wanted her blood to churn with the promise of a fight.

Four of her grandmother's journals were stacked in front of her. Dorothy took a moment to run her hand over the weathered face of the book on top, sliding her fingers down along the spines. She remembered the all-too-brief time they had occupied the house together. Two generations of Boones under one roof. Her grandmother, Eula, would leave for days or weeks at a time, although she always made sure Dorothy was looked after and well taken care of. She received a multitude of letters from all over the globe, some of which she still had in a special box upstairs.

Her favorite days were when Eula would return, face burned by the sun or bandaged from some misadventure. She would always take the time to get reacquainted with her young charge. Dorothy had basically been evicted from her family's home, although they would likely have labeled it as running away, but Eula welcomed her willful granddaughter into her home. Dorothy would list what she had learned from the tutor, and then Eula would regale her with surely-exaggerated accounts of her adventures.

Now the actual records were lying in front of her. She'd read them before, of course, and every time it felt like a violation. It was ludicrous, of course. Eula had always been willing to let Dorothy read whatever she wanted. And when Eula died, the journals were left to her along with everything else. But they were her grandmother's. They contained her private thoughts and feelings. Dorothy always needed a bit of ceremony before she could bring herself to crack the pages.

She finally picked one of the books in the center of the stack. She doubted Eula's first journey to the Mediterranean had been insightful enough to merit examination, and she wanted to begin after she'd had a chance to build some theories. Beatrice had marked the relevant sections in each book and Dorothy wondered just how long she'd spent on the project. She would have to remember to thank her properly for the effort she'd taken. She took a sip of her tea and finally began reading.

June 17, 1903

Arrived at Barcelona none the worse for wear, save for a few days' bout with seasickness coming through the Bay of Biscay. Traveling overland through Spain was worth the discomfort. I'll have to come again one day when I have a chance to appreciate it fully. This time it was simply a means to an end. Tomorrow Mateu will arrange for our passage to the islands. My convalescence has given me time to think. In fact, I was rarely well enough to do anything but think.

On my previous trip to Athens, I was told of an ancient end-of-the-world myth. The people who shared the story with me couldn't even date it. The tales were passed by word of mouth until someone finally wrote it down. It has of course now been diluted through centuries of translators and assumptions and embellishments, but I do believe there is a kernel of truth that remains. I intend to speak with as many local people as I can to see if they've heard similar tales. My hope is to combine these oral histories and mythology to see where they connect and overlap with one another. In those connections I will find the truth.

So many ancient texts have stories about massive worldwide floods. From their perspective, 'worldwide' would mean the area in and around the MedSea. Mankind may have started on a large landmass which became split in two by a great flood and we simply ignore the evidence because it's so obvious. Could the sea be a remnant of Noah's flood? Could the truth about civilization be buried beneath its deceptively pristine surface? We may never know.

Mateu and I departed–

After skimming ahead to determine Eula never returned to the topic, Dorothy put the journal aside and chose another. It was dated 1909, and she flipped through to Beatrice's marker. The suite had moved on to a more pastoral movement. Combined with her tea, it was starting to make her drowsy. She didn't want to get up and change the music to something more energetic so she simply focused on her grandmother's neat and tidy handwriting.

"Where did you go this time?" Dorothy asked, following barefoot through the halls as Eula moved toward the study. Eula, in her knee-high boots with her hair gathered up under a fedora.

"This time it was Tierra del Fuego. Do you know where that is?"

Dorothy shook her head enthusiastically, not caring about her ignorance but excited to learn. Eula pushed open the door to her study and went to the globe. She turned it upside down and pressed her finger to a spot practically on the very bottom of the planet. It seemed so distant, so impossibly far, that Dorothy reached out and traced her finger along the line of South America.

She was aware that her eyes were wet. Exhaustion and nostalgia could be a brutal combination. She had only lived with her grandmother for a few months, and the older woman's health faded quickly after Dorothy's arrival. Still, from time to time she thought that time spanned her entire childhood. She learned lessons in those weeks that she never would have gotten at home or in school. Eula Boone had made her the woman she was, and she didn't know if she had ever properly thanked her grandmother for that gift.

She steadied her breathing and focused on the 1909 journal.

February 8, 1911

It's down there. I know it is. Evidence of what came before, evidence that could prove there were civilizations even before what we consider pre-history. 'There were giants on the earth in those days.' (so says Genesis something-or-other) 'Mighty men of old, men of renown. God saw the wickedness of man was great and the thoughts of his heart were evil continually.' Who were these giants? These men of renown? Ozymandias. Look on my works, ye mighty and despair! Oh, how Dorothy laughed when I recited that poem to her. But what if the subject of the poem was one of these Evil Men that God saw fit to destroy?

God created Man in his image.

God was horrified by what Man became and wiped them off the face of the planet.

Humanity as we know it is the second attempt, the remnants who survived the cataclysm. The flood forced them to start over on a path that God found more acceptable.

Looking back over history as we know it, I can only imagine how atrocious those first humans were.

I've been searching for the better part of a decade for evidence that these civilizations existed and I believe I may have finally found something. I've combined everything I've learned from local legends, I've sanded off the rough edges, and I am certain that I could find it. If only... yes, if only...

Because as fate would have it, of course, I don't know when or if I'll be able to follow my lead. I don't know if I have another expedition in me. When I think of all the work I've done and all the work I've left undone, it breaks my heart. I need someone to finish what I started. A torch to carry into the next generation. I would have thought my son... but no, that is a ship that sailed far too long ago to correct its course now.

I need Dorothy. Sweet and brave and adventurous Dorothy. My little girl, my duplicate. I look into the girl's wild eyes and I see what my parents tried to squash in me. She breaks my heart every time I see her, I love her so much. I want to show her the world. I want to keep her safe. I want to take her hand and lead her into the dangerous corners of the planet. I want to lock her away so nothing can ever touch her. She is more precious than anything I've ever found buried in the ground. More special than anyone I've ever known. Such a glorious child with such potential. Is it wrong I would squander that potential if it meant she never knew fear or pain?

I know wonderful and awesome secrets lay waiting to be found. Dorothy deserves to be the one who finds them. I know that if the wrong person finds them, it could change the world in horrible ways. In the wrong hands, it could turn humanity down a darker path. A path which finally causes God (or whomever) to bring about another flood to wipe us out and start anew.

I will leave my quest to Dorothy. One day, I am certain she will have reason to find these journals, to retrace my steps and she will find the work was started before she even knew her destiny. I only regret I cannot be there to show you the way, Dorothy. If you are half the woman I believe you will grow up to be, I doubt you will have any trouble whatsoever.

Her hands were shaking when she put down the journal. She pushed away from the desk and went to the cabinet where she'd stored so many of Eula's things. There was a map in the safe-deposit box she opened after her grandmother's death. There were many maps, actually, but she remembered the first one she'd looked at. It was sitting right on top, right where her hand would naturally fall when she saw everything stuffed into the box.

She found it now, rolled up and protected, and carried it to the desk. She put on a pair of gloves she kept for handling some of the older items Eula had left her and she unrolled it across the desktop. "MEDITE RANEO," she muttered as she ran one gloved finger across the ancient writing. She pressed her lips together and scanned the inked lines.

"Okay, Grandmother," she whispered. "It's taken me over a decade, but here I am. I'm ready."

She made another cup of tea. *The Planets* ended and she began it again, then a third time. It seemed curious as she seemed to recall it was nearly an hour long, so she didn't understand how it could already have played in its entirety so many times. She went to the lavatory and splashed water on her face before going back to work.

As her grandmother's journals neared the end of her life, they became more detailed. It was almost as if she was planning an expedition for herself without actually going through with any of the plans. It was obvious that the plans were meant for her, and her eyes stung with tears. She was finally going on an expedition with her grandmother. There was enough information for her to begin immediately.

She picked up her tea and grimaced at its emptiness. She put it back down and rested her hands on the desk on either side of the map, brow furrowed as she stared at it.

"Ma'am?"

Dorothy started at the sound of Beatrice's voice. "You should have gone to bed hours ago, Trix. I can make my own tea. Go on, rest."

Beatrice entered the room. "I did go to bed hours ago, Dorothy. And now I'm awake again."

Dorothy looked at the window and saw light peeking through the curtains. "Crumbs."

"How many days this week do you intend to ignore sleeping?"

"I've gone a full week in the past."

Beatrice sighed. "In those instances, you didn't have someone like Virago breathing down your neck. You need to be at your best, Lady Boone. Part of keeping you safe means ensuring you don't put yourself at risk by ignoring your needs. Go upstairs, undress, bathe, and sleep at least until afternoon."

Dorothy started to protest, but she caught Beatrice's look and decided it was best to remain silent. Her shoulders sagged with defeat.

"Very well. But since you are rested, you must do something for me while I'm sleeping. I want you to make arrangements for an immediate departure. You, Miss Trafalgar, and myself. I doubt Cora will be up for the journey, but do make sure she knows I would want her there under different circumstances." She forced herself to calm down and pointed at the map. "It was all here. My grandmother left it all here for me."

Beatrice moved closer to the desk so she could see the maps and drawings. "What is it?"

"Grandmother found evidence she believes could have led her to a city from the dawn of time. If she was correct, it could change everything we know about the world. About pre-history. She gave me the means to get there myself. This is what I believe Virago is looking for. An ancient city richer and more dangerous than anything we've ever seen before. And Eula Boone left me the roadmap."

Beatrice whistled through her teeth. "No wonder you forgot to sleep."

Dorothy rubbed Beatrice's arm. "Set up our travel arrangements, Trix. Try to make it as roundabout as possible. Obscuring our destination from Virago is more important than speed."

She touched the map again.

"This city has waited eons for us to discover it. It can wait a few more weeks."

Chapter Twelve

Dust, polish, wash the dishes, sweep, put out the garbage. Beatrice never saw herself doing this sort of "menial" workload. She never envisioned herself as a housekeeper or maid, even though plenty of those were spawned from the building where she grew up. She came to London and preferred to live on the streets rather than find work she considered beneath her. Becoming a thief led her to Dorothy Boone's home and the horror of being frozen in stone by an artifact Dorothy had carelessly left out. Dorothy saved her life, not to mention her sanity, by freeing her from the statue she'd become.

She originally remained to clean and take care of household chores as a means to repay her debt and to make up for entering the house with criminal intentions. But she quickly learned to love the work. It was more rewarding than she would have expected. There was a serenity in washing the dishes, and she took pride in the way the morning light shone through spotless windows and reflected off the polished wood of the entry hall.

Beatrice now felt an odd sense of ownership for the house. There were times she was silently irritated with Dorothy for leaving clothes draped over the banister or when she tracked in mud or sand from all corners of the world. But she would dutifully clean it up and never say a word about it. The house belonged to Dorothy, after all. Beatrice was just in charge of keeping it standing.

To that end, she had to see to its security. After Dorothy finally went to bed, Beatrice made their travel arrangements and contacted Trafalgar so she would be ready to leave that night. Though earlier she had balked at being left behind to protect the building, there was no way she would leave it vulnerable now that she knew what they were up against. A person like Virago simply could not have access to anything inside its walls. But she wasn't going to leave Dorothy and Trafalgar defenseless on their trip.

She went through the downstairs rooms and paused next to each point of entry. She touched two fingers to the corners and muttered a quiet incantation to draw magic to each spot. The energy used her as a conduit and entered the wall, the joints, the very structure of the house. She could feel it building from the arch of each foot and moving up her legs like a painless electric shock. Beatrice put both hands against the front door, since the main entry point of the house would require a stronger charge.

There was a process to protecting a residence. She had to keep her mind focused on those who could pass through without harm. Dorothy, of course, and herself. Desmond Tindall. And as odd as it seemed, she extended permissions to Trafalgar as well. Dorothy had invited the woman to enter without knocking or ringing the bell, so it stood to reason she could be allowed to pass through. For so long she had been a rival, the competition, but their partnership was thriving. And the woman was responsible for saving Dorothy's life in the labyrinth, so she deserved the benefit of the doubt.

It took a lot out of her, and she paused frequently to catch her breath and dab the sweat from her brow and upper lip. After she had the house completely covered she would eat and drink, lie down for a bit, and replenish her energies. She knew she would have plenty of time to recuperate when they were en route to the Mediterranean so she wasn't overly concerned about the energies she was expending. She did pause once to make sure her tattoo ink wasn't glowing, just to be positive she wasn't pushing herself too far.

When every door and window on the ground floor had been protected by a web of energy, she moved up to the second floor. The energy wouldn't kill anyone who tried to gain access to the house. First there would be a mild sense of unease that would set any solicitor or milkman back on their heels. Anyone who persisted would experience mild discomfort. If there was a sincere, concerted effort to enter the home without permission, all the energy would converge on that spot with enough force to push whoever it was back out into the street.

"And hopefully into the path of an oncoming tramcar," she muttered.

She knocked lightly on Dorothy's bedroom door before entering. Dorothy had changed into her pajamas and lay half-curled in bed, one leg stretched out behind her and both hands under the pillow. She wore an eye mask to block out any ambient light. She was absolutely and completely unconscious. Beatrice smiled and moved on tiptoe to the bedside. The blankets were pushed down enough that she could lift them without disturbing Dorothy. She drew them up over her body, tucked it tight around her, and bent down to press a kiss to Dorothy's cheek.

Dorothy could go days on just cat naps and quick dozes, but once she finally crashed she could sleep through anything. Beatrice rested two fingers on Dorothy's temple and expended a little magic to ensure the next few hours would be restful and populated by only the sweetest of dreams. She let her touch linger for a moment before she went to the window and added protection to it as well.

Beatrice allowed herself a final lingering look at the woman lying asleep on the bed before she left to finish her work, shutting the door softly behind her.

They left London just after sundown. Dorothy's reasoning was that Virago would most likely expect them to begin a trip in the morning. Leaving later also meant they could sleep for the first part of the journey and wake upon arrival in Spain. Dorothy wanted to match her grandmother's travel as much as possible considering it was her roadmap they would be following. She dressed in a leather jacket and a skirt over knee-high boots, her hair French-braided underneath a tweed beret. Trafalgar wore a belted gray dress under her usual coat and a pair of gloves, while Beatrice dressed in her standard uniform of gray vest, black tie and matching jacket with a bowler hat.

Cora wished them luck and departed for Wraysbury once again. Dorothy hadn't told the others, but her secondary concern on this trip was finding some way to soothe her friend's addled mind. Be it finding the creature who took her team or only discovering where it had come from, she wanted to return to London with some kind of news that might return the strength and vivacity she remembered.

Desmond accompanied them to the train station, which they would take to the ferry docks in Portsmouth. From there, a sea voyage through the English Channel and the Bay of Biscay before arriving in Bilbao, Spain. They would make arrangements there for an overland trip to Barcelona. And that, after nearly traveling two thousand kilometers, would be the true beginning of their trip. Trafalgar expressed surprise they weren't using the *Skylarker*, but Dorothy explained she didn't want to abuse Captain Crook's generosity. Besides, using a slower sea route would further confuse Virago and hopefully slow any pursuit she might engage in. The journey would take a little longer, but it would give them time to prepare.

"It will also give Virago an opportunity to catch up with us once she figures out what we're doing," Trafalgar said from across the aisle. She was sitting by the window, while Dorothy and Beatrice were sharing the bench opposite her. Beatrice had the window seat but was sat far enough back that she didn't obscure Dorothy's view.

"We have a secret weapon." Dorothy held up the books and papers she had brought with her. There were more in the trunk Beatrice had muscled onto the baggage compartment. "We will not travel idly. While we are making our way to the southern shore of Spain, we will be seeking the most likely place to begin our search. Even if Virago somehow beats us to the sea, she will be frozen in place with no clue where to go next."

Trafalgar said, "I am sure she will have some clue. I believe we should have taken the airship and dealt with whatever consequences arose. Slowing our own arrival can only benefit Virago."

"Or she will be curious about why we chose such a meandering route. She'll wonder if there is something we know that she doesn't. She'll assume we came this way because we had no other choice."

"You're making a great many assumptions about someone you've only met once."

"Twice," Dorothy said, "once when she beat me up and again when she was bathing. Those are two times when one's personality is laid bare."

Beatrice said, "Among other things. You saw her bathing...?"

Dorothy smiled. "Jealous, Trix?"

Beatrice harrumphed and looked out the window, hands folded in her lap. Dorothy laughed and rearranged the books on her lap.

Trafalgar said, "Well, whether this is the wisest course of action or not, it is already underway. We'll simply have to deal with whatever comes next when it comes. How long shall it take us to reach Barcelona?"

"All told," Dorothy said, "it will be four days before we're in Bilbao. Then we shall see about the quickest route to Barcelona. Perhaps a week."

Trafalgar nodded and settled in. "Then I shall not feel bad about stealing an hour of sleep on the way to Portsmouth."

"I'll try to read quietly," Dorothy promised.

As Trafalgar dozed, Dorothy looked out the window at the city speeding past them. Portions of the track rose above the streets so as not to disturb traffic or pedestrians, and on this stretch it felt as if they were taking to the air. She could imagine them flying just a few dozen meters above the ground, weaving between rooftops and rustling trees with their passage. Not long ago, motorcars and airplanes were fantastic ideas, and now she could see at least five or six of the former tooling along the industrial lanes of Vauxhall. Who knew what the future held? Perhaps one day soon they would be able to skip across the Channel to Barcelona in the space of a day or a few hours.

The thought made her dizzy. To live at such a speed would cause people to become hurried and lazy. She was fine with the slow and measured pace the world currently had. When change came, as it inevitably would, she would make the necessary adjustments. That didn't mean she would have to like or anticipate them.

She glanced at Beatrice to see she had fallen asleep, and she smiled. She didn't know what Beatrice had done to protect the house, but whatever it was left a very noticeable frisson in the air. Dorothy almost felt sorry for anyone who tried to break in while they were away. Then again, Beatrice had entered her life as a thief. She looked again at her sleeping companion. If she hadn't been uncharacteristically sloppy with her artifacts, or if Beatrice had the foresight not to handle it without gloves, their relationship would have been far different.

I would have hunted her down, Dorothy admitted. *I would have brought the full force of the Met down upon her, saw to it that she was an example to others. My foe, turned to my friend and lover and confidante.*

She looked across the aisle at Trafalgar, who was also asleep at that point. Another foe, an enemy she'd actually exchanged blows with before their partnership got off on its first shaky legs. There had been days when she'd fantasized about humiliating the woman who now shared her train car. They had been more than enemies. She'd considered Trafalgar to be her nemesis. "Foolhardy, slapdash. Hardly worthy of the title 'explorer'."

And now friend. Now partner and coconspirator. Her equal.

She shook her head and sighed. As she'd thought earlier, the future was unknowable. Best to let it happen on its own and deal with the changes as they presented themselves.

CHAPTER THIRTEEN

TRAFALGAR DIDN'T much care for the sea. She first saw a vast body of water when she was a girl, taken from her home by men with nefarious plans for her and the other girls from her village. The men put her on a boat and tried to use her as a host for some undersea monstrosity they worshipped. She managed to escape them and their intentions, but even decades later she found herself uneasy when out on the open water. Travel to Spain would take an entire day, and she was wary about spending so much time on a ship. But the route kept them within sight of land at all times so she would often go out on the garden lounge so she could reassure herself by watching the shoreline.

She was also throw by the opulence of their transport. The ship was massive, an ocean liner which was merely stopping at Bilbao before heading across the Atlantic to America. It was as if the most spectacular hotel in London had been lain on its side and then had a ship's hull built around it. She was worried about getting lost, but she kept her wandering to a specific area and quickly found herself familiar with that particular part of the ship.

During the day, they would meet in Dorothy's stateroom to go over what was coming next. Trafalgar sat on one side of the bed with Beatrice across from her, and Dorothy perched on the pillows with her legs crossed in front of her. In front of her were maps hand-drawn by Eula Boone and the journals of her many trips to the shores of Greece, Italy, Egypt, and points between. Dorothy had drawn her own map so she wouldn't have to deface the original with her markings and Trafalgar took a moment to admire Dorothy's skill. Cartography was a means to an end for Lady Boone, not even something she considered a hobby, but her drawings were exquisite.

"We know where to find two creatures who have existed beneath the earth for thousands, perhaps millions of years. The Minotaur and the beast Cora escaped." She had marked those points on her map. "In that regard, we have more information that my grandmother had. But she was so close when she died. She spent decades planning the trip we're on now. She laid all the groundwork for us."

Trafalgar said, "If you'd asking us to take this on in her honor, I would be glad to agree."

"Thank you. I hate that she left this undone. All of her work enabled me to forge my own way in life. If it wasn't for the inheritance or the interest she took in me... well. This is the very least I can do for her." She looked at Trafalgar. "We. The least *we* can do."

"Where do we begin?" Trafalgar asked.

She put her finger on the Cyclades. "We're going to begin at Delos. Hardly revolutionary, I know, but there's a reason every culture has fixated upon it. The island was originally home to a culture called the Carians. They were a wealthy, seafaring people at the very beginning of recorded history. No one knows where they originated, where their wealth came from... they were just simply there. 'In the beginning, God created the Heavens and the Earth. The Earth was without form, and void, and also the Carians were there.'"

Trafalgar said, "You think these people were remnants of the race wiped out by the great Flood?"

"I believe they might be. Unfortunately Delos is not the place to find much about them. The Athenians purified the island for their own purposes and relocated the bodies buried on Delos to other islands throughout the Cyclades. Grandmother believed this archipelago was the key to understanding what came before the Flood. She believed the Carians relocated the Delos after their original home was destroyed by the creation of the Mediterranean.

"She traced where the Carians showed up throughout pre-history and made a note of every reference, every anecdotal appearance, and she tried to pinpoint where they might have originally come from. She researched references to the giants of old, those evil men that God sought to wipe out in the Bible. She was of the belief that these evil men were the Nephilim. Offspring of women who lay with the 'children of god.'"

Beatrice said, "Angels?"

"Angels or something a primitive recorder might consider to be angelic. It could simply have been more advanced civilizations. It could have been the earliest purveyors of magic." She rearranged the maps. "According to basically every myth she found, the Nephilim were larger than the average man."

"Goliath," Trafalgar said.

Dorothy nodded but then she waved. "Yes and no. Goliath was not considered giant. He was just... tall. Taller than most. So she started looking for evidence of burial sites for people who were taller than average. Eight, nine feet. She found a few sites in Turkey, Jordan, Greece, Lebanon, et cetera." Dorothy smiled, gleeful at her grandmother's ingenuity. "Then she began looking deeper."

Trafalgar said, "How do you mean?"

"Underwater. She was looking for cemeteries that would have been covered by the Flood."

Trafalgar's eyes widened. "And she found one?"

"She found what she called a necropolis. Just here, north of Mykonos." She drew a circle on her map. "There are undersea cliffs here where the water is barely one hundred meters deep, but then it plummets to six, seven, eight hundred meters. Grandmother found a spot that was one thousand meters deep. She was positive there was something down there. She sent down probes and she found a cave system. The probes were unmanned, so she couldn't investigate as thoroughly as she would have wanted, but it was enough to pique her interest."

Beatrice said, "That's where we're going? A thousand leagues under the sea?"

"I believe that's a book," Trafalgar said, "and it was talking about distance, not depth." She focused on Dorothy. "A thousand meters is impossible. No human could travel that deep and survive, not without..." She straightened. "That's what you intend to acquire in Barcelona. The means to descend as far as we need to go."

"To the very bottom of the Mediterranean," Dorothy said. "Deeper than anyone else ever has before. There is a certain amount of risk involved..."

Trafalgar scoffed. "I suppose 'infinite' does count as a certain amount, yes."

"As I said. But I have faith that the reward will be more than worth the risk."

Trafalgar chewed her bottom lip and looked at Beatrice. She could tell the other woman was waiting for her opinion, but she also knew where the girl's true loyalty was. She sighed and nodded slowly. It went against her better judgment, but Eula Boone was a legend. If she believed there was something there worth finding, then Trafalgar was willing to risk it. Even though the idea of feeling all that water above her was terrifying, she knew she had to see it through to the end.

"Wherever this leads, I shall follow."

Dorothy said, "Thank you."

They had dinner together in the dining saloon before retiring to bed. They would arrive at Bilbao before lunchtime tomorrow, and then begin their trek across Spain. Trafalgar wished Dorothy and Beatrice a good evening and retired to her stateroom early. She left the lights off so she could see the onyx bay outside her window. The moonlight and the stars reflected off its surface and she suppressed a chill before it could take hold of her. A night so long ago, one of her earliest and strongest memories: a stone in her mouth, at the mercy of men from a world she couldn't even begin to understand at that point, and a whirl-pool that heralded the arrival of some eldritch beast that she was meant to host.

Her stateroom shared a wall with Dorothy's, so she heard when her traveling companions finally returned from dinner. Dorothy's voice seemed to drum softly against the wall while Beatrice's was slightly more than a murmur and barely audible over the sound of the engines. Dorothy laughed, and then there was the sound of a weight dropping onto one of the beds. Trafalgar moved closer to the wall even as she told herself she wasn't intruding; she was simply preparing for bed. She changed into pajamas since she wasn't comfortable sleeping in the nude aboard the ship.

To their credit, Dorothy and Beatrice seemed to be trying to keep it down. A soft murmur, a rhythmic shifting of cloth against cloth at a rhythm that could have been attributed to the rocking of the ship. Trafalgar gave up the pretense and closed her eyes. To achieve that rhythm, Beatrice - or whoever was in the dominant position - would have to be moving extremely slowly. She could picture Dorothy on top of Beatrice now, shoulders hunched, Beatrice's fingers curled into claws in the small of her lover's back. She saw Dorothy's pale skin and the freckles she was certain spread across her back and upper arms. Her hair would be loose and...

She pushed away from the wall and shook her head, pressing her fingers to her temples as she retreated to her bed. She wasn't going to take advantage of the fact she could hear what was happening next door. She wasn't even certain she was intrigued by the idea of two women making love. Adeline had been of that persuasion, but she was always shy about bringing her lovers home or spending the night with them. Trafalgar once assured her she was welcome to have guests, but Adeline had merely shook her head and told her she was anxious enough because of her skin color. "Don't want to give people another reason to look down on me."

Trafalgar put the pillow over her head and hoped she would drift off quickly.

The grounds of King's College were quiet and abandoned when Desmond finally left his office. He had his books bundled under one arm, his satchel hanging heavy on the opposite shoulder. It banged against his hip when he walked. London felt odd without Dorothy Boone in it, he mused, as if a small piece of its soul had been siphoned off and released elsewhere. He would put her absence out of his mind and focus on the smaller problems at hand. Whether to catch a tram or walk, whether he would find a restaurant or eat at home. If Carter Marsh was available for a game of dominoes or to listen to the radio.

He was pondering these small but monumental decisions when he became aware of a woman walking toward him on the sidewalk. She was wearing a black dress with voluminous white sleeves, her face partially covered by the brim of a hat. He lifted his head to offer her a genial smile and she dipped her chin to him.

"Evening," she said.

"Ma'am." She brushed his arm as they passed each other and something dropped to the ground at his feet. "Oh, miss. You dropped something."

He shifted his books to his other arm and stooped to pick it up for her. She stopped and turned, looking down as he retrieved the lost item as any gentleman would have done. It was just a small packet of cigarettes, compressed and wrinkled at the edges where it had been gripped tightly in a hand. Odd that something held so tightly would fall accidentally, but he placed it against her outstretched palm with his right hand. He felt her fingers close around his in a surprisingly unrelenting grip.

"Professor Tindall," she said in a charming and melodious Irish accent. "So this is your dominant hand, is it?"

Someone slammed into him from behind hard, as if he had been dropped from a great height onto the ground. Arms that seemed as thick as his torso closed around him as an unbreakable vice. His left arm was stretched out parallel to the ground. The woman stepped forward, her face still obscured by darkness.

"Where is Lady Boone?"

"What? I'm..."

She clucked her tongue and pressed a finger against his lips. "I know you're a sodomite. I know you have no romantic interest in your supposed wife-to-be. But I also know you have to keep up appearances. I know Lady Boone and her new assistant, Trafalgar of Abyssinia, are no longer in London. The townhouse on Threadneedle Street is empty and... frustratingly well-protected." There was enough light for him to see her grimace. "So. One chance, Professor. Where is Dorothy Boone?"

"I believe she said something about taking some fresh air. A leisurely train trip through the countryside."

The woman nodded to the man holding Desmond. He rearranged his position and closed his fingers around Desmond's left hand.

"I hope you appreciate the fact that I ascertained your dominant hand before doing this."

The man squeezed and the woman clapped her hand over Desmond's mouth to muffle his scream of pain. The bones in his hand compressed and then began snapping. Desmond went limp, but his attacker kept him standing even as sparks of light danced in front of his eyes. He'd never felt such pain before, and he trembled, the woman's hand clamped hard over his mouth and keeping his scream silent.

"I'll ask you again, Professor Tindall. Where is Dorothy Boone?"

He knew she would break his other hand without a thought. The pain was so agonizing that it was like a shining beacon in his brain. It had turned the straight line of his thoughts into a twisted gyre leading down into blissful unconsciousness, but he focused on his enemy. Giving away what he knew would spare him some pain, but it would also cost Dorothy, Trafalgar, and Beatrice their lives. He could feel the blood spreading into his face and knew he had turned a purple-reddish color.

"She... didn't... tell me," he growled through clenched teeth, "for precisely this reason."

The woman held his gaze for a moment, then nodded to the man holding him. Desmond collapsed to the sidewalk and instantly folded himself around his damaged hand. The woman bent at the waist and looked down at him.

"You'll want to find a doctor, and soon." She dropped a card onto the ground in front of him. "If Lady Boone contacts you, please give me a call. I'm ever so eager to talk to her."

She stepped over him and, along with her mountain of a brute, walked away. Desmond wanted to watch them go, partially to identify his attacker but also to ensure they were really gone, but turning around would take too much effort. Instead, he blinked away the tears of pain and looked at the card the woman had dropped. His eyes cleared enough to read a single word, confirming his suspicions. Six gold-leaf letters on a black background.

VIRAGO.

Chapter Fourteen

The ship delivered them to Bilbao safe and sound the following morning. They had brunch at an outdoor cafe that catered to tourists before Dorothy headed off to find transport to Barcelona. There was no discussion about leaving Trafalgar and Beatrice alone together, and neither of them found it odd until Dorothy was already gone and they realized they had no buffer between them. Trafalgar shifted uncomfortably, while Beatrice stared silently out at people passing by. Trafalgar wore her normal jacket over a plain brown blouse and trousers. Beatrice had eschewed her standard uniform for a white blouse and a calf-length skirt. Several other diners were casting sideways glances toward their table. After a moment Trafalgar realized they were trying to figure out who was the master and who was the servant. She didn't know how to dissuade them from their notions, but she did know how to ignore them. She looked away from them and focused on the water.

There were boats in the bay and she tracked them with her eyes. The sounds of conversation drifted over to them as if trying to fill the space left by their awkward silence. Finally she decided that sitting there silently until Dorothy arrived would only make it appear as if they were both servants waiting for their mistress to return.

"May I ask your honest opinion?"

Beatrice looked startled, but she disguised it well. "Depends on the topic. I'm not guaranteeing I'll give you an answer."

"Fair enough. The topic is Lady Boone." She gestured toward the water, indicating what they had been told on the ship. "In your opinion, how much of this quest is wishful thinking?"

"What do you mean?"

"Fulfilling her grandmother's final mission. It's laudable, of course, and I'm more than happy to lend my assistance. And I have the utmost respect for Dorothy's acuity in these matters. But I can't help but wonder if she's so focused on solving the mystery her grandmother left behind that she's lost sight of her objectivity."

Beatrice considered the question. "I would say at first glance it may be as much as fifty percent wishful thinking, but that percentage only covers motive. Her purpose may be split between solving the mystery her grandmother left behind and stopping Virago from reaching it first, but her deductions are sound. She wouldn't see potential where there was none. With Miss Hyde's recollections and Eula Boone's maps, I have faith that we really are on the cusp of finding something spectacular."

Trafalgar nodded slowly. "Thank you, Miss Sek. I appreciate your opinion on the matter."

"Do you?" Trafalgar looked at her oddly and Beatrice held up a hand. "I mean no disrespect. But you and I haven't exactly had the time to bond the way you and Dorothy have. Part of me still sees you as the competition. I'm sure a part of you still sees me as the gatekeeper. Lady Boone's muscle."

Trafalgar smiled slightly. "I have been trying to stay on your good side, it's true. But you've been with her for years. I have faith you can intuit her moods and the subtext of the things she does. You may know her true intentions even better than she does."

As if summoned, Trafalgar spotted Dorothy walking toward them. By the time she arrived they had settled the bill and joined her on the street. She had changed into a dark brown turtleneck under a tan jacket that was belted at the waist. The brim of her hat was turned up to show off her face, so she blocked the sun with a pair of violet pince-nez sunglasses.

"There's a train leaving for Barcelona in just over an hour. I took the liberty of booking us passage on it."

Trafalgar said, "You know you don't have to pay for absolutely everything on this trip, right?"

"You paid for breakfast," Dorothy said as they began walking.

"You know what I mean. The ship and now the train."

Dorothy said, "True. But I have the means. The whole point of partnering is to avoid the need for a patron. You would prefer to go broke simply to maintain equality?"

"No." Trafalgar grimaced. "I'm not sure why I even brought it up. I simply wanted you know I was aware of the imbalance. Hopefully I can make it up to you at some point during the expedition."

"You're here for your expertise, your intelligence, and your ingenuity. Paying for your tickets is simply my fee for having you with me." She adjusted the cuffs of her sleeves. "And if we require a bit of a bribe when we arrive in Barcelona, I will gladly allow you to toss in a few dollars."

Trafalgar said, "Bribe?"

"I found someone who could arrange a meeting with a facilitator. He can give us what we need for the expedition, but he sounds like an odd one. It's always nice to have a little cash to help things go more smoothly."

"I'll be more than happy to help out," Trafalgar said.

"Splendid. If that's settled, we should get to the station. Our luggage was supposedly sent ahead from the harbor, but it's always best to double-check before getting underway."

The three of them walked along the pedestrian promenade toward the train station, their journey across Spain only just beginning.

The men stood motionless near the door of Emmeline Potter's front room. Their faces were formless now, the bodies under their suits as hard and steadfast as a mountain. They were good for brute force and shows of strength but otherwise they just got in her way. She was seated on the floor in the center of her main room. She was still naked from her bath, her skin scrubbed until it was pink and almost bloody. She was fresh and completely clean. She had fasted the entire day. She flattened her hands on the floor in front of her in the center of the pattern she'd drawn there. Energy thrummed through the wood and up into her arms. She closed her eyes and whispered incantations she'd learned as a child, summoning the energies to her.

She knew she was abusing the power. She knew that if the beings in charge - if they still existed, if they ever turned their attention to this plane - would be furious with her. So far she had been untouched. She had created her golems and used magic to cause harm with no consequences. She had grown richer, stronger, more adept at her practices, and it served to prove to her that there was no authority other than what people placed on themselves.

When she felt the power reach its peak, she lifted her hands. Tendrils of energy followed her as she moved. She picked up the wafer she'd prepared earlier. She didn't have much in terms of a totem, but it didn't take much. There was a smear of Dorothy Boone's blood on the face of the cracker, saved from their scuffle. She breathed it in even though there wasn't a detectable odor, then she placed it in her mouth. She bit the cracker in half and wrinkled her nose at the taste. But she forced herself to swallow.

The energy wrapped itself around her like a blanket on a cold morning. She felt it settling into her pores and filling her empty spaces. It found the tenuous link to Dorothy Boone and locked onto it.

She smelled sea air and sewage, then the familiar scent of food being cooked in the open air. She could feel the warm Mediterranean air on her skin as the scene formed on the back of her closed eyelids. Mud-colored buildings with flashes of blues and greens and gold. She saw a sea of dark-haired people with skin that was tan, not pink, and she could hear bursts of their speech.

"Barcelona," she whispered.

Virago smiled and opened her eyes. The ribbons of magical energy dissipated all around her once it had achieved its purpose. She stood up slowly, weak now and trembling. Her skin was drenched with sweat. She knew she would have to wash herself again. She swept her foot through the design; it would have to be redrawn for another ritual anyway, and it would be tempting fate to leave an old drawing behind for others to stumble over.

She went to the golems and woke them. Their bodies came to life and faces appeared on the blank canvas of their heads.

"Prepare my bags," she said. "We're going to Spain."

She turned and ascended the stairs, gathering her hair for her bath. As she lifted the curls it exposed the tattooed lines that ran from shoulder to shoulder. The inked lines created the image of a storm-lashed sea, the waves reaching up toward her neck. As she reached the second floor landing, the last of the magic dissipated, and the lines of her tattoo stopped glowing.

Though Trafalgar had never been to Spain, the six hundred kilometer train ride across its eastern border convinced her that a more leisurely visit was definitely in order. Perhaps when political temperatures were a bit calmer, if such a time ever arrived. Every man they encountered seemed aghast at the thought of three women traveling on their own to Barcelona. Trafalgar couldn't speak Spanish, but Beatrice told her that every newspaper was filled with stories of bloody riots and anti-church demonstrations. The current unrest had Barcelona rumored as one of the bloodiest and most extreme cities in all of Europe. Assassins lurked to defend the interests of business owners against unionizers, and the population was growing exponentially every day as more factories opened and jobs became available. The entire coast seemed like a powder keg waiting for the proper match.

Dorothy had been trying to read the newspaper, allowing Beatrice to translate for her as necessary, but after a few paragraphs she gave up on it.

"Virago is tearing apart history to pay for Ireland's war. We're keeping our heads down because of the unrest in Spain. I thought the war was supposed to have ended two years ago!"

"That was the world's war," Trafalgar said. "It left behind all the small, personal wars everyone has been fighting for decades, if not longer."

Dorothy sighed and nodded her agreement. "The UK is at peace. I suppose we can take comfort in that for as long as it lasts."

They arrived at the Barcelona train station and were met with further skepticism that they were traveling alone to the anarchist's "rose of fire." Dorothy had her gun tucked into her belt, hidden by her jacket, and Trafalgar's emei piercers were the flick of her wrist away. As for Beatrice... Dorothy feared for any man who considered her unarmed. They assured their would-be knights that they would be just fine on their own and departed the train station.

Beatrice escorted their bags to the hotel under protest. She wanted to be present for the meeting just in case it went wrong. Dorothy assured her it would be fine. The man they were meeting with was an unknown quantity, but he had come highly recommended. The suggestion was offered with a warning that the man was 'unusual' and it might take a few minutes for them to understand just what exactly he was all about. Dorothy was intrigued by the description and didn't get the whiff of danger from the man's suggestion they meet in one of the nicest restaurants in Barcelona.

When they arrived, the hostess sat them at booth with a curtain that would afford them a bit of privacy for the transaction. Dorothy and Trafalgar sat together on the side of the booth facing the front of the dining room so they could see when their contact arrived.

Ignacio Mata was a middle-aged man with salt and pepper hair, a face shaped like an inverted pentagon, and a beard so light that at first it looked as if the shadows were falling over the point of his chin in an unnatural way. His eyes were shaded by a heavy brow that would have been imposing if it wasn't for the beaming smile he offered them as he weaved through the tables to where they were waiting. He wore a rumpled suit, the shirt open at the collar, and he was carrying a large metal case. He tucked it under the table when he arrived and dropped into the seat across from them.

"Welcome back to Barcelona," he said, breathless and speaking quickly through his accent. "It's wonderful to see you again, Dorothy. Trafalgar. How has life been treating you?"

Dorothy glanced at Trafalgar. "As well as can be expected, Mr. Mata."

He laughed. "Why so formal?" His smile wavered and his eyes skipped between them. "Wait. How many times have we met?"

"We've never met you before this moment, Mr. Mata."

His jovial expression collapsed. He fell back against the cloth of the booth and stared at them as if they'd revealed his family was lost at sea.

"Yes. Yes, of course. Of course..." He ran a hand over his face. "I apologize. It's my fault. Not yours. Lady Boone, then, and Miss Trafalgar."

Dorothy said, "You called me by name rather easily, Mr. Mata. As if you've done it many times before. There must be a reason for that."

"There is. Yes." He was speaking slowly now, a completely different man. "I'm sorry. You must understand that from my perspective, the three of us are asso-

90

ciates. Friends."

"How is that possible?" Trafalgar asked.

He sighed. "I experience memory in reverse."

Dorothy furrowed her brow. "Explain."

"Years ago, I discovered a djinn. He granted me any wish I could imagine. I asked to know the future." He smiled mirthlessly. "Never make a deal with a djinn. They will give you what you desire, but they exact a precious cost. They gave me foresight at the cost of memory. I remember the future and forget the past.

"My mind works the way yours does. Simply in reverse. Think about when you wake up in the morning. You remember the day before, but not what is to come. When I lay down in bed at night, I forget the day that is just ending and I remember tomorrow. I know how I will die, but I don't know how I was born. I remember a long and fruitful relationship with you both, but I was unaware that relationship started right now, today, at this booth."

Dorothy said, "You can see the future?"

"I can remember it. And my memory is hazy at times, as you can tell from the fact I was wholly unprepared for this news. Think about conversations you had yesterday. You might remember the gist of them, but not every word that was said. You can remember events from a few years ago, but not with crystal clarity or perfect recall. Do I know things that will happen? Yes. But I won't share the information with anyone. There are some things people just shouldn't know ahead of time."

Dorothy thought he looked at her after he said that, but it could simply have been her mind playing tricks on her.

Trafalgar said, "If you forget the past, how are you aware of the way in which you were inflicted?"

"Part of the curse, I suppose. If I wasn't aware of my affliction, I'd be in a state of constant and utter confusion. It also seems to pick and choose what I will remember for delightful moments such as this." He shook his head and waved at the air over the table as if to clear away the conversation. "But enough of that. We can discuss it later. For now, I have everything you will need for your upcoming expedition."

"You... have..."

He smiled. "Yes. It's one way to ensure repeat customers. The next time we meet, you will tell me what you needed the last time. I'll remember it and bring it with me."

Dorothy said, "So we take this case on our expedition. And the next time we hire you, we simply tell you what was in the case?"

"Yes. And I will have the supplies you'll need for that expedition."

"That's impossible," Dorothy said.

"So is much of my life. And yet, it is how I exist." He bent down and retrieved the case. "In addition to what's in the case, I have the submersible you will need. It was difficult to find one with the exact specifications you'll require, but I managed."

Dorothy laughed. "So we simply have to remember the specifications of what you found..."

"And tell me the next time we meet so I can remember and find it again."

"This is making my head hurt," Trafalgar said.

Ignacio smiled sympathetically. "Imagine how my head feels. I simply know what I need to bring to our meetings because I have it in my head."

"Remarkable," Dorothy said.

"It's a curse. But one I have been able to make use of." He slid the case across the table. "As for payment..."

"Yes, we've made arrangements~"

He cut her off with a sweep of his hand. "Please, Lady Boone. You may not remember what we mean to one another, but I certainly do. You and Miss Trafalgar are two of my most beloved clients. I..." He looked at Dorothy again, and this time there was definitely something hidden behind the look. "I am very sad that this will be our final meeting. So in honor of everything we have meant and will mean to each other, please. Take this with my blessing."

"We couldn't," Dorothy said. "The submersible alone must have cost you dearly."

"I won't hear of payment for it. Consider it a goodbye gift. One day you'll understand." He reached across the table with both hands and gripped Trafalgar's right hand and Dorothy's left. "Remember this. Because the day will come when I won't remember you. When I treat you like any other client. I hope this gift helps you forgive me as I appear to slowly lose my trust in you."

"We'll remember you like this," Trafalgar said. "A kind man who made us feel like heroes."

He smiled and nodded. "That will do. Thank you, Miss Trafalgar. And you, Lady Boone."

Dorothy said, "Please, call me Dorothy. It would seem you earned it."

Trafalgar smiled. "And that is why he called you by your given name when this meeting began. Because last time you did not object to the familiarity."

Ignacio shrugged. "So it is. I wish I could stay longer, but we never linger after our transaction is finished. Well..." He dismissed whatever he was preparing to say. "Never mind. But I wish I could stay. I wish we could spend this entire afternoon sharing stories. But you have none, and all of mine would be information it would be best for you not to have. So I shall bid you both adieu."

He stood and smoothed down his jacket. Dorothy watched him, and a thought occurred to her.

"There must be a final meeting." He looked down at her with sad eyes. "Eventually there will come a time when one or both of us doesn't return. You know when that happens, don't you? You know which one of us will die first, and you know when."

Ignacio smiled at her in a way that both answered her question and told her he would never reveal those truths. "Good day, Dorothy. Trafalgar. It has been an honor knowing you both. And I look forward to knowing you again."

He turned and meandered back through the sea of tables, leaving Trafalgar and Dorothy behind him trying to decide whether they had just been given a bright glimpse of a long partnership or the grim threat of potential doom.

Chapter Fifteen

Part of Dorothy's travel arrangements included the private rental of a steamship that could take them from Barcelona to the Aegean Sea. The ship would also serve as a launch and base of operations for their descent. They took the case from Ignacio and returned to the hotel to await word it was ready for departure. Dorothy was impatient to leave. Reserving the private ship meant they wouldn't be forced to make stops at Rome or Malta or the other tourist spots that might have delayed them further, but it would still be at least four days before they were finally at their destination.

She was growing more concerned about Trafalgar's comments on Virago. If somehow she did discover where they were headed, there was every chance she could get to the Aegean before them. They might arrive to find another ship squatting over their prize. She sat in her hotel room with her feet up on the desk, her chair angled so she could look out the window. Her room faced the wrong way to see the harbor but she imagined she could hear the stevedores working to prepare their vessel.

Ignacio's case was sitting on the bed. It was incredibly heavy, made of a thick metal that brought to mind a vault rather than valise. Carrying it had strained the muscles of her arms and back, but she'd managed. She had yet to open it, and when she suggested Trafalgar sort through the items the other woman had stiffened and shook her head. Dorothy knew she could open it and get an idea of what they were going to face. If Ignacio was telling the truth about his curse, then he would know exactly what they would need. She might not understand the context of every item, but she could gather enough for an educated inference. Medicine. Bandages. Weapons. The temptation was far too great. She didn't want to know. Knowing anything in advance would lead to confirmation bias, would make them question their choices, and could doom the expedition. She would just keep the case close to hand and, if an insurmountable obstacle arose, they would break it open and hope the solution was inside.

Beatrice had gone for a quick jog that ended up lasting most of the afternoon. Dorothy wasn't surprised. After spending days cooped up on a boat and a train, with another long journey ahead of her, she knew Beatrice was eager to stretch her legs as much as possible. When she returned she immediately stripped down to her underclothes to change into something more casual, only noticing Dorothy's doldrums when she sat on the edge of the bed to tie her shoes.

"Are you all right?"

Dorothy sighed. She knew she must have looked a ruin. Her hair was down, her blouse unbuttoned to reveal the chemise underneath, and her stockings had runs in them. "I fear taking this route could have dire consequences. Virago is a crafty opponent. She may have already discovered what we're up to. She could be in Athens right now chartering a vessel to take her out to her prize. She may be long gone by the time we finally arrive."

Beatrice stood and went to stand behind Dorothy's chair. "Sit up straight, for God's sake." Dorothy complied, and Beatrice began massaging her shoulders. "You did what was necessary. You needed to plan, to prepare, to get us here. To make yourself ready for what's going to happen. Do you remember what you used to say about Trafalgar? How she would rush ahead without a plan in place? She was headed for disaster. I would much rather take a few extra days to ensure we're ready for a thousand-meter descent into the Aegean. Let Virago rush. Let her be crushed like a dry leaf."

Dorothy reached up and stroked Beatrice's arm. "Thank you, Trix."

"And if she does beat us to the punch," Beatrice said, leaning down next to Dorothy's ear and lowering her voice to a conspiratorial whisper, "we will simply have to break into her home and steal back any priceless artifacts she may have absconded with."

Dorothy laughed and turned her head, capturing Beatrice's lips in a kiss. Beatrice slipped her hands into the open front of Dorothy's blouse. Dorothy shifted in the chair to get a better angle, dropping her feet to the floor as she reached up to loosen Beatrice's hair. The door opened and Trafalgar entered. She only took one step before seeing what she had intruded upon and turned so quickly that the tail of her coat flipped up like a bird's wing.

"My apologies."

"No need." Dorothy turned away and did up the buttons on her shirt. "Where have you been?"

"I went for a walk and decided to check out the boat. I regret complaining about you paying for everything on this expedition. That can't have been cheap."

Dorothy said, "No, but it was necessary. I'm not going to risk failure or defeat simply because of the expense. I owe it to my grandmother."

"I wish I'd known her," Beatrice said.

Trafalgar said, "I was vaguely aware of her, but our paths never crossed the way yours and mine did. I know she was very respected in our field."

Dorothy nodded. "She was one of the best. And one of the first women to do this sort of thing without a man endorsing her or taking the lead. But beyond that, she made me who I am today. I was not encouraged to be an adventuress. Hell, I wasn't encouraged to get my clothes dirty. But Grandmother brought me books. She told me I had more to look forward to than suitors and marriage and a house full of babies. When the time came to choose between what my parents wanted for me and what I wanted for myself, Grandmother was there to give me a place to go. I owe it to her to finish what she began. I'm just terrified I won't measure up to her. That I'll fail in the attempt and prove that she was wrong to have faith in me."

Beatrice said, "You're more than worthy. I have faith in you."

"As do I." She snorted and shook her head. "I'm about to go a thousand meters under the sea for you when I have a difficult enough time aboard a boat."

Dorothy smiled and leaned forward. "Thank you for the pep talk, ladies. I believe now it would be best if we have an early dinner and get to bed at a reasonable hour. We'll have a few days on the boat, but that time will be spent learning how to operate the submersible. Might as well get all the rest we can while we're still on dry land. I believe I saw a restaurant in the lobby. It will be Trafalgar's treat." She winked at Trafalgar as they gathered their things and filed out of the room.

When they reached the lobby, a man behind the front desk called out to her. "Lady Boone? A telegram has arrived for you, from London."

Dorothy changed course and retrieved the paper from him. She slipped him a coin and skimmed the contents of the message, then read it again slowly as Trafalgar and Beatrice joined her.

"What is it?" Trafalgar asked, knowing from Dorothy's expression that the news was dire.

She handed the message over to Trafalgar and explained aloud for Beatrice's benefit. "Desmond had a run-in with Virago. She shattered his left hand."

"Dear God," Trafalgar said.

"Is he all right?"

Dorothy said, "He's confident it will heal. He got medical attention. And he says he didn't reveal anything about our plans to Virago. But..."

"But she won't have given up that easily," Trafalgar said.

"Precisely. Virago is coming." She took the note back from Trafalgar and turned to the desk clerk. "I'd like to send a message back."

Trafalgar said, "I assume dinner is off?"

Dorothy nodded. "We mustn't waste any more time. We have to depart as soon as possible. I have no doubt Virago is already on her way to intercept us."

\#

The ship was the SS *Cervantes*. It was a paddle steamer seventy meters long with a ten-meter beam. A tall mast rose from its foredeck to help the ship adjust for winds or rough seas. The new steam turbines they were putting into ships meant that the *Lusitania*'s once-impressive top speed of twenty-five knots was now considered the standard for all passenger vessels. At that speed they would reach the Aegean in four days; Dorothy hoped it would be enough to beat Virago to the prize.

She was more intrigued by the addition Ignacio had requested be added to the ship's starboard deck. The submersible was much smaller than she had envisioned. She hoped claustrophobia wouldn't be an issue. It was shaped like a gray teardrop lain on its side, with the point coming out the back and angling up. That housed the main engine and was also where the winch connected to the side of the ship. Lights mounted at the one- and eleven-o-clock positions around the viewport would provide light once they had descended farther than the sun could reach. It had been the first thing added, so pushing their departure up by twelve hours wouldn't affect it. The front of the vessel was all glass, and through it she could see two chairs set amid a wall of dials, screens, and controls.

Someone approached from behind and she looked at the reflection to see a man dressed in standard sailor gear. He had a broad chest and a heavy beard that left everything but his nose and eyes concealed.

"It's not that hard, once you know what to push and when."

Dorothy said, "You know what all those buttons do?"

He laughed. "Not even half of them. But I know which ones do what I need, and I know when to push them. That's good enough."

"I suppose you're right." She turned and realized the reflection hadn't done him justice. He was massive, a full head taller than her. She covered her shock and extended her hand. "Lady Dorothy Boone. It's a pleasure to meet you, Mister...?"

"Mister? No thanks." He took her hand. "Name's Huey. Huey Conway. But you can call me Huey or 'hey you-ee' or anything in between and I'll come running."

Dorothy grinned. "I shall endeavor to remember that. Will it be your job to teach me and my associate how to use this contraption?"

"As well as I can in four days. Be easier if I could just take it down with you, but... well. You see it only fits two. One plus a half-of-one, if I'm included. And to be honest, the captain tol' me how far down you were going and I'm not too keen on getting that far away from the air. 'Specially not in something I could wear like a hat."

Dorothy laughed. "Trafalgar and I are quick learners, I assure you."

"You'd better be, Lady Boone. Not to frighten you, but something like this, I think a little fright can be a good thing. Once you get in here and start going down, you have a little leeway. If it starts leaking or you think the pressure is too much, we can haul you up. But once you get down to a certain point, there's no quick way out."

"Your warning will be taken to heart," she said. "And if you are to be Huey, then I must be Dorothy."

"Doesn't work that way, ma'am. But I appreciate the thought, just the same."

Dorothy said, "Very well. I'll retrieve Miss Trafalgar and we can begin our first lesson."

"Right now? Ship's not even setting out for another hour."

"I'm aware. But as you said, time is of the essence. We don't have much, but the clock is still ticking down with every moment."

\#

As the *Cervantes* was pulling away from Barcelona's docks, fifteen hundred miles north, Virago was preparing to leave London. She was not particularly fond of the man she'd been forced to ask for help, and he was no fan of her. Captain Willard Baker, a scoundrel and drunkard she ordinarily wouldn't give the time of day, who considered her to be a woman of low morals. But strange bedfellows and all that rubbish, and she was paying him plenty to put up with her for a few days. And she was more than willing to suffer his presence in exchange for his marvelous submarine.

It was shaped like a jellyfish, with a bulbous main compartment broken up into individual rooms. The engines extended rigidly out behind the body of the vessel and but also contained tendrils that could move with the ocean currents to increase its speed. He was inspired to create the ship after reading Jules Verne's remarkably dull book, a tome Virago had never been able to force her way through, but she was grateful for the author's inspiration now. The *Mobilis* was one of the fastest ships in the world, capable of achieving over fifty knots. She hoped that would more than make up for any lead Trafalgar and Boone had gotten on her, even if they were forced to go the long way around to Gibraltar.

She entered the bridge, a ludicrously gilded dome which gleamed with the ambient light coming through the front glass. They had been towed out to the North Sea and were now submerged to begin their journey. The command console formed a half-circle in front of the glass and it was here that Baker sat upon his throne. An image of Neptune was carved into the back of the chair to greet everyone as they came onto the bridge, a none-too-subtle reminder of how the man at the controls saw himself. Virago stepped around the ostentatious chair and rested a hand on top of Baker's head.

"Has the journey gotten off to a good beginning, Cap?"

"Yes," he muttered.

"I trust we're making good time." She bent forward to look at the readouts. "Excellent. I know you're worried about burning out the engines by going at full speed for so long."

He swallowed hard. "No trouble. Engines is engines. You can always fix 'em or buy a new one."

"That's the spirit, Willie!" She patted the top of his head hard enough to make him cringe. When she enlisted his services, he had suggested things they could do together to pass the time. It had been mild innuendo at best, nothing she hadn't heard a thousand times outside a bar or walking down the street. But she was about to embark on a week-long journey under the sea with the man. She didn't need him getting any ideas about what she would consider acceptable behavior.

She had been very clear about what she would allow. And now she was certain Baker would behave himself. He would sit in his sad little throne and he would keep his lecherous hands to himself, and she would have a nice subaquatic journey. She would fill her time plotting against her adversaries. If they were already in Barcelona they had a daunting lead on her. She knew Baker's ship was fast, but still she was worried it might not be fast enough.

"Take us up to fifty-five knots."

Anger flashed across his features. "That isn't~"

Virago locked her eyes on him, not blinking.

"That isn't... too far outside the realm of possibility, Missus Potter."

She smiled, showing her teeth. "Good boy, Willie." She pursed her lips in a mocking kiss and left the bridge in his capable hands. She would reach the Aegean when she reached it. If she beat Lady Boone, fine. If not... she would make sure that her rivals never returned from their watery tomb.

Chapter Sixteen

It was the second day of the journey before Trafalgar was forced to excuse herself from the training and retreat to the front of the boat. It wasn't necessarily seasickness, though the symptoms were basically the same. The sway of the deck under her feet reminded her of the day she killed Enoch Solomon. Her tongue felt heavy and she could taste the stone he'd put in her mouth to draw whatever entity he'd summoned into her body. She was queasy and unsettled as she gripped the railing and looked south toward the African coast, drawing in slow breaths of fresh air to settle her nerves.

"I wish I could say it gets easier," a man said from behind her, "but it doesn't. Not always, not for everyone."

She turned and saw a man whose name she didn't remember ever hearing. He was as tall as she was, but broader in the shoulders. He had a kind face that was prematurely aged by the sun and salt of the sea. He smiled as he approached.

"Some people get used to it. Others go their whole lives getting on ships and spending the whole journey bent over the rails. There are some tricks to it, though."

"Oh, really?"

He stretched out one arm and pointed two fingers across the water. "Focus on the horizon. Keeps you grounded, a bit. Helps your brain figure out what's going on and that settles the other stuff. You could also, um..." He patted the pockets of his jacket until he found what he was looking for. He held out a cellophane wrapper that contained a small white lozenge with twists of red along its edge. "Peppermint. I don't know how it helps, but people swear it does."

Trafalgar took the candy from him. The plastic crinkled as he passed it to her.

"Thank you. I'm Trafalgar."

"I know. Bert Carroll."

She unwrapped the candy. She hesitated to put it in her mouth, fearful it would only intensify the memory of the stone. But she put it on her tongue and was surprised by the sharp and pleasant flavor of it. She moved it over between her cheek and gum. The tang actually helped suppress the memory. Instead of the flat, earthy taste of the stone, she could only taste the peppermint.

"Thank you very much, Bert. I can already tell it will help."

"We have loads more down in the mess. Just ask and someone will get them for you." He shifted his weight and said, "There's one other thing I could do, but I'd have to touch your hand. If that's all right."

She considered saying no, but she couldn't think of any reason to refuse. She held out her left hand to him. He took her hand in his, then pressed the thumb of his other hand to a spot just below the crease of her wrist. He applied gentle pressure to the skin between the tendons.

"Don't ask me why," he said. "Man who taught me this little trick never bothered to explain it. But it helps. Like the peppermint. Some of the power might be in just thinking it will work."

"I wouldn't be surprised. And yes, it does seem to be working." She didn't know if it was the pressure or the act that he was touching her that was helping calm her nerves. The power of touch could be an incredible thing. "Thank you. It really wasn't necessary for you to help, but I'm glad you did."

Bert shrugged. "I'm happy to pass along tips when I can. Especially for someone like you."

"Someone like me?"

"Sure. Miss Trafalgar of Abyssinia. We heard about you a lot these past few years. There was the incident in Turkey. Istanbul. There was, ah… let's see. Brazil."

Trafalgar laughed. "Have you been keeping tabs on me, Mr. Carroll?"

"Inadvertently, maybe. I confess, I always hoped one day you would charter our vessel for one of your adventures. When the captain said Lady Boone was looking for passage, I convinced him to accept. I knew that the two of you were working together now. I feared it might be my only chance to meet you."

He was still massaging the inside of her wrist. She didn't have the heart to tell him that the nausea had passed. To be honest, it felt too nice for her to want it to stop.

"Our adventures don't always have happy endings."

"True. But what's life without risk?"

She returned his gaze and found herself unaccountably uncomfortable. Not in a bad way, not in a way she wanted to stop, but in a way that was simply unfamiliar.

"I believe you've struck upon a cure for what ails me, Mr. Carroll."

"Bert, please. And what did it? The peppermint or the massage?"

Trafalgar smiled. "The company."

"Huey Conway is a bloody madman!"

Trafalgar twitched at the sound of Dorothy's voice, her hand slipping most of the way out of Bert's grip. She moved her arm to free herself the rest of the way and turned to watch as Dorothy stalked toward them. There was sweat on her forehead and upper lip, and she shook her hair free from its braid as she neared the railing.

"He locked me in the submersible! Can you believe that? He locked me in and refused to let me out until I had completed his interminable tests. I know. I know that once we're underwater we won't be able to just jump out whenever we want. But it's a far cry between that and being locked in a tin can secured on the deck of a ship."

She exhaled forcefully and looked at Trafalgar, then turned her gaze on Bert as if she had just realized he was standing there.

"Who is this?"

"Bert Carroll," Trafalgar said. "He's a member of the crew."

Dorothy looked between them. "Oh. Oh!" Her eyes widened. "I apologize. I had no idea I was intruding."

"You're not intruding," Trafalgar said at the same time Bert said, "Nothing to intrude upon." He was already backing away from the railing. "If you need anything else, Miss Trafalgar, there are some other curatives we could try. Just come find me."

"I will. Thank you, Bert."

He smiled to her and nodded to Dorothy before he turned his back to make a retreat. Trafalgar wasn't aware she was watching him go until it was too late. Dorothy had noticed her watching and was smiling an insufferably knowing smile.

"Stop that."

"I will not. It's nothing to be ashamed about. A bit of flirtation helps pass the time." She turned and rested her arms on the railing. "To be honest, I was getting a bit worried for you. I've never seen you with a suitor. I didn't even know if you preferred men or women."

"Neither," Trafalgar said. Dorothy looked at her curiously. "I mean I don't have a preference for one or the other. Each has their... appeal..."

Dorothy laughed. "I suppose they do."

Trafalgar sighed.

"Oh, come on. We have two more nights on this rig. I plan to spend at least one of them with Trix. Why shouldn't you have someone to warm your sheets?"

"I'll likely never see Bert again after this expedition."

"All the more reason to take advantage of the opportunity. Look, you know that Trix and I have an understanding. When I'm away, when I'm in the Philippines or Jordan and she's home in London, I take lovers. It's not because I'm a hussy. Although I suppose by some definitions, I certainly qualify. No, it's because I understand that everything could be lost at any moment. Every expedition could be our last. The ship could sink, the submersible could fail when we're too far down to be rescued, the world could erupt in another war and we could be caught unawares by the enemy."

"So sleep with whomever and damn the consequences?"

"No. It's not about sex, it's about intercourse. It's about being vulnerable and open with another human being. It's as much about the sleeping together as it is the mechanics of the act. Skin to skin, sharing breath and sweat, enjoying one another, spending one... blissful moment with one another." She chewed her bottom lip as she looked out over the water, eyes narrow. She tapped her fingers on the railing before pushing away. "I think I'm going to go find Trix. Take a break from the training."

Trafalgar smiled. "Have fun."

"I shall." She touched Trafalgar's arm. "I suggest you do the same. You never know when you might get another opportunity."

"I'll consider it," Trafalgar said with a weary sigh.

"Good girl. I should hurry before Huey comes looking for me."

She left Trafalgar alone on the deck considering her advice. She had never been one for casual flings, but it would certainly help with some of the stress and anxiety she'd been feeling for the past week. If a simple touch on the wrist could elevate her spirits, she could only imagine what a more involved massage could do. Bert fit the bare minimum of requirements she had for a lover. He seemed strong, he was kind, and he was tall. She liked being with tall men. And judging from the way he'd held her hand, he certainly seemed willing.

"Oh, Lady Boone," she sighed out over the water. "You are clearly a terrible influence on me..."

She rolled her eyes and left the railing. Her stomach was quiet enough that she could wander the ship for a while until she decided what to do with the rest of her night.

The submersible was technically called a bathysphere, a research vessel originally invented by Otis Barton during the Great War. His original design was unpowered, but recent technological advances had allowed him to provide a motor. Trafalgar hoped to use the engine to putter around whatever they found on the floor of the Aegean. She sat in what she considered the command chair, on the port side of the vessel, and ran her fingers over the console. The space was cramped, with her knees awkwardly folded out to either side to accommodate the yoke. Not the most comfortable conveyance she'd ever used, but it was not the worst, either.

Night had fallen quickly. The rest of the crew was below decks either having dinner or settling in for the evening. Huey had declared it was too dark to see the controls, so there was no use trying to train them. Trafalgar wasn't interested in the dials and levers that filled the compartment. She wanted to get comfortable in the device itself. She wanted to learn how it felt to be inside, to feel the walls curving all around her. It was so compact that every inch was filled with some necessary piece. Spending time in the machine would help her feel like one of those pieces.

Through the glass, she saw someone coming toward the submersible along the railing. From his height, she could tell it was Bert. He slowed and craned his neck forward, squinting through the glass. Trafalgar flashed her lantern and he held up his hand in greeting. She unfolded herself from the seat and reached up to open the hatch in the top of the submersible. She was climbing down the side when Bert approached.

"To be completely honest with you, Miss Trafalgar, that thing sort of makes me shiver. It looks like a giant eye sitting here."

Trafalgar looked at it again. "Good heavens, I suppose you're right. I'll never get that out of my mind now."

"Apologies."

"No, no. It's fine. And please, just Trafalgar is more than fine."

He nodded. "I was afraid maybe you were suffering more of that seasickness. Thought I'd come and offer you some more peppermint, if you needed it."

"How sweet. But no, I've been fine since our last encounter."

They stood together looking at the submersible. Trafalgar could hear Dorothy in her mind urging her onward, telling her to take the initiative.

"We should be where we need to be by day after tomorrow," he said. "Think you'll have a handle on this thing by then?"

"What I don't know, I'm sure Lady Boone will be able to cover. I hope. That seems to be the way things go with us. She fills gaps I wasn't aware I had."

Bert chuckled. "Best kind of partner there is." He adjusted his coat and looked out over the water. "Well, I suppose… I mean, if you're fine, I don't want to impose…"

"Wait," Trafalgar said. He turned toward her, and she realized she had no clue what she was going to say next. So instead of saying anything, she stepped closer and kissed him. He pulled back in surprise and broke their contact. When she opened her mouth to apologize, he craned his neck forward and resumed the kiss, his hands moving to her waist. She arched her back and pressed against his chest, grabbing handfuls of his shirt and pulling him with her as she moved. She fell back against the curved side of the submersible.

"This isn't the sort of thing I normally do," she said against his cheek, feeling the stubble there against her lips. "I want you to know that. I usually prefer a bed."

"I got one of those," he said, breathing heavily.

"No," she said. "Here. Right now."

He nodded and gasped, "Yeah, okay," and moved his hands between their bodies. Her pants were undone first, pushed down and left gathered around her calves. She did the same to him but only pushed his pants down as far as she needed them to go. She pressed her palm against the base of him, wrapped her fingers around the shaft, and groaned with approval at what she found. Her other arm slid around his shoulders while his hands cupped her ass.

Bert lifted, Trafalgar rolled her hips forward, and her hand guided him to her. She sank down onto him, her knees tight around his waist, holding tightly to his shoulders. They fit together well, and between the cold hull of the submersible and his strong hands supporting her, she was able to focus on moving her body against his.

"Good lord, how have I waited..." she groaned, moving her lips to his neck. He felt wonderful inside of her. She curled her fingers into claws and dug the nails into his shoulder. Bert moved faster, knocking her against the submersible, breathing heavily. They both pulled back at the same time and kissed. He grunted and trembled, turning his head so that his lips were next to her ear. He whispered something and she nodded.

They moved breathlessly, and she dropped to her knees in front of him. As she took him into her mouth, she put one hand between her legs to finish herself off. She climaxed with her lips around the head of his cock, feeling it throb as he reached his own orgasm. His groan of completion seemed to reflect off the side of the submersible and echo up and down the deck of the ship, but Trafalgar was beyond caring. She swallowed and touched the tongue to the sensitive tip. She smiled at the way it made him twitch.

When she stood, Bert touched her cheek. "I didn't expect that. I was just being nice."

"I know. That's what made you deserve it." She kissed the corner of his mouth. "I hope you also understand that this was just..."

"Oh. Yeah. If anyone understands what just happened, it's a sailor. Trust me, I don't expect anything more. Except... well. You're not reaching land for another forty-eight hours at least. Hopefully somewhere in that time we can make it to a bed. I can show you what I'm really made of."

Trafalgar laughed. "I shall have to make the time in between training."

She could see the moonlight glinting off his teeth when he smiled. They kissed once more and then helped each other back into their clothes. Bert walked away toward the bow while Trafalgar took a sternward trajectory. Just before she reached the door that led below deck, it swung open to reveal Dorothy and

Beatrice. They were both in their nightclothes under heavy coats, their hands clasped tightly. Dorothy stopped short when she saw Trafalgar and released Beatrice's hand. The shame in that movement made Trafalgar feel sorry for them.

"It's just me."

"Oh," Dorothy said. "I was just going to show Trix the submersible."

"In the middle of the night. In your pajamas."

Dorothy grinned. "Well."

"I see." Trafalgar stepped to one side. "Don't let me keep you. I was just about to retire."

Dorothy stepped closer and examined Trafalgar. There was just enough light from the corridor for her to make out details.

"You look a bit... disheveled, Miss Trafalgar. Your hair... it can't possibly be that windy out here, can it?"

"Those Mediterranean winds."

Dorothy smirked knowingly. "They can be nefarious. Well. Good night, Trafalgar."

"And to you. Enjoy the submersible."

"We plan to." Dorothy took Beatrice's hand, leading her outside as Trafalgar went below. When the door closed behind her, she chuckled and shook her head. With everything they were certain to face in the coming days, she could think of worse ways to spend their evening. She just hoped Dorothy and Beatrice were cautious in their "exploration." It wouldn't do to have a sailor notice what was going on in the cramped compartment. But she had suspicions about a few crewmembers. If anyone made a fuss she would simply bring up their predilections. She was confident her new friends would be safe for the time being.

She just hoped that safety continued when they reached the far more treacherous depths of the Aegean.

Chapter Seventeen

It looked like two monstrous men were hanging from hooks on the ceiling. The bodies were a combination of leather and rubber. Attached to the front of each suit was a manual control that trailed tubes to the bulky machinery attached to its back. More hoses stretched up to the helmet to make it look as if a man's head had been replaced by an octopus or squid. There was a window on the front of the helmet, much like the one on the submersible.

"We don't actually have to wear those," Dorothy said.

Huey smiled. "It's more comfortable than it looks, I swear." He walked over and patted the arm. "It doesn't quite conform to your body, but it sort of feels like an ill-fitting suit. The mechanics at the back help keep the suit pressurized so you don't have to worry about the bends. And of course you have the independent air supply."

Dorothy said, "But the plan is to remain in the submersible at all times. We can tool around whatever we find, but its environmental controls will be enough to protect us."

"Sure," Huey said, "if everything goes perfectly. But what if there's a leak and the compartment starts filling with water? You want to try getting into this thing in that cramped ship?"

Dorothy recalled the night before last, sitting in the copilot's seat with Beatrice on top of her. It had been difficult enough getting out of their nightgowns. She didn't want to think about trying to dress while her life was on the line.

"And if it does fill up with water, you just clap the helmet on and hook up these tubes. That will give you a few extra minutes of oxygen while we're hauling you up. Could mean the difference between drowning and getting up on deck."

"I suppose you have a point," Dorothy said.

Trafalgar arrived and looked at the suits. "We don't actually have to wear those, do we?"

Huey chuckled and pinched the bridge of his nose. "You do if you want to survive."

They allowed Huey and one of the deckhands to help them into the suits. Huey wasn't lying about the fact it was more comfortable than it looked, although it would honestly have to be. For the sake of comfort, visibility, and maneuverability, they didn't have to wear the helmets unless they became necessary. The collar where the helmet would attach was an iron ring around her throat that felt oddly like a yoke, and she found herself tugging at it to see if it would give a little more. They followed Huey out onto the deck with their heavy boots clunking with every step.

Beatrice was waiting to accompany them to the submersible, carrying Ignacio's case in her right hand. Dorothy still hadn't looked inside and, as far as she knew, neither had Trafalgar. She still wasn't entirely convinced it would deliver what he'd promised, but she wasn't going to risk being caught without it if something unexpected arose.

"Everything all right?" Dorothy asked under her breath so Huey wouldn't hear. Magic was very well known, and the practitioners weren't shunned, but she didn't know who aboard the *Cervantes* was trustworthy. Any one of them could have been bought off by Virago. That was another reason she wanted Beatrice to remain on the surface; she wanted at least one person she could count on by the controls.

Beatrice nodded. "The magical protections I placed on the ship are holding. I don't want to be too optimistic, but it should prevent any unforeseen mechanical failures."

"Thank you, Trix."

A small group of midshipmen were hovering around the submersible like a colony of ants that had found a toffee apple. They were moments away from arriving at the coordinates from Eula's map, according to the crew, but Dorothy was mystified at how they could determine that fact. The sea was featureless in every direction save for a hint of land far behind them. Ahead and to all sides, the sky was perfectly clear and the water was like glass. There was hardly any line at the horizon, just a hazy area where the two shades of blue faded and mixed into a pale white.

Huey stopped next to the submersible. "I didn't think it was possible, but you two are fast learners. I still wish I was the one going down there with you, but I'm confident you can handle it. When we start lowering you down, we'll have a short window of opportunity where we can pull you up if anything goes wrong. But once you get past the point of no return... even if you contact us immediately and even if we react as quickly as humanly possible, you're going so far down that we may not be able to rescue you."

"We understand," Trafalgar said.

Huey said, "Then what are we waiting for? You ladies have been sitting around long enough. Time to start your work."

"To the bottom of the sea we go," Dorothy said.

They climbed up the ladder, an act more difficult given their current outfits, and slid in through the hatch. Trafalgar had asked Dorothy to take the pilot seat so she could have a bit more legroom, so Dorothy angled herself to straddle the yoke. Trafalgar passed down their helmets and Ignacio's case, then followed her in. At one point her boot nearly clocked Dorothy on the side of the head, but she swatted it away and leaned to the side until Trafalgar was safely inside. They strapped themselves into their seats and checked the instruments to make sure everything was on and functioning properly.

"Look at us," Dorothy said. "One might think we actually knew what we were doing."

"Don't we?"

"We're about to ride this metal bubble a thousand meters under the sea tethered to the surface by a spool of steel thread."

Trafalgar said, "When you put it that way…"

Huey stepped in front of the ship and nodded at them through the glass. They both raised their thumbs as someone on top of the submersible shut the hatch and began to process of sealing it. Dorothy looked up at the only exit and tensed so that she wouldn't shudder.

"Well, I suppose there's no turning back now."

"Your grandmother would have been very proud of you right now, Dorothy."

She looked at Trafalgar, touched by the gesture. "Thank you. I hope you're right."

Metal screeched as the winch was activated. Dorothy braced herself against the wall as the submersible was lifted off its platform and moved carefully over the edge of the ship. They could see through the glass when they crossed over the railing and Trafalgar shifted uncomfortably in her seat.

"Doesn't seem natural, that's all," she said in response to Dorothy's unasked question.

"It's ridiculous. We've both been underwater before."

Trafalgar nodded. "This is no different. Just deeper."

"Right. Deeper… much deeper."

They reached the water and, after a moment of resistance, began to submerge. Dorothy kept an eye on the instruments Huey had taught her how to read. Everything had seemed so simple on the deck; now she was questioning everything she had learned. Trafalgar watched for any signs of leakage, checking the monitors but also scanning for tell-tale drops or evidence water was seeping in through the seals. Everything was currently shining blue ("blue means good," Huey had told them multiple times over the past four days, "yellow means bad. Red means... well, you'll never see red."), so Dorothy let out a sigh of relief and looked out the glass.

"Nowhere to go but down," she said.

Trafalgar nodded.

Dorothy turned on the engine and felt it rumbling to life behind them. They had a range of a few hundred meters in every direction, but they'd been warned not to get overly adventurous. The submersible was lowered at a decent clip, just fast enough to be safe and not overtax the mechanisms on the ship or the engine. Dorothy took the opportunity to take out her camera and prepare the film. Taking pictures was all they could do for the time being, but she was anxious to get the best possible shots. Depending on what they found, it might be their only chance to get a look at the untouched site.

"What in the world is that?"

Dorothy looked up and Trafalgar pointed. She spotted a darker area of ocean that was currently far to the west of their current position but closing fast. Its movement was linear and unnatural, meaning it could only be a submarine of some sort.

"Virago."

"How can you be certain?"

Dorothy glared at her.

"Fair enough." The ship was closing in at a good clip. Soon it would be at the *Cervantes'* position. "I'll signal the ship to warn Beatrice about their approach."

"Or..."

Trafalgar looked at her.

"She could spot us, move to intercept, and sever the line. If you chose to signal the ship and ask them to bring us up, I wouldn't argue with you."

"Is that what you want?" Trafalgar asked.

Dorothy looked out the glass. "We're so damned close. I'm not sure what I want. All I know is that it's a risk. Continuing down could cost us our lives. I wanted to let you know I'm open to taking the safe route. I leave the decision up to you."

The ship was now close enough for them to see details of its shape. It was closing fast on the *Cervantes*. Trafalgar unhooked the radio microphone and turned it on, searching for the proper signal before she spoke.

"Captain Mederos, this is Trafalgar. You're about to have company, coming from the west. It's a submarine, so you most likely won't see them until they're right below you." She gave him the bearings as best she could figure from the instruments. "Judging by the speed, they'll be there inside of ten minutes."

There was a squawk of static before a man responded in broken English. "Shall we reel you in?"

Trafalgar shook her head. "No. We're continuing down as planned."

"Good luck with you, Miss Trafalgar," he said.

"To you as well."

She ended the connection and they both looked out as the underwater ship inched ever closer to its target.

"We can't do anything to help them from down here," Dorothy said. "Focus on the task at hand."

"Right."

Dorothy took the yoke in her hands even though they were only going straight down for the time being. It helped give her the illusion that she had some measure of control over whatever was going to happen next.

Beatrice happened to be passing by underneath the bridge when Captain Mederos pushed open the window and began shouting to his men in Spanish. It irritated her because she knew he could speak English. Choosing not to at this moment meant he was trying to keep her from overhearing the news. She would have to take him to task for that, but at the moment she had more pressing concerns. She understood enough to glean his message: there were pirates approaching.

She immediately broke into a run, stripping off her jacket and letting it fall to the deck behind her as she ascended to the bridge. Mederos looked surprised to see her, grimacing and turning his back on her to focus on the screens. She walked up behind him and put a hand on his shoulder so he couldn't pull away from her. When she spoke, her words were in Spanish.

"Where is the attack vessel? I didn't see anything."

He stared at her for a moment, startled that she knew the language, but she was scanning the horizon. "The women saw a submarine." He pointed at the radar. "Big one, too."

Beatrice said, "Damn big. Trafalgar and Boone?"

"They said they didn't want to be brought back up."

She had to switch back to English. "Then we abide by that. Tell your men to get weapons."

The captain shifted languages as well. "We know how to deal with pirates."

"Normal pirates, maybe. These aren't going to lie down easily." She turned to leave the bridge. "Make sure your men are prepared. It's going to be a tough fight."

She returned to the deck and ran forward until she found Huey. He saw her coming and closed the distance between them.

"We should pull them back up."

"They said not to."

Huey said, "If anything happens to that wire~"

"They said not to," Beatrice said again. She was entirely aware of the dangers involved, but she wasn't about to drag either of them up against their will. If they believed they could continue with the mission, then Beatrice intended to honor that. "We need weapons."

"We have weapons."

She followed him along the port deck. She could see the submarine's wake now, a massive bullet-shaped wedge in the water riding up alongside them. She was watching to see if it would surface when someone grabbed her arm. She turned to see someone vaguely familiar from the past four days aboard the ship but she couldn't put a name to him.

"Bert," he said to her confused expression. "Bert Carroll. Trafalgar and I~"

"Right," Beatrice said. "You want to help. We're on our way to get weapons."

The rest of the crew was preparing for the submarine's arrival by securing the access points below deck and posting guards around the engine room. Beatrice grabbed one of the men and ordered him to put a guard around the winch. If this was Virago - and she saw no possible way it could be anyone else - she didn't want to give the woman any leverage.

Huey led them to the weapons locker and armed himself and Bert with a rifle he called a Smiler. "SMLE Rifle. Stands for short Magazine Lee-Enfield," he explained as he handed it to Bert. "We've had these lying around since the War."

He also gave them a Mauser and a Smith & Wesson. Beatrice took one of the handguns, a few grenades, and a Filipino bolo knife. She tucked the weapons into her belt. She preferred close-quarters combat to long-range options, but she also hoped they could hold off Virago's people from boarding the *Cervantes*.

"Man in the water!" someone shouted from the foredeck. "We have men in the water!"

"What?" Beatrice muttered. She and Bert left the armory and ran in the direction the shout had originated from. Men were leaning against the railing and stretching their arms out to point into the water. Beatrice joined them at the edge and peered down. The submarine had broken the surface and hung beside them at a sharp angle. A hatch was open on the top and, as impossible as it was to believe, large shirtless men had jumped from the side of the ship into the teal Aegean waters. Two of them were currently swimming toward the *Cervantes*, while one was already gripping the anchor's chain.

Bert said, "There's something wrong with those men."

Beatrice had seen it, too. The one climbing the chain had a blank look on his face, the look of a wooden toy or a drawing. His body seemed unusual as well, as if being in the water had made him less solid. As the thought occurred to her, a clump fell from his shoulder and plunked loudly beneath him.

"Golems," she said. "Virago is sending us golems."

Bert said, "Witchcraft."

"Magic. You should be used to it by now."

If he wasn't, he was about to get a crash course in it. Knives and guns were all well and good, but there was no way she could defeat Virago and her golems without using some magic of her own.

Chapter Eighteen

Beatrice could see the crew preparing for battle further down the deck, arming themselves with the same war leftovers she had been given. Rifles and bayonets wouldn't do much against the mindless drones Virago was sending up. A golem could sustain a startling amount of damage before it even started to slow down. They were strong and mule-headed. But she also knew they were generally made from earth materials; clay and stone, dirt, mud. Dov had called her an earth elemental, and she doubted there would ever be a better time to test the theory out.

"Bert," she said, "hold onto me."

"Uh..."

Beatrice was already climbing onto the railing, so Bert wrapped his fingers around the Y formed by her suspenders in the center of her back. She stood up straight and gathered energy into her cupped hands, waiting until she could feel it tickling her wrists and forearms before she let loose. She hit the golem on the anchor chain first, splitting him in half. The center of his torso was blown away, causing his legs to plummet and hit the golem beneath him. He dangled from the chain with a blank expression, still trying to achieve his goal. Beatrice thrust out her other arm and destroyed its head.

"More difficult than anticipated," she said, "but not impossible."

"*Canastos,*" Bert muttered. "How did you do that?"

"Very carefully," Beatrice said. She was standing with the top rail against her knees. She knew that if she lost her balance, she would most likely tip forward into the water. "Do not let go."

Bert tightened his grip and used his other hand to grab her belt. Beatrice gathered more energy and focused two blasts at the golems still in the water. She broke the arm off one, but their buoyancy helped them absorb the blasts with minimal damage. She grimaced.

"I'll have to wait until they start climbing the chain to destroy them."

"Picking them off one at a time. Can you do that?"

She shrugged. "I'll have to try."

Huey joined them and looked down at the creatures. He watched as Beatrice wound up like a baseball player and hurled another burst of energy, knocking off the next golem's head. His body fell lifelessly back into the water and joined the pieces of his cohorts. The limbs and broken bodies were beginning to fall apart and expand as they took on water.

"Huh. That's not something you see a lot of," he said in a quiet voice. "I guess that's why Lady Boone is always calling you Trix, huh?"

Bert said, "Tell the men to aim at their heads. Whatever these things are, it ain't human. They don't have to worry about killin' anything 'cause I'm fairly certain they were never alive to begin with."

"But they are strong," Beatrice said "A good headshot is the only way to stop them."

"I'll spread the word," Huey said.

Another golem had begun its ascent. Beatrice hit just below its shoulders and knocked it back into the water. Her fingers cramped and she could feel sweat on her forehead and upper lip. She counted four more creatures in the water. She didn't know how many remained on the ship, but there had to be a finite amount. Virago couldn't very well have filled the entire submarine with enough clay and mud to create an infinite army.

She was waiting for the next clay man to begin his ascent when Bert suddenly pulled her backward. He fell to the deck and she landed on top of him, her elbow digging hard into his gut as she struggled to get up.

"What in the blazes~"

Her question was cut off by the ping of a bullet striking the hull above their heads. The gunshot echoed over the water and she realized he had most likely saved her life by pulling her back.

"Thank you, Bert."

"Sure," he said. "She came up out of the hatch with the rifle. I didn't think you saw her."

Beatrice said, "I did not."

He remained crouched next to her on the deck. "I didn't know it was another lady."

"Is that a problem?"

"No, no. Not a problem at all. I've just never seen so many dangerous women in one place."

Beatrice said, "Spend enough time with Dorothy Boone..." She took out the gun she'd been given and checked to make sure it had been loaded. "What's the range on this thing?"

"Not as much as you're going to need."

"I'll need one of your long arms."

He rose up enough that he could see the submarine below. "She's not in sight. But stay low."

Beatrice moved in a crouched position, staying close to the wall. The chain rattled and swung against the hull as the golems began climbing unchecked. More gunfire from the ship, and then something clanged against the railing. Beatrice thought it was just a poorly-aimed shot until Bert shouted for her attention. She looked back and saw two metal hooks attached to the rail.

"She's put up a ladder."

Beatrice growled. She summoned more energy and pushed it toward the hooks, trying to lift them up and off the rail. They had just started to lift when Virago's hand closed on the railing and she began hauling herself aboard.

"Damn it." Beatrice urged Bert to go on. "Protect the submersible at all costs. She can't be allowed to take control of it or this ship."

"What about you?"

"I'll be dealing with her."

Bert hurried off as Beatrice got to her feet.

Virago was dressed in a white blouse under a heavy maroon coat. A pair of gun belts crossed her hips to form an X. Her wind caught her hair and lifted it up, exposing her neck in a way that Beatrice found particularly exploitable. Virago grinned wickedly as she shed the coat and tossed it aside.

"You must be Beatrice Sek. I've heard a lot about you."

"You're the woman who hurt Lady Boone." She curled her hands into fists and cracked her knuckles. "I've been looking forward to this for a long time."

Virago hissed and lunged forward. Beatrice dropped into a crouch, slapped her hands on the deck, and gave herself enough of a magical bounce to achieve a five-foot vertical jump. She swung out her leg to kick Virago across the chin. The other woman stopped short, grabbed Beatrice's foot, and pulled. They both tumbled, but Virago was the first to recover.

"I don't often get the opportunity for an evenly-matched fight," Virago said. "I've been quite looking forward to this."

"I hope I don't disappoint."

Near the stern she could hear the shouting of crewmembers; the golems were starting to get aboard. Virago held her arms out to either side, fingers spread so that Beatrice could see the yellow-orange energy sparking between them even in the sunlight. She mimicked Virago's stance and demonstrated the crackling blue light of her own power.

"That's a lovely color on you," Virago said.

"Let's see how it looks on you."

They lashed out at the same time, both with their right arms, and the energy met and twisted together at the halfway point. Beatrice was weak from using the golems as a shooting gallery, but she could sense she was the stronger of the two. Virago also seemed aware of her shortcomings. The cocky grin left her face and she brought up her other hand to increase her output. Beatrice backed up a step as the orange energy doubled in strength.

"Not bad," Virago said. "Where did Dorothy find you?"

"Don't bother looking. I'm one of a kind."

She raised her own hand but, instead of strengthening her attack, she aimed a small burst at the foot Virago was resting her weight on. She stumbled and her energy dissipated. Beatrice ran forward and brought her energy down like a club to flatten her opponent to the deck. Virago fell flat, arms splayed out to either side as Beatrice landed on top of her. She scrambled to reposition herself so she could straddle Virago's hips and pin her arms.

"You've made it this far," Beatrice said, "so I'm sure Lady Boone won't mind revealing what she found on the seabed. But you're going to be held in the brig. When we get back to~"

The punch took her completely by surprise, knocking her to one side so forcefully that only the railing kept her from continuing over the edge into the water. She ended up on her stomach and pushed herself up onto her knees as the golem closed his hand around her throat and hauled her up. Her feet dangled and her head felt like it would snap off the top of her spine, but she managed to cup her hands around the golem's head. She sent a burst of power between her palms and turned its head to pulp. Without the life to give it strength, she was able to pry its fat fingers from her throat and dropped back to the deck.

Virago rushed her and slammed into her from behind. Beatrice couldn't aim properly over her shoulder and had no defense as she was slammed face-first into the wall. Once there, however, she twisted in Virago's grip and punched her hard across the face. Close-quarters magic was too risky; they both didn't want to accidentally get hit by their own energies. Virago punched Beatrice in the stomach, and Beatrice grabbed a handful of Virago's hair to pull her head back.

"Not bad for an old woman," Beatrice said.

Virago laughed. "The cockiness of youth. I knew I could count on it to rear its ugly head."

Beatrice could hear the sounds of fighting from all over the ship. Someone's scream was cut off in a sudden and alarming choke. She swept her arms out to break Virago's hold and simultaneously threw her head forward. Virago tried to duck out of the way, but Beatrice's forehead cracked on her chin. Both women cried out in pain, but the move had served its purpose. Virago stumbled back just enough to let Beatrice get free. She grabbed the knife from her belt and slashed at Virago's midsection. Virago saw the flash of light on the blade and retreated further to avoid it.

"Do you think you can hold us off forever? Do you think you can fight us all while protecting your very vulnerable friends down below? One word from me, and that submarine will dive with a singular purpose. It will find and destroy the submersible Trafalgar and Boone are in. All it would require is a small puncture. The sea would do the rest. They'd be crushed by the pressure in a matter of seconds."

"If they die, my life's work would become your slow and painful torture until you finally pass away of old age. And as you draw your last peaceful breath, I will plunge a blade into your heart."

Virago laughed. "Oh, Beatrice Sek, I do like you. It's a shame we're meeting as enemies." She grabbed the blade of Beatrice's knife and squeezed. Blood rose up between her fingers as she reached out with her other hand to grab the lapel of Beatrice's shirt. She pulled her forward and their bodies slammed together. Beatrice stiffened, very aware of the wickedly sharp blade between them. It was a hard weight against her abdomen, held there by Virago's body.

"Go on," Virago said. "No magic, no scheming, just two women holding a knife. Are you strong enough? Eh? Go on, then. End me. End me, and my golems die as well."

They were both straining to get control of the knife. Virago's other hand was still gripping Beatrice's shirt, but Beatrice's left hand was free. She slipped it into her pocket and pulled out something long, thin, and metallic. She held it out to the side and let the ring on one end dangle from her finger. The glint of sunlight on the slender spike drew Virago's eye, but her hold on the knife didn't waver.

"What is that?" she laughed. "Go ahead and stab me with it. It would be a minor irritation at best."

"Sure," Beatrice said as she let the pin drop to the deck. It was a struggle to speak while counting in her head. "You never saw one of these in Ireland, did you? Germans used them in the War. Called them Kugelhandgranates." She pulled the ball from her pocket. It looked armored, with a checkerboard of small black squares. Beatrice reached "three" in her countdown and tossed the grenade straight up. Virago's eyes widened with fright and she retreated immediately. Beatrice also retreated as the weapon tumbled back down.

It exploded in the place they had just been standing, high enough to avoid serious damage to the ship but low enough that it would have killed either of them if they'd still been standing there. As it was, the explosion made Beatrice lose her footing. She fell hard and landed flat on the deck. Her ears were ringing and she was battered, weak from using too much magic too quickly, but she managed to stand. She stumbled and reached out to the wall for balance as she turned around to see how Virago had fared. The smoke was still clearing, but she could see her opponent standing on shaky legs just on the other side of the blast zone. Her face was bloody; apparently she'd hit her head when she fell. Beatrice considered that a win.

"You want to play with fire? So be it."

Virago crouched and held her arms out with her hands cupped as if she was planning to lift something heavy. Beatrice felt the entire ship sway underneath them and her panic surged. The tendons on Virago's neck stood out like steel rebar, veins rising to the surface across her face as she lifted what seemed like an impossible weight. Something crashed against the side of the *Cervantes* and Beatrice realized too late it was a wall of water.

The wave retracted, but a sweep of Virago's arm brought it back around. It was just like a child creating ripples in the bathtub but on a massive scale. Beatrice summoned what energy she could and shot it across the deck like an arrow. She hit Virago center-mass and knocked her off her feet, but the damage had already been done. The wave Virago had been manipulating had no option but to follow gravity. Beatrice turned and ran for the nearest doorway.

"Tidal wave!" she shouted, unsure of how else she could warn the crew of what was about to happen. She reached the door just as the water crashed aboard. She was hit hard enough to be knocked off her feet, but then the wave caught her and carried her along with it. Beatrice hit walls, doorways, the ceiling, and finally was tossed like a forgotten toy onto the ground.

She struggled to rise, but fighting back against Virago combined with the wave and destroying the golems had taken everything out of her. She collapsed on the deck and let the water wash over her as a physical manifestation of her fading consciousness.

Chapter Nineteen

The instrument panels went dark. It was only thirty seconds before they came back to life, but Dorothy doubted she or Trafalgar breathed during that half-minute. She swallowed her panic and leaned forward in her seat to look up at the surface. The submarine hung near the *Cervantes*, and she could see what looked like dismembered corpses floating in the water all around. She reported to Trafalgar what she'd seen as she returned to her seat.

"Good lord. They may require our assistance."

"Or surfacing now could be a distraction that leads to Virago gaining the upper hand."

Trafalgar said, "What's to say she doesn't have it already? We could be the distraction Beatrice is hoping for."

Dorothy considered their options. "How deep are we?"

"Six hundred meters," Trafalgar said. "Two-thirds of the way down. We're going to continue on."

Dorothy said, "You're not putting it up to a vote?"

Trafalgar said, "You can't vote. Choosing between your grandmother's legacy, and saving the woman you love? Whichever decision you make, you'll regret not taking the other option. Both are valid, both have their pros and cons, and you'd never be satisfied no matter what eventually happens. So I'm taking the choice out of your hands."

"Thank you," Dorothy said softly.

"Of course. You would do the same for me. Besides, the *Cervantes* crew has dealt with pirates before, and Beatrice can handle whatever Virago throws at her."

Dorothy nodded. "Of course you're right."

Her anxiety wouldn't be easily quieted, so she focused on what they were seeing outside the glass. The depths in this area had fluctuated so wildly on the maps but she truly hadn't expected anything quite so mountainous. Schools of fish that appeared black in the submersible's lights swarmed around them, bumping up against the glass before letting the current sweep them up and over the curved dome of the ship. They had to adjust their course several times to avoid alighting on a plateau, continuing deeper into the sea. Soon the teal waters gave way to blue and then violet. The streaks of sunlight grew thinner and their visibility diminished with each meter.

"Eight hundred meters," Trafalgar said softly, her tone giving the moment its proper reverence. The ship groaned and strained around them as if in response to her comment. They both scanned for evidence of leakage but found nothing alarming.

"Beginning to regret your decision?" Dorothy asked.

Trafalgar said, "Absolutely not."

Dorothy smiled and looked at her instruments. The radar pinged on a system of caves below them. They had seen other caves on the descent, yawning mouths in the side of cliffs and scattered across the foothills of mountains they had left hundreds of meters above them. These opening, however, seemed to extend further into the rock. She reached out to the controls and angled one of the lights to shine into the opening when they were near to it.

"What is it?" Trafalgar asked.

"I don't see the back wall. It could be a tunnel."

Trafalgar shrugged. "I suppose..."

"How far are we?"

"Eight sixty."

"So we have a bit of leeway on the tether. We could pause the descent and use the engine to scoot over, see what's in there."

Trafalgar hesitated. "What possible value could that have?"

"Inscriptions, artifacts, road signs. If there is a civilization to be found on the sea floor, we might find evidence here."

"I suppose it could be worth a quick look. But we shouldn't waste too much time. We have no idea what is happening on the ship, and I don't want to be a hundred meters into a cave if they start reeling us back in."

"Understood."

Dorothy guided the ship over, holding her breath as the lights filled the opening with a pale shine. Creatures unaccustomed to such bright lights swarmed out of the cave's mouth. Dorothy was grateful that Trafalgar had the foresight to pick up the camera and snap off a few shots. The sea life wasn't their primary goal, but she knew it would be considered valuable information to someone.

She paused on the threshold of the cave and moved again to the edge of her seat, leaning close to the glass to see as much as possible.

She so was focused on the walls and the arch that made up the opening that Trafalgar had to say her name twice to get her attention.

"What is that?"

Trafalgar was pointing deeper into the cavern, toward the curved roof. At first it appeared to be a flat silver object affixed to the rock, but when Dorothy tilted her head to the side she could see that it was rippling slightly with the current.

"That's... not possible," she said.

"An underwater cavern?" Trafalgar said. "Not so unbelievable."

Dorothy chewed her bottom lip and stared at the mysterious spot. "It might be nothing."

Trafalgar looked at the instruments. "Huey said that if we wanted to make a quick excursion, it should be possible. The suits will protect us from the pressure for a short amount of time."

"Even at this depth? It would crush us like a dry leaf if we opened the door. Or... if that *is* a cavern, then would the pressure in the cave be low enough to survive?"

"I haven't the slightest idea," Trafalgar said. "Huey was more concerned in teaching us how the suits work than the mechanics of ocean pressures. None of us really believed we would have cause to leave the submersible. But either way, these suits have an internal mechanism that keep us at a safe level. It might become uncomfortable, but we'll survive."

Dorothy said, "I'm not certain the reward would be worth the risk." But her hands were shaking. She wanted to know what was on the other side of that pool.

Trafalgar turned on a radar screen and sent out a ping to determine how far away the pool was. "Fifteen meters. The suits will protect us for a trip that short. We open the hatch, swim out, poke our heads above the surface, and swim back. Huey showed you how to drain the ship if we were forced to open the hatch, right?"

"We're not being forced, we're choosing to," Dorothy said in a distracted monotone.

Trafalgar picked up her helmet and turned it in her hands until it was aligned properly. "I believe this is precisely what your grandmother was searching for. You can either come with me now, or you can look in six months when your brain has refused to let you sleep until you know what's on the other side of that pool. Put on your helmet, Lady Boone."

Dorothy did as she was told. They were able to make the connections on their own masks but, just to be safe, they turned and checked each other. Confident that everything was proper, Trafalgar twisted a key and opened two nozzles at the bottom of the compartment. A controlled flow of sea water began rising around their feet. Dorothy looked back at Ignacio's case, the one that supposedly carried everything they would need on this expedition.

"It will be difficult to carry both that and the camera," Trafalgar said.

"Right. If we need it, we can come back to the ship. The camera is more important."

Trafalgar nodded and sat patiently until the compartment was full. The mechanisms were all protected from the water, though Dorothy couldn't quite understand how. Huey had put her fears at ease by spilling an entire cup of water over the console. "I don't know how, either," he admitted, "all I got to know is that it does."

A blue light came on, and Trafalgar reached over her head to open the hatch. As she was hauling herself out, Dorothy entered a code that would lock the submersible's commands until they returned. It would be a disaster if they came back to find it had been reeled back to the ship without them aboard. She pushed up out of her seat and drifting out through the hatch. Trafalgar was standing on the curved edge, one hand against the stone wall to keep herself steady as she waited for Dorothy to follow her. Their suits had a pressure gauge on the wrist that would alert them of imminent failure, but neither was even close to the red.

"That's impossible," Dorothy said. Trafalgar didn't respond, so Dorothy looked up and saw she was examining the cave leading to the pool. Her lips were moving behind the glass of her helmet, but Dorothy couldn't hear a word. She reached out and tapped her glove against the viewport. Trafalgar looked at her. "I can't hear you. And you can't hear me. And... it's ridiculous that I'm speaking aloud right now."

Trafalgar mouthed, "What?"

Dorothy shook her head and pointed toward the pool. Trafalgar nodded and gestured for her to lead the way. Dorothy pushed off the side of the submersible and swam forward. Her heart pounded so hard she thought she could hear it echoing through the suit. She was aware of the pressure, but it was nowhere near as strong as she had feared. She reached the pool and positioned herself underneath it, gazing up into what appeared to be a large open space.

"This is impossible," she said again, and she dropped her hands. She pushed herself up and broke the surface, the water cascading down the front of her mask. The opening was wide enough that she had to stretch her arms out to either side to grip the edges.

She had emerged into an open room that appeared to have been naturally formed. It was a cathedral of stone and what appeared to be coral, porous trunks and branches that stretched from the floor all the way up to a vaulted ceiling thick with stalactites. Some of the rock formations were as thin as needles, while others looked to be thicker than her torso. The room was at least a hundred yards wide, vast enough to make her feel puny in the center of it. It reminded her of the theater that had so impressed Clara the Librarian, but on a much grander scale. The entire space was lit with a pale green glow that she couldn't immediately find a source for. Directly in front of her, the stone floor sloped downward to a wall broken into a series of arches that looked to have been hand-carved. Her pulse raced as she looked at them, staring in slack-jawed wonder.

Trafalgar slapped her hip and Dorothy realized she was blocking the exit. She crawled up through the opening, careful not to snag her suit on the edges. She turned around and bent at the waist, taking Trafalgar's hand to help her up and out as well. Once they were out of the water, the hum of their respirators was impossible to ignore. Oxygen hissed through their suits to keep the pressure constant and the echo seemed to make it even louder.

Dorothy was looking at the arches, so she didn't notice Trafalgar removing her helmet until it was already halfway off. "No!" She reached out to stop her, but the damage had been done. Trafalgar looked at her and then held up her wrist to show her gauge. Dorothy saw the blue light indicating the environment was safe. Though she couldn't count the number of times she'd said the word in the past minute, again she said, "Impossible."

"The air is breathable," Trafalgar said, breathing deeply. "Not the freshest, granted. It feels... thin. But it's definitely not fatal."

Dorothy unhooked her own tubes and reluctantly took off her helmet as well. "That was incredibly reckless."

"This whole endeavor is reckless. And look what we've discovered. My God..."

Dorothy had to admit that point. She put down her helmet so she could use both hands for the camera. Their voices were echoing from the rock formations, the dying echoes still ringing even as they responded to one another. She followed the slope of the ground to the archways. They were carved into a stone wall which blocked the mouth of the cavern. Inside she could see other arches leading into more corridors. She was shaking, her mouth dry, her eyes wide and unblinking as she took in the sights.

"Look at this," she whispered reverently. "This is not natural. This was made by someone."

Trafalgar said, "Yes."

"This chamber serves as a... an antechamber for the rest of... whatever this is."

"The Eula Boone Antechamber."

Dorothy looked at her and smiled, tears in her eyes. "Yes."

Trafalgar smiled and moved forward. She looked at the section of stone between the archways. There were no markings, nothing to identify who had made it or what its purpose had been, but there were blatant tool marks on the openings. At the threshold to the antechamber was a thin line, a paper-thin gap separating the exterior and interior. There was no denying that the antechamber had been created by humans at some point. She took off her glove and brushed her thumb over the stone.

"It's smooth."

"Perhaps it's not always above water level," Dorothy said. "We may have arrived at the perfect moment to see it revealed." She passed through one of the archways. The blue-green glow was present inside as well, just dimmer than in the main room. "Can you see any source for this light? It's gorgeous. But this entire chamber should be pitch black."

Trafalgar turned and moved back up the slope. She took out her flashlight and aimed it at the stalactites. "There's some kind of algae on the stalagmites. It appears to be some sort of bioluminescence."

"Tites."

"Pardon?"

"Stalagmites are on the ground. Stalactites are the ones in the ceiling. Because they must hold on tight to remain in place."

Trafalgar laughed softly. "That's one way to remember."

"I've never forgotten." Dorothy saw something gathered in one section of the antechamber. She turned her light toward it and gasped as a pile of skeletons were revealed. "Bloody hell!"

"What is it?"

"It would appear we aren't the first souls to find this place after all." She walked over to the remains and crouched in front of them. They couldn't be as old as the chamber, but they were by no means new. "A few other explorers seem to have met their end here."

"Perhaps we should~"

The rest of her suggestion was drowned out by a roar of stone sliding on stone. The floor under Dorothy's boots shifted as if there was an earthquake, and she had to fight to keep her balance. The entire antechamber was moving counter-clockwise and the archways were lining up with the solid stone.

"No, no, no..."

She ran, tripping over her boots as she tried to move in a straight line on the spinning ground but she could tell she would come up short. Trafalgar was running as well. By the time they reached the wall, the opening was less than six inches thick. They stared at each other, Trafalgar horrified and Dorothy terrified as the final gap closed. As soon as every entryway and exit was blocked, the spinning ceased. Dorothy fell to her knees and flattened her hands against the wall.

"Crumbs," she gasped, her bottom lip trembling.

"Dorothy?" Trafalgar's voice was hollow but audible through the stone.

"I can hear you," Dorothy said. Tears burned in her eyes. "I'm... I'm here."

"Can... you..." Trafalgar sounded panicky, desperate. "Are there any markings?"

Dorothy had already looked, but she shined her flashlight over the wall again. "No. There's nothing. There's... there isn't anything."

Trafalgar was silent.

Dorothy turned and put her back against the wall, legs out in front of her, gaze locked on an empty spot in front of her. If there had been a puzzle, if there was some clue she might have overlooked, or some clever escape... but the room was completely featureless. She felt cold.

"Ignacio's box," Trafalgar said suddenly. "I could... there might be something..."

Dorothy laughed. "You don't really believe that, do you?"

Trafalgar said, "It's... it's worth a shot."

"No, it isn't. I looked in the box our third day at sea. Boxes of ammunition, rope, a first-aid kit, rations. Nothing that could remotely be useful in this predicament."

Trafalgar laughed mirthlessly. "You lasted a day longer than I did."

Dorothy closed her eyes. "I knew we would never sabotage ourselves that way. The future. Everything we would need, laid out at our fingertips. But we both know what would have happened."

"We would peek," Trafalgar said.

"And we would conform our actions to fit the contents of the box. We would have made different choices based on what we thought we would do."

Trafalgar said, "So you believe in free will?"

"I don't know," Dorothy said so softly she was certain it wouldn't pass through the wall. "I believe there are no free rides. There is no easy answer. No psychic ready to hand you a magic wand. His recall is flawed. Who is to say giving us a jackhammer wouldn't have changed the future?"

More silence. Then finally, "What do you want me to do, Lady Boone?"

Dorothy had no idea. But she was saved from answering by another sound. At first she thought it was the stone moving again, but the floor remained stationary beneath her. Then she felt it, a wetness against the underside of her suit. At first she thought it was the residual moisture from swimming up through the cave, but then she saw that there was a thin layer of water covering the entire antechamber.

"Oh, crumbs." Her voice broke when she said the word.

Trafalgar said, "Dorothy..."

"The water is rising."

"I know. The same thing is happening out here."

Dorothy felt choked. Her entire body was trembling. She aimed her flashlight at every wall, every flat surface, but there was nothing she could see that could assist in her escape. She looked at the skeletons and the mystery of how they had come to be there was suddenly very clear in her head. The water was rising up through the cracks in the ground, the same cracks which had allowed the antechamber to turn and trap her inside.

"There must be some way to get you out of there," Trafalgar said, her desperation raising her voice to a level Dorothy had never heard.

Dorothy aimed her light at one of the skulls across the room for her. "I believe there might be," she said, "but it might take you awhile. And I believe it would technically be a recovery, not a rescue."

The water continued to rise.

Chapter Twenty

THE WATER rose slowly. In a way that was worse than if the chamber had filled quickly. The slow rise gave Dorothy time to examine her options and find herself utterly helpless. She moved along the edge of the room and looked through the churning water to see where it was rising through the cracks. They were too narrow to even fit her fingers in. She couldn't see how she could possibly push the entire room back to where it had started while she was standing in it. There was nothing on any of the walls, no ancient riddle or rhyme she could decipher to save herself.

"This room was meant to kill," Dorothy said. "It's not a test of wills or worth. It's a death trap, pure and simple."

Trafalgar said, "That doesn't mean it's inescapable."

The water was nearly to Dorothy's knees. "There aren't a hell of a lot of options here, Trafalgar. I'm not the sort to just give up, but..." She held her arms out to either side and then dropped them. "I'm standing in a room that has no entry, no exit, and it's filling with water just slowly enough for me to understand what is about to happen."

"I can... I can go back to the ship and bring Beatrice back down. She can use her magic..."

Dorothy said, "Even if you did bring her down and she freed me in time, the submersible only seats two. There'd be no room for all three of us to go back up without making multiple trips. Besides, you're forgetting the ship is currently under siege. If you go back to the surface, Virago would simply take you hostage as well. You may well be able to fight her off, but not before this room has completely filled with water."

On the other side of the wall, Trafalgar was pacing through ankle-deep water. There was far more area, so it was taking longer to fill. Soon, however, she would be forced to put on her helmet and cut off all communication with Dorothy. Her mind was racing. Dorothy couldn't save herself, fine, then it was on her. She was the one with a complete suit, she was the one with access to the submersible. If there was a solution, she would have to be the one to find it.

"Trafalgar." The stone wall between them made Dorothy's voice sound hollow. "You should go."

"What?"

"This trap is still standing eons after it was created, and it still works. If there was a way to escape it, then someone would have found it. I'm looking at a pile of skeletons that tells me that isn't the case. Meanwhile, Beatrice and the crew of the *Cervantes* are facing an incredibly smart enemy. You would be better served helping them."

Trafalgar said, "There must be some way to save you. I won't leave you."

"Look around. Do you see any way to break the stone? Anything that could help you cut through rock? This room was built to kill."

"That's not possible! Whoever built it must have had a way to pass through to the other side. This entire place was carved from stone. They must have had a reason. There must be a purpose to this room besides trapping their enemies."

Dorothy said, "Perhaps it was an execution chamber. They brought their enemies here to get rid of them. It would explain the lack of ornamentation. This is a charnel house and I'm merely their latest victim."

"I refuse to believe that."

Trafalgar paced back toward the pool where they'd entered. Their helmets were now bobbing on the surface of the water and Trafalgar scooped them up so they wouldn't get cracked against the wall. She refused to believe Dorothy would never wear the helmet again, just as she refused to even picture herself taking the submersible back up alone. She saw her reflection in the facemask of one helmet.

"Besides, I can't go back to the ship without you."

"Why not?"

"Because Beatrice would murder me the second she discovered I left you down here alone. I'm terrified of that woman."

Dorothy laughed. "We are in agreement there. Oh, Trix... Trafalgar, when you do leave, tell her that I was fortunate to have her in my life."

Trafalgar said, "She loves you, you know. She absolutely adores you."

Dorothy said, "I know. But it's nice to know it's so obvious to others."

"I would have thought the opposite. If it was known you were~"

"I don't care. I won't announce my sexuality to the world, but... I won't be ashamed of wearing my love for Beatrice as a beacon."

Trafalgar cursed under her breath and moved quickly back to the wall. "There must be some way to break through! If these blasted walls are thin enough we can hear one another, then it stands to reason they must be thin enough to break! Perhaps there is a blunt instrument in Ignacio's case..."

"There's not."

"I know there's not!" Trafalgar snapped. "But... there has to be something!"

Dorothy said, "We both looked inside. Why are you so certain we overlooked something so crucial?"

"Because if we didn't, it means I've let you die *twice*. It means that I stood here and walked away, then went to Ignacio and didn't ask him for that damned hammer or a pneumatic drill or something that could save your life. I refuse to believe that. I refuse to believe I would choose your death over some vague idea of truth or honor."

Dorothy said, "If there were any way out of here..."

"I would have asked for it," Trafalgar said.

Dorothy rested her forehead against the cold stone. The water was now to her waist, the current lapping against her stomach. "I understand now, Trafalgar. This past year, we haven't been working toward a partnership at all. I was learning who you were, seeing how you operate. I was becoming comfortable with the idea of letting you carry on when I'm gone."

"Enough of that talk."

"If not now, when? All the explorers we've spoken to in the past months about creating an alliance, none of them hold a candle to you. None of them come close to your skills or ingenuity. None of them combined come close to your strength of will. Someone has to take on my legacy. It might as well be you. I would like very much for it to be you. The townhouse, everything within, my accounts. It's all to be yours, Trafalgar."

"Stop talking like that."

Dorothy sighed and closed her eyes. "You've become a very good friend, but I don't regret the years we spent butting heads. It's made us both stronger people. Thank you, Trafalgar."

Trafalgar said, "Thank you, Lady Boone. You saved me from an ignominious end to my career after Adeline died and Leola left. I don't know what I would have done if you hadn't brought me in."

They were silent for a long while, and still the water continued to rise. Outside, it had just reached Trafalgar's mid-thigh. Dorothy was now letting her hands float on the surface, heart pounding at how close it was to her face. Soon she would have to start treading water, then swimming. How long could she keep that up? She had the tank of oxygen on her back, so she could conceivably just put the tube in her mouth and breathe until that was gone. And then...

"How can you just give up?" Trafalgar asked.

Dorothy scoffed. "I don't see much choice. There's literally nothing for me to work with in here. I'll suck the last of the air out of my tank because it would be stupid to die with it left in reserve, but after that... I choke and drown."

"How can you say there's nothing to work with? There's your mind! How can you die with a mystery unsolved?"

"What mystery?"

Trafalgar shouted, "What the hell is this place?" Her voice echoed off the stone and the water. "The place that killed you when everyone and everything else failed. You've survived your whole life. You fought off anyone who tried to kill your spirit and became the woman you are today. You fought off anyone who said you had to love and marry a man to be whole. Goddamn it, Dorothy, do not die with a question in your mind. Know what kills you."

Dorothy closed her eyes. "I didn't see enough to get... to know even where to begin."

"Then find the most likely answer. Who built this? The Greeks? The Romans?"

Dorothy sighed. "No. They wouldn't have had the technology to descend this deep. It would have to have been carved before the Flood. The Athenians or the Carians." She felt buoyant and lifted her feet off the ground. She was floating now. "Most likely the Carians. If it was built before the Flood..."

"Or?" Trafalgar said.

"The Athenians or Carians," she muttered. "Carians were here first... but the Athenians stole their land. Tore their ancestors from sacred burial grounds and moved them to other locations around the Cyclades." Her heart was pounding as she swam toward the wall. She rested her hand against the stone and tried to organize her thoughts. "That would mean this isn't nearly as old as I thought it was. Still unbelievably ancient, but... not Biblical."

"Dorothy?" Trafalgar shouted, and Dorothy realized she had been muttering.

"I'm here! I'm just thinking." She chewed her bottom lip. "The Carian cemeteries were desecrated for the Athenian religions. If that happened to you, what would your response be when your people continued to die?"

Trafalgar said, "I would put them somewhere I was certain they wouldn't be disturbed."

"Underwater," Dorothy said. "In a necropolis fronted by a trap no one was supposed to survive. There must have been a way for the Carian people to protect themselves so they could visit loved ones or bury someone new. But this chamber existed in case the Athenians came back, or if any future civilizations tried to disinter their ancestors. It's a cemetery. This is just a security measure."

Trafalgar said, "Well done, Lady Boone."

Dorothy sighed. "I thought you said solving this mystery would make me feel better."

"I'm sorry."

"Don't be sorry." She was swimming now. The ceiling looked to be seven or eight feet above her now, and she could see there were no openings to grant her a last minute reprieve. "My time is counted in minutes now. You should return to the ship. I'm sure Beatrice could use your help."

"You need my help."

"I'm beyond help."

Trafalgar sighed. "Your chamber will be filled before mine is. When you can no longer speak, then I will... I'll leave."

Dorothy said, "I suppose that would be acceptable." She felt tears welling up, but forced them away. "Thank you."

"Of course."

Trafalgar said, "Use the tubes and your suit to stay alive as long as possible. Just in case one of us has a flash of inspiration. Give yourself every second. Promise me, Dorothy."

"I will."

They remained silent, unable to find the words to say everything that remained to be said. The water had risen to Trafalgar's chest. Soon she would have to put on her helmet.

"Dorothy."

"Is it time?" The water was nearly to the domed roof.

Trafalgar said, "I believe so. I'm very sorry."

"There's nothing to be sorry for. I'm honored to have a partner who would fight so hard against impossible odds. But there is no recourse."

Trafalgar was surprised to discover she was crying. "Goodbye, Lady Dorothy Boone."

"Goodbye, Miss Trafalgar of Abyssinia. It was an honor working by your side. I just wish our time had been longer."

With great effort, Trafalgar managed to push herself away from the wall. She pushed through the water, waves of it splashing over her shoulders with her movement. She fitted her helmet on and made the connections blind. It felt like years since she and Dorothy had checked each other's seals. Once she was sure it was on properly, she ducked down under the water level and swam forward. It was only then that she realized she hadn't been panicking about the water or her own danger of drowning. She had thought the idea of being in a room slowly filling with water would paralyze her. Dorothy had given her something else to focus on so the fear never had a chance to grab hold.

Another thing I owe her for, she thought miserably.

She reached the opening - no longer a pool or a pond, just a hole in the rock floor - and pushed her way through. The submersible sat where they had left it eons earlier, silent and dark. As she swam toward it she thought about Dorothy's theory about the Carian people. The cemetery, the trap for Athenian bastards come to steal their dead. It was brutal, but she could understand why they had felt the need to protect their ancestors.

She stopped in front of the submersible and opened the hatch. They'd left it flooded when they left, so she would have to climb in and close the hatch, then...

Drain the water.

Trafalgar stared into the submersible, currently filled like a fishbowl. She couldn't see the drains the ship would use, but she knew they were there. What if a Carian funeral delegation showed up and there were a bunch of Athenians drowning in the antechamber? There had to be a way to drain the water so the cemetery could be used. She wet her lips behind her mask and tried to think, crouched on top of the submersible.

There had been nothing on the walls in the main room. There was no evidence of a way to control the antechamber or drain the water from within. But there had to be a way. The water flooding in couldn't have been a natural tide; the timing was far too perfect. No, somehow the Carian people had found a way to spin the room and begin filling it with water. That meant there had to be a way to reverse the process.

Trafalgar abandoned the submersible, clutching Dorothy's helmet to her chest with one arm as she swam back. She prayed Dorothy would need it again soon.

CHAPTER TWENTY-ONE

THERE WAS a girl. Blue eyes that seemed too big for her face, pale save for her freckles. Messy red hair that is tied up behind her head to keep it out of her face. The girl had a stick that she used to poke holes so she could see what kind of creatures would come out. Sometimes the little cat following her would give chase to the animals the girl flushed out. Her pants and shirt are too big for her, rescued from the trash even after she told her mother she didn't mind hand-me-downs. "Girls don't wear trousers," her mother had said. But she also wasn't allowed to get her dresses dirty. There really wasn't any other option.

The girl who was now a woman floated face-down in the last room she would ever enter. She wore trousers under the protective clothing, and a lavender tie, and her hair spread out around her head like a spray of blood. Before the room completely filled with water, she had figured out how to cover her nose and mouth with a plastic cup from her suit pockets. She threaded the hose between the edge of the cup and her mouth, and now the last gasps of air in her tank were being fed into the small pocket of air she'd created.

She was going to die.

Dorothy could hear the tank alarm sounding through the water. She was almost out of air. She closed her eyes and pictured the lovers she had known, the women she'd taken to bed and those she'd only kissed or held hands with. She remembered their lips on hers, their hand at the nape of her neck, and their breath on her throat. Her thoughts drifted then to Beatrice and she smiled. She had been Beatrice's first female lover, and their first few times together had been awkward. But Beatrice was a quick and enthusiastic student.

She wished she had written a letter to Beatrice. Something to tell her how she really felt, to make sure it was never questioned. She also wished she could apologize to Desmond. He would need someone else to protect him, a new beard for his true relationships. Just someone else she'd let down. Like her grandmother. But at least Trafalgar would finish her grandmother's final mission. People would know what was waiting to be uncovered beneath the Aegean Sea.

Her eyes drifted closed. She was quickly running out of air. Going to sleep seemed like the most peaceful option, so she let her consciousness slip away while holding on to thoughts of Beatrice and the way she made her feel. As last thoughts went, she could hardly think of anything that would be better.

Beatrice jolted awake. She tried to pull her arms forward, but they were trapped behind her back. She was seated on the floor in drenched clothes, various aches and pains registering throughout her body. Some of it was from behind thrown around the deck, while she knew others came from overuse of her magic. She could feel the throbbing start of a migraine behind her right eye and tried to ignore it as she examined her surroundings and took stock of the situation.

One, her arms were bound behind her by metal cuffs. She was resting against a pipe, and she assumed that was what her arms were wrapped around.

Two, she was on the bridge. Captain Mederos and his crew were lined up along the opposite wall in various stages of beaten and bleeding. Huey was conscious and looking at her. He nodded when he saw she was awake and she returned the nod. Bert was next to him looking frightened but ready to fight.

Three, her heart was broken and she was on the verge of tears. She didn't understand that and chose not to examine it.

Four, Virago and a man she'd never seen before were standing at the controls. Two golems were standing guard outside the bridge doors.

Virago turned and saw Beatrice was awake. "Ah, there she is. My worthy opponent. Don't feel too badly about being defeated. After all, I had to use the entire sea to take you out." She crossed the room and straddled Beatrice's legs before dropping down to face her. "If I'd known how special you were, I would have approached you back in London."

Beatrice glared and said nothing.

"I suppose you're wondering what I mean. Your shirt burned a little bit. I noticed it when my dummies were dragging you to the edge of the deck. They were about to hurl you into the water, but I was curious. Aren't you the lucky one?" She sat down on Beatrice's lap and put a hand on her neck, fingers slithering like snakes to peel back the collar of her shirt. "I took a peek while you were unconscious. Don't worry, there was no untoward peeking." She winked. "But I saw your tattoo."

Beatrice's lips curled into a sneer.

"Oh, don't be like that. It's a gorgeous work of art. Had it since you were a baby, right? I assume you know it ties you to earth magic, given the way you went after my boys."

She withdrew her hand, reached up, and pulled open her own collar. She twisted and leaned forward, revealing her own back. Beatrice intended to feign disinterest, but her breath hitched at the sight of the water tattoo.

Virago laughed. "I thought that might get your attention. That's how I was able to use the ocean to sucker punch you. Sorry about that, by the way. Again, had I but known what Dorothy Boone was hiding away, I would have treated you with the respect you deserved. I've been looking for you a very long time, Beatrice." She reached out to stroke Beatrice's cheek.

"Don't touch me."

"Come now. We're practically family, love..."

Beatrice glared at her.

Virago stood up. "You might want to rethink your position. When your current employer and her partner get back to the surface, I'm going to find out what they discovered and then I'm going to kill them both. You, though. I could never bring myself to destroy something as precious as another elemental. I'll make you a fair offer of employment."

"I'll accept," Beatrice said, "if just so I can kill you in your sleep."

Virago pursed her lips. "If you're in my bedchamber, I hope you find an activity we could both enjoy. But there will be time for that later. And don't bother trying to use magic to break free of those cuffs. They were made special from some kind of stone which absorbs magical energy. Anything you try to conjure up to escape will just make the chains stronger." She walked back to the controls. "Any change, Captain Baker?"

"The submersible is still locked, mistress."

She sighed and rested her hands on the controls. "I'm torn, Miss Sek. I grow impatient for them to return. But the longer they remain stationary, the better chance there is that they're exploring something magnificent. It's a struggle, to be certain."

Beatrice was also torn. The longer Dorothy and Trafalgar remained on the seabed, the more opportunity she had to turn the tables and subdue Virago. But the more time they spent underwater, the higher the chances something had gone horribly wrong. She still felt that horrible hollow ache in the center of her chest, the sudden sharp pain that had drawn her out of unconsciousness. She looked out the window at the deceptively still sea and wished she knew what was happening under the surface.

Later she would struggle to describe it, finally settling on the sensation of waking up and being punched in the stomach at the same time. She coughed violently and spit up water, and someone rolled her onto her side so she wouldn't choke. Her ears were ringing, but she was aware of someone speaking. She coughed again as she was put on her back again. Her chest was heaving as she sucked in the gorgeous, thick oxygen. She stared blindly at the rock formations on the ceiling and took a moment to appreciate the fact she was alive before focusing on how it had happened.

She looked to her right and saw Trafalgar sitting beside her. She had been perched on her knees but was now fallen back into a seated position. She had one hand pressed against her mouth. Dorothy couldn't tell if the water on her face was from taking off her helmet before the water had fully receded or if she'd actually been crying.

"You kissed me," Dorothy said with a rough, weak voice.

"It's called artificial respiration."

Dorothy smiled. "You kissed me."

"See if I ever do it again, if this is your response."

Dorothy reached out and grabbed Trafalgar's hand. She squeezed hard. "I can't... I can't even..."

"Then don't. Just do the same for me sometime." Trafalgar got to her feet. "Do you think you can stand?"

Dorothy nodded but stayed where she was. "Give me a moment." She looked around until she saw the antechamber, which was once again standing open. Water dripped from every surface, and there was still a shallow puddle on the ground. "What happened? How did you get it open?"

"I didn't. When I got back to the submersible, I thought about the drains I would have to use to empty it out. I figured whoever built this would have something similar to gain access to whatever was on the other side. The fill was automatic, so I thought perhaps the drainage would be as well. If I was right, there was a chance I could revive you. But I had to be here the second the doors opened."

"You went inside to retrieve me. Dragged me out here."

"Yes."

"You risked becoming trapped yourself."

Trafalgar said, "At that point I was still wearing my helmet. I'd just discovered that the room seems to open itself up again after a set amount of time, so I was confident I would be safe."

Dorothy got to her feet. "You risked your life to retrieve me. That's not something I'm likely to forget, Trafalgar."

"Yes. Well, as I said... you would do the same for me."

"This is the second time you've refused to let me die. You dragged me out of the Minotaur's lair, and now..."

Trafalgar nodded. "If next time you could refrain from surrendering quite so easily, I would be much obliged. Saving your life should not be a full-time profession."

Dorothy smiled and turned to look into the antechamber. She could see through the room where she'd been trapped to the other archways.

"It's a shame we can't just... hurry through."

"Don't even think about it."

"I'm only saying that we've come this far."

Trafalgar said, "I just saved your life. Don't make me want you dead."

Dorothy sighed and held her arm out. "It's right there! I can run through now that I know it's a trap. And if it closes again and floods, this time I'll take my helmet with me."

"Your air tank is empty. Your suit will hold a little air, but not much. Just enough for the swim back to the submersible, in fact."

"Virago is nine hundred meters above us right now. If we leave, she'll come down here. She'll destroy this antechamber and everything on the other side will be pillaged. It will be destroyed, and every remnant of that once-great civilization will be lost so she can pay for a few more guns and a bit of ammunition."

Trafalgar said, "You risk being trapped there with it. Dying after I risked my life to save you. That's some gratitude."

"I am grateful," Dorothy said. "More than you could possibly know. But..." She turned and looked through the arch again. "How could I just walk away, Trafalgar? The path is wide open to us. How can I not walk through?"

"If you walk through there, you'll do it alone."

Dorothy said, "It's hardly suicide. It might just take longer if the room closes and we have to wait it out. The opportunity to see what is waiting on the other side is worth it! Now that we know what to expect, we can prepare. I can wear my helmet. I can move quickly instead of lingering. If I hadn't paused to examine the antechamber I could easily have made it through to the other side. And maybe there's something on the submersible we can use..." She stopped speaking suddenly as a smile spread across her lips. "Oh, Trafalgar, we are so brilliantly stupid. Ignacio's case."

"What about it? We both went through it and there was nothing that could possibly help us now."

"No, the case was full of random items. Useful in any expedition. But the case itself... it was metal. Incredibly heavy, strong metal. Strong enough that if we placed it in the doorway, it would prevent this room from closing all the way. It could prevent the entire trap from springing."

"Or the water could sweep in, knock it out... the rock could be stronger than you think it is, and the case could be crushed..."

Dorothy said, "For which I'll take extra precautions."

Trafalgar sighed. "There's no way to talk you out of this, is there?"

"I'm afraid not."

"Then I suppose someone should be here to save your life. Again." She bent down and retrieved her helmet. "Since I have more air in my tank, I'll go get the case. You stay here and do nothing. I have no idea how long you were without oxygen before I revived you. Sit down against the wall and give yourself time to recover."

Dorothy nodded. "Very well." She was feeling a little woozy and sore. She walked to the wall and sat down carefully so she wouldn't tear her suit on the stone. "Are you satisfied?"

"I wouldn't go that far. But I'll retrieve the case."

"Thank you for indulging me."

Trafalgar sighed and rolled her eyes. "Yes, yes. Perhaps I would have moved slower had I remembered what a pain you could be."

Dorothy smiled as Trafalgar reattached her helmet and descended into the pool once more. When she was gone, Dorothy looked toward the antechamber. Now that she was alone, she closed her eyes and brought both hands up to her face. It had taken everything in her not to start shuddering while Trafalgar was there. Only the knowledge that she would be back soon kept her from screaming. She had died. She'd stopped breathing, floating alone in a room with no exit or entrance. She'd made peace with the fact she would never get out.

Surviving was almost cruel. She would never choose the alternative, and she would be forever in Trafalgar's debt for what she had done. But she knew that she'd suffered a trauma that might take a good long while to get over.

Dorothy wiped at her eyes and composed herself so Trafalgar wouldn't notice anything odd when she returned. She was terrified that her idea wouldn't work and she would find herself trapped on the other side of the antechamber. But at the moment the risk of dying wasn't scary to her. She needed to take the risk before she got too accustomed to her survival.

If she was going to come that close to death, then she was damn sure going to use it to her advantage.

Chapter Twenty-Two

Beatrice tried to focus on the pain that had pulled her back to consciousness, but her mind kept drifting back to the tattoo she'd seen on Virago's shoulders. Dov had told her there were other elementals. Did that make Virago her sister? A cousin? Should they be allies or enemies? Dov had intimated that the four elementals joining forces could only have bad consequences, so maybe they should avoid each other at all costs for the sake of the world.

Huey and Bert were watching her now that she was awake. She knew they were waiting for her to give some sort of signal, or to indicate she had a plan, but she was at a loss. Virago's power was at least equal to her own, and that was only when she was at full power. Now she was weak from the fight, from being knocked unconscious, and from the energy-sapping cuffs she was wearing. She was as helpless as anyone else aboard the ship.

"What is taking them so long?" Virago asked. She had taken to pacing the length of the bridge while her associate - Captain Baker, apparently - kept an eye on the controls.

"Can't tell. They have a radio, but they haven't used it."

Beatrice said, "Of course not. They know you're up here. They're probably down there conspiring."

Virago said, "They can conspire all they want. The fact is that I have them at a disadvantage once they reach the surface. I could cut them loose right now. The only reason I haven't done it already is because I need their submersible. Once I have it, their lives will rely on what they can tell me about what they found. Hopefully it will be enough to justify not killing them."

"What do you have to gain from killing them?" Bert said. "They obviously beat you here. Can't you just let it go? Admit defeat?"

Beatrice said, "It's not that simple, Bert. She's looking to fund an army. Lady Boone and Trafalgar are two of only a handful of people who know where this site is. If she kills them all, it can be her personal bank account. No worries about historical societies or preservation. Just dive down, rip out some antiquities, sell them to the black market. Buy another gun."

Virago said, "The guns are just a means to an end. We also buy people, politicians, so we can affect change quietly. We pay rent on homes where we can have planning sessions so we're not just burning the world down indiscriminately. Money makes war so much more civilized than just scrapping in the streets. All we want is our independence. We want to cut ourselves free from you Protestant bastards."

Beatrice said, "Do I look Protestant to you?"

"Takes all kinds," Virago said. "The riches buried here can help create an independent Ireland for future generations to call home. A much better use for them than rotting in a cave hundreds of meters under the Aegean or ignored in some museum. Much more noble."

Huey said, "And that's worth killing two people?"

Virago laughed. "Much more than two people, sir. I don't see any reason to leave the crew of this ship alive when I'm finished with it. The only reason you're still alive right now is because I don't want the smell to become an issue. Although I suppose I could just toss you overboard. It would give my golems something to do."

Huey said, "All right, then." He hunched his shoulders forward and Beatrice heard the bones of his arm snap. Virago and Baker both turned at the sound, but Huey was already on his feet. Breaking his arm gave him enough maneuverability to get out of his chains. Virago gathered so much energy that Beatrice could feel it crackling in the tight space of the bridge. Huey was too massive to duck or avoid the blow, but Virago was also wary of letting it loose with so much potential collateral damage to the submersible's controls with the ricochet.

Huey didn't have to worry so much about that. He used his body as a projectile and slammed into Virago, knocking her back into Baker like dominos. Baker was smashed against the console and collapsed over it like a broken doll. Virago brought her hands up around Huey's face but he swept her hands away. The energy from her other hand burst against his cheek with barely more strength than a furious slap.

He spun Virago like a dancing partner and pinned her against his chest with one arm. With the other he groped at the pockets of her coat.

"And now you intend to take advantage of me, is that it?"

"I'm offended you think of me like that," he said, "but I s'pose when you think like a hammer, you start thinking everyone else must be a hammer, too."

He pulled the keys from her pocket and twisted to toss them toward Beatrice. "Think you can let yourself out, Miss Sek?"

She twisted and managed to get her fingers around the keys. "I'll give it a valiant effort, Mr. Conway. Well done."

Virago closed her eyes and clapped her hand against Huey's thigh. She dug her nails in hard enough that it was painful even through the cloth of his pants and he cried out. His grip loosened enough that she was able to slip free. She turned and shoved him away. His bulk worked against him then, and he tripped over his feet before tumbling toward the bridge entrance. The two golems who had been standing there stupidly staring out to sea awoke when she flicked her fingers toward them.

"Kill him!"

The first golem grabbed Huey around the throat and pulled him to the ground, while the other began pummeling him on the head and chest. "Don't!" Huey shouted. "You get!" Blood darkened his lips with each shout, and Virago smiled as he was beaten to submission. When she finally called off the clay men, Huey was barely breathing. His face was a swollen mass of purple and red. She stepped forward and put the heel of her boot on his hand, stepping down until she heard the bones break. He could only manage a weak whimper at what must have been incredible pain.

The attempted escape dealt with, she straightened her coat. "Now then, Miss Sek, I..."

She turned and saw the magic-dampening cuffs lying empty and Beatrice Sek was nowhere to be seen. Virago realized Huey had been telling her not to help, to make her own escape rather than saving him from the beating. Virago moved toward the back of the bridge and saw the open window Beatrice had crawled through. The deck was empty in both directions.

"The bitch is fast," Virago muttered.

The golems were standing still again, awaiting their next command.

"Find her. Bring her here alive. Break her arms, break her legs, paralyze the conjuror for all I care. Just bring her back."

They shuffled off to follow her commands. Virago checked Captain Baker's vitals. He was still alive, but he had taken a brutal hit. It didn't matter. If he died, she would leave his ship behind and find another way home. If Trafalgar and Boone had found what she thought they would, she could afford a luxury vessel to take her back to Ireland in style.

All she had to do was be patient. She rested her hands on the console and watched the screen, waiting for the signal that her foes were starting back to the surface.

When Trafalgar returned with the case, Dorothy dumped out its contents and tested its strength by standing on it. Trafalgar expressed doubt that her weight was anywhere near equal to the pressure that would be exerted on the case by a moving wall of stone, but Dorothy was satisfied. She placed it in the threshold with the lid open, which would provide almost three feet of clearance if the walls tried to close again. And if the walls crushed the case completely, she would have her helmet on so she could survive without needing resuscitation.

"I hope you understand that I'll be staying out here," Trafalgar said.

"Of course. But it should be perfectly safe."

Trafalgar said, "Should be."

"Will be."

"You don't know that."

Dorothy sighed. "No, I don't. But I have faith. I truly believe that no one would build this trap without a way to bypass it. Now, their methods may have been different than mine. But this is beatable. And I think having a doorstop there will work."

Trafalgar said, "Good luck, Dorothy."

"Thank you." She started forward.

"Dorothy." She turned and looked back. "I'll never leave you behind. You know that, don't you?"

She smiled. "I do."

With a deep breath to steady her nerves, Dorothy walked back into the room where she'd died. Her hair was still wet, and her throat was rough from coughing up the water she'd swallowed while gasping for air. She cradled her helmet against her chest like a talisman, a totem that reassured her she wouldn't be caught completely breathless again. She moved quickly across the floor. She told herself she didn't have to run; last time it had taken a minute or two before the room closed on her. But she still felt relief when she reached the other side of the room. She chose one of the arches at random and stepped through into a dark, narrow tunnel. She had a flashlight tied to her wrist and held her arm out to illuminate the far corners.

"Trafalgar?" Her voice echoed. "Can you hear me?"

"I'm here."

"First tunnel seems to be a dead-end. Checking the others." She retreated back to the room and moved through the next archway. Her heart was thudding so hard she was surprised it wasn't echoing as well. Again she found herself in a tunnel that appeared to dwindle to nothing. She had just stepped out when she heard the same terrifying scrape of stone on stone as the room began to move.

"Dorothy!"

"I know!"

She stopped breathing and ran to the next tunnel. A quick flash of the light through the opening revealed only darkness, so she continued to the next one.

She dived through when the doorway was half-blocked and spun around to see if her plan would work. She could see Trafalgar across the room shifting her attention between the wall and the case. Dorothy's skin erupted in sweat as the stone wall made contact. The side wall of the case sagged slightly and Dorothy sucked in air through her teeth, still not exhaling, still not breathing. If the case shattered, if it couldn't stand the weight of the stone pressing against it, she would be trapped again.

Everything in her said run, take advantage of the slight gaps remaining and save herself. But after the initial weakening of the box, it didn't give any further. The stone groaned and something within the walls creaked loudly, but there was no further movement.

Dorothy let out a relieved whoop. Trafalgar's smile was wider than Dorothy thought she'd ever seen on her face.

"Brilliantly done, Lady Boone!"

"Thank you. Now we just have to remember to ask Ignacio for that precise case when we get back."

"Just be quick," Trafalgar said. "We have no idea how long this will hold, or if the chambers will still eventually flood."

Dorothy examined the tunnel she'd ducked into a found it was an even smaller space, even more of a dead end than before. She'd have dreaded being trapped in there, even if she knew salvation was coming soon. It was far too much like Poe's prison for Fortunato. She stepped out through the gap, which was larger than she'd first thought, and moved to the next one.

"If these all wind up being dead ends, I shall be very cross..."

She slipped through the next tunnel and almost immediately found something to be excited about. She put her helmet down and took the flashlight from her wrist, placing it in her mouth as she aimed the camera at what she was seeing. The ground sloped down and away before becoming a short flight of stairs. There was a tall opening and, through it, she could see the same pale glow of bioluminescence they'd seen in the main room.

"There's another chamber."

"For God's sake, be careful," Trafalgar said.

"Sure, yes." Dorothy examined the doorway carefully and saw no line where the room could rotate and trap her again. There was nothing above the door set to drop down as soon as she passed through. She went down the stairs and gave a thorough examination of the door before she looked out into the new chamber.

"Bloody... hell..."

It was massive. The ceiling was a smooth dome covered with more glowing moss, shining a pale teal light down onto a field of stone plinths. The pale grey wedges were arranged in neat rows that faced the entrance. Each one was at least two meters in length, perhaps more, but they still looked miniscule in comparison to the rest of the space. In front of each plinth was a small altar, and when Dorothy got closer the light of her torch flickered and danced off gold and gems. Each tomb was hosting a fortune. She took pictures of them and then turned her attention to the stones themselves.

"Dorothy?"

She spun and saw Trafalgar standing at the base of the steps. She too was staring in awe at the necropolis, her hands dropping to her side as she entered.

"Is it safe for you to be here as well?" Dorothy asked.

"You didn't hear it? After you came down here, the room returned to its original position. I left the case where it was, just to be cautious, but I assume whatever mechanisms were at work have been reset. I weighed the risk and determined it was negligible enough to see what you'd found."

Dorothy smirked. "In other words, you'd come this far and couldn't resist."

"Don't gloat."

"But I love gloating when you're proven wrong. It's my favorite hobby."

"And one you can engage in so rarely."

Trafalgar had arrived at the first tombstone. "My god. Look at this." She aimed her torch at the carved letters on the face of the plinth. "It looks like Lycian...?" She looked at Dorothy for confirmation and received a nod. "I don't suppose you can read Lycian?"

"Not a jot," Dorothy said. She unzipped one of the pockets on her suit to retrieve the paper and charcoal she'd brought with her. They were sealed in a plastic bag, but she still checked to make sure they hadn't been ruined by being underwater for so long. "So which job do you want? Stone rubbing or photographing?"

"I'll take photography."

"Excellent." She handed over the camera and took off her gloves as she approached the first tombstone. The carvings were condensed to a small space, so she would be able to get everything on a single piece of paper. She placed the sheet over the etching and began to rub. Multiple clocks were ticking in her head, counting down how long they had before the trap reset and before Virago's patience ran out. She wondered if taking the time to chronicle the gravesites would have disastrous effects on the hostages waiting for them on the surface. She could only hope that Beatrice was holding off the hounds without too much trouble.

Chapter Twenty-Three

Beatrice evaded the golems by being quick and clever, not that it was hard to outwit the senseless beings. She'd spent four days aboard the *Cervantes* inadvertently memorizing parts of its layout. The golems were ignorant and imbecilic, so they were easy to avoid. When she got below deck, she went immediately to her quarters. She had guns and knives, weapons she could rely on if her magic got too unreliable. Before she left her room, she went into the lavatory and took off her shirt. The sleeves were wet with blood from where she'd cut herself getting out of the cuffs, and she didn't want to deal with the mess. There were also certain kinds of magic that Virago might be able to do if she got her hands on Beatrice's blood; better to keep it to a minimum.

She twisted at the waist so she could see her back in the mirror. The tattoo was inert. She clenched her fists and tried to force it to start glowing, tried summoning all the energy she could, but it remained stubbornly dark. She grunted with frustration and rested her hands on the edge of the sink. She couldn't believe another elemental would appear within weeks of discovering others existed. She briefly wondered if Dov could have alerted Virago to Beatrice's tattoo, but the bitch had seemed honestly surprised about it.

Maybe Dorothy was right. Maybe the war had broken something in the world. All the magic ripped things apart in a way that was only now becoming apparent. Maybe a part of that was magical entities like the elementals being drawn to one another.

Regardless of the coincidence, she had to take care of Virago before Dorothy and Trafalgar reached the surface. She was right about the fact that they would be sitting ducks in the submersible. She had to eliminate the threat before they came back. She washed her hands and left the bathroom. At the door she paused and listened to hear if the golems were nearby. The corridor sounded empty so she slipped out. The pain and exhaustion was like a wire strung between her wrists and shoulder, twisted in a throbbing knot at the bend of her elbows. She ignored it and ran for the closest deck access.

A golem was standing guard at the top of the stairs. It turned at the sound of her approach and she sent out a burst of magic to decapitate it. The creature fell backward and bounced when it hit the deck. Beatrice stepped over it and started to continue on, but she stopped and looked back at the body. Its head was mush, the point where it had been connected to the body little more than a nub. Virago had been able to use the sea because she was a water elemental. Beatrice was able to destroy the golems with such relative ease because she was an earth elemental.

She crouched down next to the body and put her hand on its chest. Whatever life Virago had put into it was completely gone. She didn't know if she could awaken it again and, frankly, she didn't want to. Creating even brainless life was too close to a brand of magic she didn't want to mess around with. If her magic was indeed stronger with clay and stone, hopefully she could use the golem bodies as a weapon without tiring herself out too much.

With a quick look around to ensure she was still alone, Beatrice stood up and compressed the golem at her feet into a flat, featureless sheet. She stepped onto it, grimacing at how similar it felt to standing in a puddle of mud, and pushed herself up. For a moment she was afraid her feet would push through, but the makeshift flying carpet strengthened. She created a gentle breeze to push herself up over the navigation deck. She took care to avoid any bridge windows so Virago wouldn't see her as she ascended.

Once she was high enough to see the majority of the deck on both sides of the ship, she leaned forward to find the rest of the golems. She spotted one near the bow, looking out over the water for some reason. She flicked her fingers and then formed a fist, and the golem's head was compressed. It fell but she pulled it forward before it could hit the deck. As it rose, she spun it into a column of clay and then smoothed it out. She added it to the carpet under her feet.

Another one near the gangplank, one hunkering by the door that led down to the cargo hold, two more standing guard by the winch that would recover Dorothy and Trafalgar. All of them were killed and added to the thickening platform under her feet. When she was certain she'd gotten them all, she lowered herself back to the deck. She exerted some force to keep the blended former golems from splattering when they landed. She could feel something tickling along her spine and assumed the tattoo was currently burning. She didn't bother to check as she drew her gun and circled around the superstructure. She aimed well above the masts and fired twice.

Virago stepped out and glared down at her, then searched the deck for her braindead army.

"Don't bother," Beatrice said. "I took care of them all. It's just you and me."

"And an entire Mediterranean full of water." Virago started down the stairs. "Maybe this time I'll just let you get swept out to sea. You may be an elemental, but you're proving to be a true poxbottle. Better off without you, I am. Of course that would deprive me of seeing your face when I finally drain the life out of you. And I am very curious about what will happen to your magic when you die. Maybe I can absorb it into myself."

Beatrice said, "You talk a lot."

Virago smiled. She had reached the deck. Her energy flickered around her hands. "You do realize I don't want to hurt you. I certainly don't want to kill you. We could be partners. We could find our fellow elementals and... oh, the power we could have then. Surely you know the rumors. We're myths and legends, you and I."

"Nah." Beatrice dropped down and to the left, sending out a flash of energy that caused Virago to leap back out of its way. She countered with energy of her own, and Beatrice scrambled around the capstan. Virago followed, but Beatrice was already running along the port side of the deck. She kept her head down as Virago launched more attacks, creating sparks of light that whipped painfully across Beatrice's back and upper arms. She didn't retaliate, just ducked and altered her course to make it more difficult for Virago to pin her down.

Virago followed her. "You're not even going to fight? At least make this sporting."

Another crackle of energy hit Beatrice's foot and forced her ankle to twist. She went down hard, stopping her fall by flattening both hands on the deck. Virago closed the distance between them, one hand raised with a ball of lightning cupped in her palm.

"You just run away? Maybe you're not an elemental after all. Maybe you're just a dumb girl with a tattoo."

Beatrice said, "Or maybe I have a better use for my magic than firing blind." She stuck her arm out to the side, curled her hand as if she was grabbing a rope, and she pulled. "Let's see how you like *my* wave."

Virago looked just as the wall of clay erupted over the bridge. She shot the energy she had gathered at the approaching tsunami, but a water elemental couldn't stand a chance. Beatrice scrambled back so she wouldn't get caught up as the clay hit Virago. She was completely enveloped in it, knocked to the ground and smothered by it, and Beatrice got up on her knees. She held her arms out in brackets and clenched her jaw as she forced the whole mess into a smoother shape. Sweat dripped down her face as she reformed it with her mind.

After a moment, Virago's head burst free. Beatrice hardened the clay around her neck and then did the same around the entire construct. When she was finished, she could taste blood on her lips. Virago twisted and fought against her prison, but Beatrice was fairly certain she wouldn't be able to break free. At least not before she and a few members of the crew had moved her to the brig. She got to her feet, every joint aching as she approached the ship's new masthead.

Virago glared, her face and hair streaked with clay. "You are going to suffer for this humiliation, Beatrice Sek."

"Maybe. But the memory of seeing you like this may be worth it."

"We could have been allies."

Beatrice walked past her to go find someone to help her move the prisoner. "Maybe so. But then you threatened to kill my friend, and I lost interest in playing nice."

She went to the bridge, still nursing her various aches and pains. Captain Baker, Virago's reluctant partner-in-crime, was conscious and slumped against the console. When he saw her, he immediately raised his hands in surrender. "I'm hoping this means you took out that crazy witch. If so, you did us all a favor. I ain't about to fight you."

"Good." Huey had been left by the door and she knelt beside him. His face was blossoming into a fairly livid bruise, one eye completely closed and his lips swollen. She only intended to check his pulse, but he surprised her by opening the one eye that could still see and focusing it on her.

"Tol' oo to go."

"I did," she said. "I got away, and I got her."

He managed a pathetic version of a smile. "Good job."

She patted him on the shoulder. "Thank you for the key. You're the one who saved us, not me."

"Agree to disagree," he slurred.

Beatrice told him she was going to free the others and then come back to check on him. She stopped by the console and looked at the control screen for the submersible. It was still stationary, still locked. They had stopped close to nine hundred meters down and hadn't moved for nearly two hours. She could only hope they'd found something spectacular, something world-changing.

"I finished the housekeeping, Dorothy," she said softly. "You can come home any time now."

She put her hand against the screen as if Dorothy could feel it, then turned to begin freeing the rest of the crew.

Dorothy finished with another rubbing and looked up to check Trafalgar's progress. She was crouched to get a close-up picture of the jewels and gold decorating the front of one tomb. Dorothy craned her neck back to look up at the fungus giving them light. Had it already been there when the Carians carved out the tunnel, or had they somehow introduced it to the environment? Were the bodies added one by one, or had this been some sort of mass grave? And what secrets would be found when they examined the bodies that were left behind? Were they soldiers or peasants, commoners, prisoners? Was the antechamber proof that these graves belonged to royalty? She could spend decades investigating the cave and she would only scratch the surface of what was waiting to be known.

"Trafalgar."

"Yes?"

"Take a moment."

Trafalgar looked over her shoulder, then stood up and ran her eyes along the row of tombstones. They were standing amid the final resting place of a nearly-forgotten civilization. One of the oldest and most obscure races that ever walked the earth, and now they had found a treasure trove of history. Each stone had a name, a date, and more information Dorothy didn't even want to speculate about. The room they were in could shine a light on one of the darkest periods of human existence. A time before the pyramids, when the Mediterranean was dry, when monsters like the Minotaur still thrived.

"It's a monumental discovery," Trafalgar said.

"A fitting cap on Eula Boone's career. She'll be remembered as the woman who resurrected the Carian race. She would have been proud of that."

Trafalgar said, "And of her granddaughter."

Dorothy nodded and wiped her eyes, leaving a smudge of charcoal on one cheek. "It wouldn't have been possible without you. I never could have finished her work if you weren't here, Trafalgar. Thank you."

"You're very welcome. Thank you for giving me the opportunity to be here to witness something so amazing." She looked around again. "I just want to photograph everything. There's not enough film in the world for it, I fear. This is the true death trap. I never want to leave."

Dorothy laughed. "I understand. But I suppose at some point we must return to the surface. We'll remain until your current roll is exhausted, and then we'll force ourselves to go back to the submersible."

"I'm amenable to that."

"It's almost a shame," Dorothy said. "This room has been untouched for the whole of human history. When we get back to London, we'll be unleashing a horde of well-meaning archaeologists, historians, and academics on it."

Trafalgar said, "They've been resting in peace for untold generations. Revealing this tomb to the proper authorities on the subject will turn it into a protected site. Once everyone knows what is here, it will be guarded from those who would simply scavenge it for what they could sell."

"One of whom is currently perched above us waiting for a signal there's something worth stealing. What say we hurry up and go deal with her?"

"I concur." Trafalgar looked at the nearest headstone. "These people helped form the ancient world. It's time they were known."

Dorothy nodded her agreement and took out a fresh sheet to begin rubbing the next engraving while Trafalgar moved deeper into the darkness to find something unique to photograph.

CHAPTER TWENTY-FOUR

WITH THE help of the liberated crew, Beatrice managed to get Virago moved down to the brig. She retrieved the magic-cancelling cuffs that had been holding her and fastened them onto Virago before freeing her from the ball of clay and securing her in a cell.

"Are you going to behave yourself now?"

Virago sneered. "You can't hold me forever. Eventually I'll be free to come after you again."

Beatrice said, "Good. I'd hate to have to go looking for you. You said we were sisters, that we were meant to find one another. You're wrong. I've never had a family. I've never had anyone I cared about. I don't know who gave me this tattoo, but I know who gave me purpose. I know who means the world to me. So listen well. If you harm Dorothy Boone, if you so much as threaten her, I will use everything available to me to track you down and make you pay. Am I clear, Miss Potter?"

"Crystal," Virago said, her lips twisting into an oddly approving smile.

Beatrice turned and walked away. She waited until she was on the stairs before she let herself sag against the wall. She was incredibly weakened from the fight, from everything that had happened, and she just wanted to sleep. But the battle wouldn't be over until she knew Dorothy and Trafalgar were safe. Once she caught her breath she used the ladder to haul herself the rest of the way up the stairs and trudged forward to the bridge. Bert and Captain Mederos were standing by the radar station, and both looked up when she appeared.

Bert said, "The submersible just came back online. Engines are running and they signaled for us to start bringing them up."

It could mean anything. One of them could have been injured or left behind, they might have run out of oxygen and been returning to the surface in a panic, or any number of other emergencies she couldn't even imagine. They had a radio, and they hadn't called for medical assistance when they reached the ship, but it was turned off. For all they knew, Virago was still in control. They wouldn't announce a weakness unless they absolutely had to.

"Bring them home, Mr. Carroll."

The process of leaving their discovery behind left Dorothy depressed and foggy-minded. She went through the motions of crossing the dangerous antechamber, fastening Trafalgar's helmet and then waiting while Trafalgar fastened hers, and then swimming back to the submersible. She dropped into her seat and fastened her harness as the water was drained from the interior. Through the front glass she could see the pool that could have been so easy to miss. Just a small sliver of light in an otherwise dark cave. She was glad their helmets were still on so she couldn't voice her misgivings to Trafalgar. What if they couldn't find the graves again? What if there was a cave-in or some other calamity? She looked at the camera in Trafalgar's lap, safely protected by a waterproof bag.

When the water had fully drained, Trafalgar turned on the ship's systems and sent a signal to the surface. It took a few minutes, but eventually the lights went blue and Dorothy steered them out of the cavern and began the long rise to the surface.

"We should be prepared for an assault when we reach the *Cervantes*," Dorothy said.

Trafalgar nodded. "We'll hardly be in any position to stage an assault. We could attempt to negotiate. Use the photos and rubbings we acquired in the cave as collateral to keep her from attacking us on sight." Dorothy grimaced. "The alternative is we're taken prisoner and she takes everything anyway. Even if she sells the photographs to the press, the important thing will be that they're out."

"I suppose," Dorothy sighed. "That doesn't mean I have to like it."

"The way I see it," Trafalgar said, "we can only do harm by reacting violently when we breach. We surrender and hold back information about the death trap we discovered. She'll have to keep us alive for the trip back to London. That will give us ample time to stage a mutiny and regain control of the ship."

Dorothy nodded. "I understand the logic, and I believe you're right that it's the best course of action. But it still feels far too much like giving up."

They remained silent for the rest of their ascent. Light increased, and soon curious fish were once again brushing against the submersible's glass and peering in at these strange creatures that were invading their tranquility. Dorothy had to try navigating around outcroppings which forced them to go a bit slower than they otherwise would have, but soon they had reached the surface. Water cascaded down the glass and the sun filled the cramped space with unbelievably bright light.

"Crumbs," Dorothy said, blocking it with her hand. "Was it always so bright?"

"Can't see a blasted thing."

Dorothy squinted as they were brought up the hull. Her vision cleared enough that she could see the sun was on the horizon. The angle was just right to shine directly onto their faces. The armature swung out and magnetically attached to the side of the submersible to pull them back to the cradle.

"I suppose it's a good thing we already decided to surrender. Wouldn't be much good in a scuffle if I can't see who I'm fighting." She unfastened her harness. "I'll go out first, just in case she's in a shooting mood."

"I'm starting to think you have a death wish."

Dorothy shook her head. "Not at all. I just feel that I'm the one who antagonized her, so I might as well test the waters, as it were." She stood up and unfastened the hatch. "I'll try not to get any blood on you if she does shoot."

"That is extremely unfunny."

Dorothy grinned and pulled herself up through the opening. She held her hands up, fingers splayed, and looked down at the deck.

Beatrice was sitting in a chaise, one foot up on the winch mechanism. She was in her undershirt, eyes protected from the sun by a pair of goggles, her hands folded neatly on her stomach. She still shaded her eyes when she looked up.

"Oh. Hello. Back already?"

"Well, we didn't want to keep you waiting." Dorothy climbed out and Trafalgar, having seen Beatrice through the glass, followed her down. Dorothy looked toward the bridge as Beatrice stood up. "We were under the impression you had some sort of mishap."

Beatrice shrugged. "Just a few unannounced visitors. Nothing we couldn't handle."

Dorothy grabbed Beatrice's suspenders and pulled her close for a forceful kiss. Beatrice put her arms around Dorothy's waist and let the kiss continue until Dorothy pulled away.

"I had a bad feeling myself." She ran her fingers through Dorothy's hair. Her voice was calm because allowing any emotion to seep in would have broken her. "Your hair is wet. There is no reason for your hair to be wet if everything went according to plan."

"We can talk about that later." Movement from the bridge made her step away from Beatrice. She wouldn't have taken back the kiss for anything, but she still didn't want to advertise her sexuality to a group of strangers. "These uninvited guests you mentioned... I assume their ringleader is still present?"

Beatrice said, "Right this way, ma'am."

She led Dorothy to the stairs. "Was your day fruitful?"

"It was splendid." She touched Beatrice's shoulder and squeezed, unable to stop herself from making physical contact. Everything that happened in the undersea cave was already starting to feel like a dream. Being on familiar territory, safely aboard the ship, it was easy for her brain to file away something so fantastic as a dream or hallucination. She still needed the confirmation, however, and touching Beatrice was the best way she could think of grounding herself.

When they arrived at the brig, Virago was seated in the middle of the floor with her skirts spread out around her. Her only reaction to seeing Dorothy was to slightly raise her chin and tilt her head to one side. Dorothy stepped in front of the cell with Trafalgar taking a position slightly to her left.

"Welcome back to the land of the breathing," Virago said. "I was afraid you'd turned mermaid and simply swam away."

Dorothy said, "Hello, Emmeline."

"My name is Virago."

"You'll be arrested, charged, and tried under the name Emmeline Potter. You should get used to hearing it."

She laughed and shook her head. "I won't spend a day in jail. I'll never stand trial. Besides, who knows what a brutal English prison might do to a poor defenseless Irish lass? You would be condemning me to torture and violence. You're far too civilized for that, Lady Boone." She got to her feet and moved closer to the bars. "Tell me what you found. You were down there far too long to just be poking around. I know you found something."

Dorothy said, "You'll hear about it soon enough, along with everyone else. But for right now, you and I have unfinished business. I seem to recall a threat. You said if I got in your way, you would... ah, it's been weeks. You would kill me? Something along those lines? Me, those I love, my colleagues, et cetera. I mean, I have the gist. The details aren't important."

Virago's eyes darkened as her smile grew. "Oh, I remember the details, Dot."

"I'm here to tell you that the slate is clean. By beating you to the punch, I saved your life."

"How on earth did you arrive at that conclusion?"

"If you had gotten here first, and if you'd been able to find the same cave we did, you would have been alone. Or with your disgusting golem creations. Is that accurate?"

Virago shrugged. "I only work with those I can trust. That eliminates everyone but myself and those I have complete control over. So I suppose you have a point."

"Then you would not have survived the trip. There is a trap down there, one that I didn't see until it had been sprung. Now, maybe your magic would have given you an advantage, but I doubt it."

"You obviously managed to escape using only your wits."

"That's where you're wrong, Miss Potter. I had no idea how to escape. In fact, I didn't. I drowned. I lost consciousness and ran out of air. It's only because I had Trafalgar with me that I'm still alive. She waited for me. She pulled me out of the trap and started me breathing again. If she~"

Dorothy's rhythm was thrown by Beatrice's hurried exit from the room.

"Crumbs," she said under her breath. She focused on Virago again. "If not for her, there is no doubt in my mind that I would have died. I know the same thing would have happened to you."

Virago looked at Trafalgar, who nodded. "It's true. I don't have Dorothy's confidence that magic could have aided you in that situation. Whoever built the trap knew what they were doing. You would have died in that cave if you went down there alone."

Dorothy said, "Seeing as our reaching it first technically saved your life, I would say any revenge you planned to take should be replaced by gratitude. And since I don't think either of us could stomach that, why don't we just call it even? You won't come after us, and we won't consider you an enemy. I'm sure you have much more important matters to tend to closer to home now that your anticipated windfall isn't going to be coming anytime soon."

Virago weighed her options carefully and squared her shoulders. "You wouldn't pursue me?"

"You broke into my friend's office, broke Desmond Tindall's hand, assaulted several members of this crew and commandeered their vessel... I do intend to hand you over to the proper authorities. But I believe you when you say that you won't remain imprisoned any longer than you choose to be. But if you flee, I won't pursue. We have more important things to deal with."

"Very well. I don't share your certainty that I would have been as helpless as you were down there, but I'll give you the benefit of the doubt. You found the cave first, and there's no sense in wasting resources on hurt feelings. We'll consider this a draw~"

"The hell we will," Trafalgar said. "This was a defeat for you."

Dorothy smirked. "The woman has a point."

Virago glared. "Fine. You have nothing to fear from me, Lady Boone. At least, not in retribution. The next time our paths cross..."

"Oh, I'm certain there will be many sleepless nights due to that threat, Miss Potter." She walked away from the cell. "Settle in. There's no sense rushing back to London, and it's sure to be a dull trip from your point of view. Consider it a chance to catch up on your sleep."

She went upstairs and found Beatrice on the deck. The sun had continued its downward trek and the sky was a deep velvet color. Not quite night yet, but certainly no longer day. Beatrice was standing on the deck, her hands on the railing, looking out toward Greece. Or maybe Italy. Dorothy had gotten so turned around that even with the sun setting she wasn't entirely sure about directions. She nodded for Trafalgar to continue on and joined Beatrice at the railing.

"Sunsets are always so lovely at sea."

"You died?"

Dorothy pressed her lips together. "There was a point~"

"No games."

"Yes. I was trapped in a room with no entrance or exit. It filled with water, and I didn't have my helmet with me. I remained afloat as long as I could, but... in the end... yes. I drowned. Trafalgar remained until the trap reset itself. She risked her life to save mine. She brought me back."

Beatrice moved her hand to cover Dorothy's. "I felt it. I was unconscious when it happened, but I felt something that woke me up."

"I'm sorry I didn't tell you privately."

"You didn't have a chance to. I'm sorry I ran out the way I did. I just didn't want Virago to see me being weak."

Dorothy curled her finger and brushed the hair away from Beatrice's face. "You do look rather peaky. You must have used an awful lot of magic today."

Beatrice shrugged.

Dorothy leaned in close and kissed the corner of Beatrice's mouth. "Go to bed. I'll come join you when everything is settled on the bridge. You've done more than enough for today."

"I think I'll take you up on that." She turned and hugged Dorothy. "I'm so relieved you're okay."

"Same here." She kissed Beatrice's neck. "Go on. Rest. We really do have a long trip back to London ahead of us, and I want you to spend as much of it as possible recuperating."

Beatrice said, "I'm just tired enough to not fight you on that. Good night, Lady Boone."

"Pleasant dreams, Miss Sek."

Beatrice brushed her hand down Dorothy's arm as she retired for the evening. Dorothy rested both hands on the railing and looked out over the calm sea. The sky was even darker now and the air was so still that the breeze felt like a hand brushing through her still-damp hair. She took a deep breath and closed her eyes, holding it in until her lungs forced it back out. She couldn't remember drowning, couldn't remember those final horrifying seconds when she was trying to breathe but couldn't, and she supposed she was grateful for that. But if the experience had taught her to be grateful for a simple inhale of salty sea air, she supposed she couldn't regret it too much.

Chapter Twenty-Five

Later that night, Beatrice slipped into Dorothy's room without knocking. As expected, Dorothy was seated at the small desk under the porthole with the stone rubbings spread out in front of her. She had a book open at the top of the desk and was scribbling potential translations onto a spare sheet of paper. She looked up when Beatrice came in and smiled before going back to work. Beatrice put the leather pouch she was carrying on the foot of the bed.

"It's driving me crazy that we can't develop the pictures until we return to England. I'm terrified they won't come out properly. We had the flash, but the bioluminescent fungus might not have interfered with the exposures."

Beatrice didn't say anything as she approached.

"I wish I had brought along Weston or even Strong. This reference is fine, but it's not as..."

Beatrice slipped the pen out of Dorothy's hand and put it to the side.

"I sort of need that to work, love..."

Without a word, Beatrice marked the place in Dorothy's book and closed it. She turned off the lamp and took Dorothy's hand.

"I want to at least make a dent on this..."

Beatrice led Dorothy to the bed and began undoing the buttons of her blouse. "You've been working nonstop since this mission began. Then you went underwater and drowned. You died." Her voice broke, and she took a moment to compose herself before continuing. She slipped the blouse off Dorothy's shoulders and ran her fingertips over her freckles. "We have at least a week before we're back in London. That's a lot of time to fill. You'll have plenty of time to make headway on the translations. But I believe you've sacrificed enough of yourself to this mission for one day."

"And what about you?" Dorothy asked. "You went to bed over an hour ago, and yet you don't look like you've slept at all. Your day was as harrowing as mine."

"I kept reaching over to find you." Beatrice undid Dorothy's belt. Her pants hit the floor a moment later. "After everything that happened, this will be more restorative than sleep."

"I think that's fair." Dorothy leaned in and brushed her lips across Beatrice's. "While I was down there. When my oxygen was running out..."

Beatrice flinched. "Please don't."

Dorothy brushed the back of her hand over Beatrice's cheek. "I only wanted to tell you that my last thought before losing consciousness was of you. All I cared about was making sure you knew just how important to me you are."

"I know."

She took off Dorothy's underclothes and took a step back to admire her, biting her lip before guiding Dorothy onto the mattress. Dorothy moved the pillows to prop up her shoulders and to get a better view of Beatrice as she undressed herself. As she dropped the last article of clothing, she picked up the package she had put down as she entered the room. She opened it and withdrew a contraption made of straps and buckles. Dorothy perked up at the sight of it.

"Well. I had no idea you'd packed that for this trip."

"Tropical locales, the sense of danger, I thought it might be fun if we had the time." She stepped into the harness and reached between her legs to press one of the three pouches inside herself. She grunted quietly at the sensation, then tightened the leather straps on her hips. The golden buckles caught the moonlight coming in through the window as she crawled onto the mattress. Dorothy spread her legs and put her hands on Beatrice's shoulders.

The device was one of her own creation, something she couldn't commission out to Threnody or any of the other craftsmen she knew. The phallus hanging from the front hung limp until Beatrice cupped the other two pouches and began massaging them. The fluids within were released into the limp leather shaft and gave it girth. Warmth made the compound harden into a serviceable prosthetic, so Dorothy wrapped her fingers around it and began to stroke as Beatrice hovered over her.

"I always forget how big it is," she whispered, angling her head to kiss Beatrice's neck.

"Do you need me to go down?"

Dorothy shivered. "Well, a bit of lip service couldn't hurt."

Beatrice moved down Dorothy's body, letting her lips, tongue, and fingers take full advantage of the trip before settling between her legs. Dorothy opened her mouth slightly in anticipation of the touch, lifting her shoulders off the pillow when it finally came. She'd never met anyone as skilled as Beatrice when it came to this particular skill, an oddity when she remembered that Beatrice had never had a female lover before Dorothy introduced her to the possibility. She had to be a natural talent, and Dorothy prided herself on discovering it.

It didn't take long before Dorothy was wet enough to continue. She whispered to Beatrice that she was ready. Beatrice returned to her first position and slipped her hand between the small of Dorothy's back and the wrinkled sheets, gazing down at her as Dorothy guided the tip of the phallus into her. Beatrice rolled her hips forward as Dorothy sank down. Dorothy curled her toes and put her free hand on the back of Beatrice's head as she was filled.

Several of her past lovers had considered the phallus with apprehension, wondering why she felt the need for penetration if she wasn't interested in men. Dorothy thought it was an ignorant question. If it was just about penetration, she could achieve it with her fingers or certain items from the garden. It was about the connection. It was about feeling someone she loved inside of her, being connected to them more intimately than with any other interaction. Cunnilingus was one thing, and having Beatrice's fingers inside of her was divine, but nothing compared to being joined at the hip and intertwined with another person.

The phallus was designed to mimic a physical cock, the pouch inside Beatrice squeezed and massaged by her muscles to push more of the fluids out of the other two pouches. That would make the compound within the shaft throb and the cock to become harder and thicker. Beatrice moved slowly to make it last as long as possible. She moved her hands over Beatrice's body, tracing the curve of her breasts and the line of her throat. Beatrice turned her head and closed her lips around two of Dorothy's fingers.

The waves gently moved the boat, affecting Beatrice's rhythm to the point where Dorothy held her still and just let the sea do the work. Beatrice put her face in Dorothy's hair and returned her hand to where her body curved, just above her ass.

"Hold," Dorothy whispered. "Hold, hold... h-hold..."

Beatrice nipped at Dorothy's ear. A few seconds later Dorothy's grip tightened and her breath washed over Beatrice's shoulder as she came. It wasn't a violent climax, but it was glorious and cleansing and precisely what she needed. For the first time since waking up in the cave with Trafalgar kneeling over her, Dorothy finally felt like she had survived. She felt the sweat on Beatrice's back and shoulders. She felt the way Beatrice's breasts moved against her when they breathed. She closed her eyes and opened her mouth to thank Beatrice, but all that came out was a sob.

"Sh," Beatrice said, withdrawing the phallus and rolling onto her side. She pulled Dorothy to her, rocking her gently as she wept. "It's all right. You're safe. You survived." She kissed Dorothy's forehead and held her until the tears passed.

Trafalgar watched the sea roll by through the porthole. There wasn't much to see at night, but occasionally they would pass another ship or a steamer that would light up the world. The lights were off in her cabin so the glare wouldn't interfere with the view. She was still trying to wrap her mind around where she and Dorothy had spent their day and the darkness helped clear her head. The air in the cave shouldn't have been breathable, and yet. The people who made it shouldn't have had the capability to dive so deep, to create something that would still be operational all these centuries later. And yet. She could still feel the rough stone under her fingers. The sight of the bioluminescence was burned onto the back of her eyelids. She couldn't have slept even if she wanted to.

She had left the rubbings with Dorothy because she would have a better shot at translating them. It was unlikely they would make much progress until they got back to London, but she'd learned it was best not to discourage Dorothy Boone when she got focused on a task.

There was a light knock on her door, just barely loud enough to be heard but not so loud it would wake her if she was asleep. She smiled, assuming it was Bert dropping by for a late-night visit. She checked her hair in the mirror and opened the door without asking who it was, a risky move considering the takeover a few hours earlier.

But her only surprise was a pleasant one, as she discovered Beatrice standing on the other side of the door. She was wearing her normal clothes, but something about her seemed disheveled and unkempt.

"I hope I'm not disturbing you," Beatrice said.

"Not at all. Is everything all right?"

Beatrice said, "Yes, everything is fine. Thanks to you. Dorothy told me the entire story about what happened down there. She told you to leave, but you remained behind. You risked your own life on the off chance you could save hers."

Trafalgar said, "Of course."

"It's the second time you saved her. The labyrinth wasn't... she was still conscious and mobile when you refused to leave her behind, so it didn't hit her as hard as it did this time. It hit me hard as well. The fact that you remained..." Her voice trailed off and she looked down at her feet. After a moment to compose herself, she looked up again. "This past year, I've considered you a necessary presence. Dorothy wanted you around, so I didn't object. But you were still an outsider in my eyes. I wish I could have seen your value without making you prove yourself so dramatically."

Trafalgar shifted awkwardly. "I... I never felt excluded, Miss Sek."

"Be that as it may. I would have fought for you if it benefited Dorothy, but I wouldn't have put my life on the line for yours. That changed today. Whatever

Lady Boone expects of me, you can expect it as well."

"Well... not *everything*."

Beatrice smiled slightly. "Your loss."

Trafalgar laughed. "I'm sure."

Beatrice held out her hand. "I was Dorothy's majordomo, her protector. I am officially extending that to you."

"I would be honored." She took Beatrice's hand. "Thank you, Beatrice."

"You can call me Trix. If you're so inclined."

Trafalgar said, "Another honor. But I think that is something best left for Dorothy."

"Perhaps you're right." She gave Trafalgar's hand a squeeze before she let go. "Again, sorry for disturbing you."

"Not at all. Your visit was very welcome indeed."

They wished each other goodnight and Trafalgar closed the door. She hadn't expected gratitude from Beatrice, only because she didn't think it was necessary. But it was definitely a gift she had no trouble accepting. Beatrice was fiercely loyal. Earning the respect of someone with that quality was hard to do. She smiled as she returned to her perch by the window. She didn't know what the future held when they returned to London, what the community would think about their discovery. She also hoped the photographs came out clear and beautiful and not murky, questionable, and disappointing.

In the end she decided it didn't matter if their discovery was touted as a world-changing event or dismissed out of hand as a hoax. She and Dorothy knew what they'd seen. They knew where they had stood and, even if they weren't certain of its significance, she knew it was a key to understanding the world history had forgotten. There was also one other key development she hadn't even realized until she sat down and started looking out at the ocean.

She wasn't scared of the water anymore. She had dived to the submersible to retrieve the case, she had stayed underwater waiting for the trap to reset, and never had she panicked. Never had she felt the urge to look for the monster that had been haunting her for twenty years. She rested her forehead against the glass and felt how cold it was. She could hear the waves and now they soothed her, like a lullaby.

There was another knock on the door just as she was about to fall asleep. It was quickly followed by a hushed, "Miss Trafalgar?"

She smiled at the sound of Bert's voice. It would seem she wouldn't be going to bed alone after all. With one last look out at the water, she got up to let her new friend in.

"A DROWNED NECROPOLIS DISCOVERED!" screamed across the top line of the newspaper above one of Trafalgar's photographs. It was a beautifully framed shot of a tombstone with the gold-tipped pillars framing it on either side. Another picture was one Dorothy barely remembered posing for. Her hair was wet and she had a slightly dazed look in her eyes. She regretted there were no pictures of Trafalgar, but when she brought it up, the look of terror in Trafalgar's eyes revealed the lack of portraits hadn't been an oversight. She wasn't interested in seeing herself on the front of a newspaper. And now that Dorothy could see her own bug-eyed stare, her wet hair smoothed down on one side while the other stuck up insanely, she could understand why.

She tossed the paper back onto the desk where Beatrice had left it with the rest of the mail. They'd been back from the Mediterranean for five months, and the time was spent going back and forth between translators and experts on ancient Greece, the Carians, and the Cyclades in general. There was a hefty amount of skepticism from all corners, as expected, but as their claims were confirmed, a general buzz of excitement began to grow.

The newspaper article was the first official announcement of their adventure. Dorothy had been obliged to sit for interviews with a cavalcade of reporters. Some of them requested Trafalgar's presence as well, and those who didn't found her present regardless. Cora also sat in on several of the interviews, although she insisted privately that she didn't feel she had done anything to merit inclusion. "I did some of the legwork," she said, "but I put it all together incorrectly. You, Trafalgar, and Eula Boone are the ones who deserve to go down in history."

Of course now they would have to suffer the ignominy of fame. Such a big

deal was being made about them - female explorers! An African adventuress!
- that Dorothy was afraid it would overshadow their actual accomplishment.
Then again, having a bit of clout also had its advantages. For months, she and
Trafalgar had been trying to gather support for a federation of people in their
profession. Their adventure in the labyrinth was enough to get them in the
room, but none of the people they contacted had ever followed through on the
offer.

Now, though, within a month of the first whispers, Dorothy was fielding calls
and summons from all over London. She'd been too busy with the actual work
of their discovery to respond. And yes, full disclosure, she did quite enjoy making them wait for a change. She realized she had been staring at the newspaper
for a full minute, so she picked it up again and skimmed the article. She was still
reading it when the door opened.

"Ma'am?"

"Listen to this, Trix. 'Lady Boone and Miss Trafalgar of Abyssinia.' Why do
you suppose they put my name first?"

Beatrice said, "You're more well-known, you have a title, your picture was
featured with the story. Any number of reasons, I presume. Why?"

"I'd like to hope it doesn't have anything to do with race. But I know that's
naive." She sighed and folded the paper. "Besides, Trafalgar and Boone sounds
much better, wouldn't you say?"

"It has a certain ring to it, yes."

Dorothy put the paper down and turned to face her majordomo. "I assume
you're here to tell me lunch is ready."

"No, ma'am. Your meeting."

She looked at the clock, startled. "Oh, you're right. Where would I be without
you, Trix?"

"Perpetually late and pleasuring yourself every night."

Dorothy gasped in horror. "The horror!" She brushed her hand down Beatrice's arm as she left her office. Beatrice followed her downstairs where Desmond was waiting. He looked dapper in his work clothes, his beard neatly
trimmed. The hand which had been crushed by Virago's golem had long ago
healed but occasionally she still caught him flexing his fingers and massaging
the palm with his thumb. She had apologized profusely for her part in the injury, taking him to dinner and paying for his medical treatments, but Desmond
insisted she had no reason to feel guilty.

"The woman found out where you were going anyway, though how I have no
idea. I only wish I'd done a better job distracting her so Beatrice could have been
spared some pain."

"You're a saint, Desmond Tindall," she'd said, and took him out for another
fine meal.

Now he was offering his chauffeur services to get them to their meeting 'to give Beatrice a chance to enjoy the sights instead of driving for a change.' Beatrice was willing to take the afternoon off, so Dorothy had agreed.

Desmond stood as Dorothy reached the base of the stairs. "You look much more ravishing in the flesh, my dear."

She scoffed as he helped her into her coat. "Compared to the drowned rat on the cover of the *Post*, I should hope so."

She had chosen a special outfit for the occasion; blending her typical masculine style with a softer, feminine flair. She wore a linen shirt and a lavender tie under a silk waistcoat, covered with a green velvet coat. Instead of the trousers she would ordinarily have worn, she was wearing a conservative black skirt. She wanted to make everyone she was meeting feel comfortable, and not all of them would take kindly to a woman being in charge. She hoped her fashion aesthetics helped put them at ease.

They went out to Desmond's car and he helped them into the backseat. He pulled away from the curb and eased into the road. Dorothy folded her hands in her lap and watched the people outside the window. Their route took them past shops in Cripplegate and the industrial warehouses of Clerkenwell. They followed narrow streets that had been carved out long before anyone had anticipated the need for motor vehicles. They inched along between the classical buildings and green parks.

"I'm loath to bring this up, but have you heard the news from Ireland?" Beatrice asked, breaking into her reverie and drawing her attention back into the car.

"I stopped reading the paper as soon as I saw my fish-eye stare gazing back at me. I assume there was a flare-up with the war?"

Beatrice nodded. "The IRA assassinated a group of British agents in Dublin. The Irish constabulary retaliated by attacking a rally that killed three civilians. Three IRA fighters were taken into custody and beaten to death."

"Bloody hell," Dorothy said.

"There's worse. The article I read this morning had sketches of some of the people involved in the violence. One in particular..."

Dorothy closed her eyes and groaned. "Oh, don't tell me."

"In the flesh."

Dorothy sighed and shook her head. Virago had escaped from custody as promised not long after they returned to London. Beatrice had assisted Scotland Yard with the search of Virago's usual haunts, but they came up empty. The police eventually declared she had fled to Ireland, and the new developments seemed to support that theory.

"Well, at least she also kept her word not to come after us. That's something, I suppose."

"I can't help but feel like it was all left unfinished," Beatrice said.

"You?" Dorothy said. "You got to have all the fun. I got beaten up by her and never got a second round thanks to your heroics."

Beatrice brushed her finger over Dorothy's cheek. "Poor darling."

Dorothy turned and snapped at Beatrice's finger. Beatrice snickered and looked out her window. "I'm sure you'll get another chance to best her. Someone like that doesn't tend to retreat for long."

"Mm," Dorothy said.

Their destination was an unassuming three-story building surrounded by a brick wall. The gate was standing open and Desmond pulled in to a cozy courtyard with tables and chairs to the left and a parking area to the right. There were other vehicles present, including drivers who had taken advantage of the seats to smoke and read newspapers as they awaited their passengers. Desmond parked among the other cars and Beatrice looked out at the other chauffeurs and hired men.

"Sure you don't mind waiting out here with the rabble, Professor Tindall?" Beatrice asked with a teasing smile.

"If they're anything like you, Miss Sek, I'm certain it will be an extremely educational way to pass the time." He winked at Dorothy and held the door for them to step out. Their arrival had gotten the attention of the small crowd, and some of them began to whisper and nod their heads in Dorothy's direction. She bit back an exasperated sigh and followed Beatrice to the entrance.

The building had once been a tavern, though its signage was long gone, Dorothy knew the name. The door was standing open to air out the large main room and let in some sunlight. Trafalgar had taken the boards off the windows but the musty sawdust smell lingered. The built-in elements, like the booths and the bar, were still present, and every five or ten feet a support beam interrupted the otherwise open space. Some of those who had gathered were sitting in the booths, two were behind the empty bar, and the rest were spread throughout the empty room. Dorothy took off her gloves and looked to make sure everyone was present.

Cecil Dubourne, the son of Gerald Dubourne, a victim of the Weeks' brothers. He had taken over his father's work. He was young and brash, but he had been trained by a good man. Dorothy had met him once or twice and knew he had potential to do his father proud.

Cora Hyde, of course, had come back from Wraysbury at the end of summer. She had yet to take any new commissions of her own, but she was consulting with the others by appointment. She smiled at Dorothy; she was one of the few present who knew what Dorothy was going to say and she'd already thrown her support behind the idea. Dorothy hoped the others were as agreeable.

Abraham Strode was a bit of a dandy. He didn't like the dirty aspects of their job, preferring to remain in his pristine office and libraries while hiring students to actually visit dig sites. He looked enormously uncomfortable in the dusty bar, arms crossed as his pale eyes darting about in search of a clean haven to settle.

Leonard and Agnes Keeping were the ones behind the bar. They apparently had decided to provide alcohol for the meeting, and Agnes was mixing the drinks. The Keepings looked posh and unremarkable, but they were both well-trained in both martial arts and weaponry. Dorothy knew for a fact that Agnes was able to hold her own in a fight with Beatrice, while Leonard had proven skilled with a sword. She didn't want to think of them in terms of bank account, but it didn't hurt that they were also well-off. If her proposal was accepted, it would be good to know she could rely on someone else to help fund the endeavor.

Rounding out their group was the member Dorothy thought would prove the most controversial: Ivy Sever. A year earlier she had been employed to kill Abraham Strode. She'd been prevented from succeeding and, judging by his lack of attention to her, the event seemed to have been forgotten by both parties. Ivy was still invisible so far as Dorothy knew, but she was dressed and made up to appear as fleshy as anyone else. The only clue to her true nature were the goggles she was wearing; there was still no way for makeup to mimic the human eye.

Trafalgar was waiting to one side of the door. She'd arrived early to let everyone else in and let them know Dorothy would be there shortly. Beatrice took a position to the other side of the door as Dorothy moved to the center of the room.

"First and foremost, I'd like to thank you all for agreeing to come. It took a while for you all to get onboard, but I believe it was time well-spent."

Abraham Strode said, "I'm sure you could have chosen a more appropriate meeting place than this, Lady Boone. Had I known you would be exposing us to the plague, I may have had second thoughts about accepting your invitation."

Dorothy said, "Oh, come now, Abe. It may not be much now, but the Inkwell was once home to great poets and scholars." She pointed to a booth in the far corner under a moon-shaped window. "Marcellus Griffin spent an entire fortnight in that seat translating Greek journals. Dr. Lincoln was hired for the Antarctic expedition at a table that once stood right about here. And my grandmother, Eula Boone, made her first money as an explorer at that bar, when she was hired by a man who was too drunk to realize he was talking to a woman."

Agnes took a drink and ran her thumb over her lip. "That's a wonderful history lesson. Honestly, I want to go over and sit in Griffin's booth to see if I can feel his ghost. But what does that have to do with us?"

"Everything. We've spent too much time bickering with one another. Competing and conspiring against each other. I'm guilty of it myself. Some of you remember when Trafalgar and I got into a fight in the middle of the street just last year."

Dubourne said, "My father used to tell me something about a submersible in Turkey."

"Istanbul, actually," Trafalgar said. "Lady Boone stole it while my camp was sleeping. At least, she attempted to."

"Technically, I succeeded in stealing it," Dorothy muttered. "But since then, we have become partners. We've worked together and, through that cooperation, we've discovered absolutely amazing things. We wandered the labyrinth and faced the Minotaur. We stood in the graveyard of an extinct and nearly-forgotten race. Not only would those things have been impossible without Trafalgar, I wouldn't have survived either of them without her. I believe the truly great things are yet to come, but I also believe the times ahead are going to be incredibly daunting.

"The magic unleashed during the Great War scarred this world. Never before had so many practitioners pulled so much energy from the veil at once. There were bound to be consequences. We're just scratching the surface of the mess that has to be cleaned up. More creatures from prehistory, more enemies we can't hope to fight alone. Our only chance to defeat them is to know they're coming and prepare ourselves properly for their arrival."

Abe Strode said, "So we all join forces with you and Trafalgar? We become a horde of explorers all focusing on one site at a time?"

Dorothy shook her head. "No. That would be disastrous. What I'm suggesting is a federation of people with a common interest. We would all remain autonomous, taking our own jobs and using our own resources for expeditions. The difference would be our cooperation with one other. Sharing information. Being transparent with one another."

Cora said, "Dorothy has been giving me credit for the necropolis she found. But the truth is, even though I did much of the research, I applied it incorrectly. I was hundreds of kilometers off and never would have known without her input and the journals her grandmother left behind."

Dorothy said, "Who knows what we could accomplish if we simply shared with one another? Last year, two men nearly wiped us all out simply because we didn't trust each other. I was willing to believe Trafalgar had tried to kill me. Mr. Keeping, you put a sword to my throat when I came into your home to warn you of the threat. Mr. Dubourne, your father died in that attack, along with several other adventurers.

"I purchased this tavern with the intention to revive it so we could use the upper levels as a meeting place. We can foster relationships, perhaps even collaborations, we can share information with each other on neutral ground, and we can prevent anyone from ever again using us as weapons against ourselves. We can also hopefully spot patterns and warning signs of future catastrophes. We can stop them before they can do unspeakable damage."

Trafalgar said, "And should something arise, we would trust each other enough to join forces to stop it. Those who cannot remember the past are doomed to repeat it. So it falls to us to ensure history is not forgotten in order to preserve the future."

Dorothy said, "I believe the people in this room are the best suited to not only see the threat coming, but to stand up against it when the need arises."

Ivy had remained silent for the entire speech, but she lifted her hand now. "No offense taken if anyone is wondering what the hell I'm doing here. Considering the qualifications to get in the room... I'm a spy."

"And assassin," Strode murmured, glaring at her from the side of his eye.

Ivy nodded toward him. "That, too."

"You're a private investigator," Dorothy said, "and you have the extraordinary power of invisibility. There are enemies like the Weeks brothers or Emmeline Potter who would choose to join forces with the darkness. They would sacrifice the world for a taste of a dark power. We need to know who those people are, what they're planning, and where they can be found. You would be one of the most important members of our group."

"I don't work for free."

"We'd keep you on retainer. I'm sure everyone contributing a bit every month would make your prices bearable."

The Keepings looked at one another and silently considered. Dubourne had leaned forward with his elbows on his knees, forefingers steepled in front of his face. Strode began to pace. Cora had already agreed to the proposal and was watching the others to see who would join in.

Cecil Dubourne broke the stalemate. "I'm just getting started with this profession. My father left me a lot, but it would be a huge help to have something like this group to watch out for me. I'm definitely willing to join."

Leonard Keeping said, "Lady Boone, you've never steered us wrong before. And with your recent track history, we'd be fools not to be in your corner. You have our support."

Strode waved his hand dismissively. "You'll clean this place up before we have any meetings here, right?"

Dorothy smiled. "I don't know... it kind of has a cozy, lived-in feel." He glared at her. "But for you, I suppose we could have a maid come in."

"Fine."

Ivy shrugged. "And I'm here as long as I'm getting paid."

Dorothy grinned. "Fantastic. Thank you all. I have a feeling that we're going to do great things together." She went to the bar and picked up one of the glasses Agnes had filled. She lifted it to the room. "Welcome to the charter members of the Mnemosyne Society."

"Nema-sin-ee?" Strode said. "Whazzat?"

"Greek personification of memory," Trafalgar said.

Strode snorted and shook his head. "I'm never going to remember that..."

Dorothy grinned at Trafalgar, who gave her a nod of approval. It had taken over a year of work, cajoling everybody one at a time just to get them into this room. The job was done, and now they had the framework for a group that she believed could take a stand to protect the world against the growing wave of darkness. She knew there were still rough patches ahead, and she knew their disparate personalities might cause friction, but they could deal with that when the time came.

For now, the most difficult part was over. Now the real work could begin.

Trafalgar and Boone

will return

in

TRAFALGAR & BOONE
AND
THE BOOKS OF BREATHING

ABOUT THE AUTHOR

Geonn Cannon lives in Oklahoma. He is the author of several novels, including the Riley Parra series which is currently being produced as a webseries for Tello Films, and an official Stargate SG-1 tie-in novel. Information about his other novels and an archive of free stories can be found online at geonncannon. com.